LAST SALUTE

by

Tracey Richardson

Bella
BOOKS

2013

Bella Books, Inc.
P.O. Box 10543
Tallahassee, FL 32302

Printed in the United States of America on acid-free paper.

First Bella Books Edition 2013

Editor: Medora MacDougall
Cover Designed by: Judith Fellows

ISBN: 978-1-59493-372-1

Other Books by Tracey Richardson

Blind Bet
The Campaign
The Candidate
Side Order of Love
No Rules of Engagement
The Wedding Party

Acknowledgments

It takes a village to raise a writer, and there are too many people to thank who have generously and unconditionally offered me support, encouragement, advice and joyous distraction over the years. Every single one of your actions has manifested themselves in my words. Every emotional connection I have ever made in my life resonates in these words also, and for all of that, I am thankful. My editor, Medora MacDougall— you rock! I am indebted to Bella Books for their loyalty and professionalism. You won't find better quality books for women anywhere! And readers, thank you for spending a few hours of your time with me…you are the inspiration behind my work. My biggest thanks goes to Sandra for her love and rock steady presence. Okay, *and* for putting up with me when I'm in my writing mode!

About the Author

Tracey is the author of six other Bella novels, including the popular *No Rules of Engagement*, *The Candidate* and *The Campaign*. She has been a winner of /or finalist for several lesbian fiction awards, as well as newspaper awards. Tracey works as a daily newspaper reporter/editor and lives in southwestern Ontario with her partner and two very busy chocolate Labrador retrievers. When not writing or news reporting, Tracey enjoys playing ice hockey and golf and is trying to re-learn how to play the guitar. Please visit *www.traceyrichardson.net*.

Dedication

To my friend Lynn, who was taken too soon. And to those who have served and continue to serve.

CHAPTER ONE

Pamela Wright never thought it would happen again. Only much later, the myopia of grief having blurred, did she marvel at the cruel swiftness with which her world had crumbled with a simple, unexpected knock on the door. She never saw it coming, never expected it, though she probably should have. She'd been visited by tragedy before, had learned that hard lesson a long time ago. Her mistake had been in thinking it couldn't happen again, that lightning never strikes twice. Allowing herself to be cradled in a false, flimsy sense of security was inexcusable and was something she vowed would never happen again.

It began as one of those days in the ER of Chicago's University of Illinois Medical Center—the kind that made Pam ache to race home and lie around in her pajamas, watch one of her old romance DVDs, indulge in the forbidden comforts of a bag of artery-clogging chips and a glass or two of wine.

She had almost—but not quite—felt guilty about her little plan as she climbed the steps to her two-bedroom townhouse, the day thankfully behind her. If it'd been one of those crazy, adrenaline-infused ER shifts of car crashes on the Lakeshore or gang shootings from the South Side—the kind of tragic stuff that was fertile ground for medical heroics—she'd still be jacked up. Jacked up and throwing on her jogging shoes instead of rooting around in her fridge for leftover spaghetti and meatballs and trying to decide between *Sleepless in Seattle* or *While You Were Sleeping*. But there'd been no such luck. Instead, the day had been a dreary, soul-sucking one, and her exhaustion was more mental than physical, because she'd finished her shift with zero sense of accomplishment, zero sense of having helped anyone in a meaningful way.

Hmm, she thought, *Meg Ryan or Sandra Bullock?* Both were cute and wholesome and girl next door-ish—exactly the kind of woman Pam secretly pined for but never had the time, the energy or the brazen confidence to pursue. A dog could be cute and wholesome too, and she had a much better chance of sharing her life with a chocolate Lab than a Meg or a Sandra, she mused. Pathetically, that idea was okay with her at the moment.

Pam placed the plate of spaghetti in the microwave and poured a glass of cabernet merlot, silently saluting the fact that tomorrow would be a much-needed day off. It'd give her plenty of time to cast off the agitation of her shift, which had started out with Mr. Shiffler, a long-time two-pack-a-day guy with a bad case of emphysema. He was on a dozen or so medications, but he'd decided days ago that he was tired of the pills, so he quit them. Predictably his breathing had deteriorated and he was in her ER early this morning, wheezing and coughing like a man gasping his last breath—which in all likelihood he was. She'd filled him with steroids, antibiotics, given him a nebulizer treatment, and after all that, he still needed to go on a ventilator. Totally frustrating and futile. Then a fifteen-year-old kid had come in by ambulance—alcohol poisoning. Following that there were three successive patients complaining of mysterious back injuries and could she please just prescribe them some OxyContin and they'd be on their way. "Just a few pills doc, to get over the worst of it." And those were the highlights of the day.

Definitely a Meg Ryan night, Pam decided, slipping the DVD into place and retrieving her plate from the microwave. Tomorrow she'd go for a three-mile run along the lake, maybe take in the annual kite flying competition in Lincoln Park, write her sister Laura that inexcusably long overdue email. And who knows, maybe she'd finally take that cute little social worker, Connie Mayfield, up on her open-ended offer of a date—she'd been bugging Pam about it for three weeks now. In any case, she'd recharge her batteries and enjoy her days off and get over the fact that days like today made her feel as though all her training and education, all the hours she put in as an emergency medicine resident, were good for little more than patching up people and sending them back to their self-destructive lives.

Self-pity wasn't normally Pam's nature. If she wanted to be a true hero doc, after all, she'd have followed her older sister Laura into the army, where she could be helping sick and wounded soldiers and villagers in Afghanistan right now, all while trying not to get her ass shot off. But she didn't have the stomach for that brand of glory. No way. And she'd never been too proud to admit it was the part about trying to avoid getting her ass shot off that had kept her out of uniform. Her self-preservation was simply too firmly entrenched. She was no Laura.

She shook her head and smiled as she remembered Laura teasing her about taking her residency in Chicago, about there being as many guns in the city as there probably were in all of Afghanistan. At least I'll be armed when someone tries to shoot at me, Laura had said, her smile lacking any joy. "I worry about you, little sister," she'd said. Ironic though, because it was Pam who worried about Laura.

Pam shifted her attention to the movie, felt her body relax with the first soothing sips of wine. Meg Ryan was listening to the little boy on the radio show pleading for a girlfriend for his lonely dad when Pam's doorbell rang. *That's odd*, she thought. Her hours at work were so unpredictably long that anyone who wanted to see her knew enough to text her or call her first to make sure she was home. Maybe, she thought with a smile, some little kid somewhere was trying to set her up with a hot but lonely widow, like the kid in the movie, and the hot widow was right now on her doorstep begging to come in. *Yeah, like that fairy tale stuff is ever going to happen to me.*

Still smiling, she opened the door to a man and woman in full army dress, their brass buttons shining beneath the porch light, their ties perfectly straight, the crease in their pants sharp as a knife's edge. The detail of their faces didn't much register, but they weren't smiling—that much she noticed. Friends of Laura's maybe? She'd seen Laura in army dress only three times—her graduation from med school, a wedding and their mother's funeral.

A funeral. Oh my God! No!

Her mind emptied to total blankness. Her knees began to tremble so wildly she was sure they'd give out. Nothing moved—not time, not these two strangers, not even traffic on the street. The background noise from the television seemed to have stilled too. Everything was silent, immovable—a black yawn of emptiness.

In a toneless voice, the woman asked, "Are you Dr. Pamela Wright?"

Pam barely managed to nod.

"May we come in?"

Involuntarily, she moved aside to let them pass, even though what she really wanted to do was send them away, the way she would some lousy door-to-door salesman. It occurred to her that if she didn't let them in, they couldn't deliver their message.

"I'm Major Rowan," the army woman continued in that flat voice of hers. "And this is Captain Mitchell. We're here about your sister, Major Laura Wright."

I know, Pam wanted to scream. *And now you're going to tell me she's dead!*

"Would you like to sit down?" Rowan asked, as if it were her home and not Pamela's. She seemed to be the one with the speaking role, which was better than the alternative, Pam decided. The guy looked nervous, uncertain, like maybe he was learning the ropes.

"No," she rasped. She would take this standing up, the same as when she was the one delivering the bad news.

"The Secretary of the Army has asked me to inform you that your sister, Major Laura Wright, was killed in action..."

Oh Jesus, no! Pam's heart thudded in her ears about a million beats a minute and she made a blind grab for the wall to stop from collapsing to the floor. Her chest heaved; she could not breathe. Her body was reacting far faster than her emotions, which was entirely a foreign concept to her. She was always so damned good at maintaining control. So practiced at being stoic, in command, no matter the circumstances. But this...this overpowered her, tossed her around as though she were a tiny rowboat in a thrashing sea. The major was still talking, but most of her words failed to register—only the part about a helicopter crash in Afghanistan, Laura not surviving her injuries—stuck with Pam.

"Go," Pam tearfully ordered when she could find her voice. "Please, I want you to leave now."

She couldn't stand to look at those dark blue uniforms and colorful medals anymore. The two didn't want to go. They offered to stay, to call a friend, someone. There was no other family, only her and Laura, and the two casualty notification officers looked like they'd been cheated out of something. Reluctantly they agreed to leave, fumbling with their caps in their smooth hands, saying someone would be in touch again tomorrow to help her with funeral details.

Pam slid to the floor as the door closed, unspooling in every way possible. So *this* is what it feels like, she thought numbly, as though she were outside herself. Many times, she'd had to perform the grim notification duties herself in the emergency department. She knew what it was like to be on that side of the news, knew too what it was like to watch her mother slip away to cancer. But this. This was different. Laura was all she had, and now she was gone. "Laura," she whispered in desperation. *Laura, Laura, Laura. It can't be true, please! No!* She clutched a hand to her mouth as though the act might somehow lessen the impact of Laura's death.

Laura was the older sister who could do everything, the one who was smarter, braver, the better athlete. She was the one full of joy and adventure. She was the invincible one, the role model, the protector. The only family Pam had, for God's sake! No, it didn't make any sense. Laura had always been in her life—distant yes, but always there. Always a phone call or email away.

Quiet tears grew into sobs. Pamela Wright had never felt more alone, more bereft, in her life.

* * *

Trish Tomlinson packed the remaining essays—she'd already graded about half of them—into her worn leather satchel. She was usually one of the last teachers at Ann Arbor's Huron High School to leave work each day, but this time she had a vague but persistent desire to get home as quickly as she could. She wondered, with only mild concern, if she was coming down with something.

She said good night to a couple of students lingering in the hall, waved to a fellow teacher and walked out the doors—the front ones this time instead of the ones closest to the parking lot that she usually took. A little walk, a little air might rid her of the tickle in her throat, she reasoned. A janitor was at the main flagpole, reefing on the rope that held the flag. She watched him for a moment before she approached. It wasn't a common occurrence to see the flag dropped to half-mast, and when it was, it was bad news of course.

"Hey, Jim," she said breezily. "What's the half-mast for?"

The older man, nearly as slender as the aluminum post, shrugged bony shoulders. "Don't know, ma'am, except that it was one of our own."

Shit. She hadn't heard any news all day, but maybe the school had just been notified. She stood a moment longer, watched Jim tie the flag in place and mentally scrolled through a list of likely candidates. Michael Ferguson hadn't been in school for a couple of days. Jarrod Murray had been gone all week without explanation. It was spring, and boys liked their cars fast, their music loud and, unfortunately, their beer warm or cold. A sure recipe for disaster, and a couple of students always succumbed every school year.

Trish started toward the parking lot, stopped, turned sharply on her Blundstone boots. If she didn't find out who had died, it'd bug her for the rest of the evening.

"Have a good night, Jim," she called out and hustled back inside.

She ducked into the office, where the remaining secretary was packing up her things for the day.

"Marla, hey."

The burly African-American woman beamed at her, gently shaking her head. "Why, Miss Tomlinson, I can't believe you almost beat me outta here! Since when do you go hightailing it before five o'clock?"

"You caught me. Decided to step out early today."

"Hot date or something?"

All the staff knew she was single, though she rarely discussed her private life. She wasn't exactly closeted. It was more like her life was too boring to talk about.

"Nah, nothing like that. Listen, I saw the flag outside just now. Somebody die?"

"Yeah, an alumnus from a ways back."

Relieved, Trish exhaled the nervous breath she'd been holding. Then her curiosity took hold again. She was an alumnus of Huron High herself, class of '93, and the only teacher at the school who could make such a claim. "A ways back" could be forty years ago or it could be someone she'd graduated with. "Do you know who?"

"As a matter of fact I do. A soldier. Just let me look up that email we got an hour or so ago."

Trish's heart skipped a beat, then another. Then it crashed to a near halt. *No, please no, don't let it be her.*

"Let me see here. A woman. Hmm, such a shame, not very old. That darned war over there. Seems like it's never going to be over."

Goddammit, just tell me who!

"Okay, here's the name. Graduated in 1993, a Major Laura Wright, thirty-eight years old. Killed yesterday in…"

Trish didn't hear anything beyond Laura's name. The secretary was still talking, at least her lips were moving, but

Trish could hear nothing beyond the blood rushing in her ears. She could not breathe. It was like choking on nothing more tangible than air—air she couldn't seem to force into her lungs.

Not Laura, not my Laura, oh God. It was all she could think, over and over, like a song skipping in place for what felt like minutes. It simply could not be her high school sweetheart, her first love, her only love. This could *not* be happening. And while her mind refused to believe it, her body had no doubt. Her legs began to quiver, go numb, and then her vision shrank until it was no bigger than the head of a pin. She was falling, spinning, shrouded in blackness.

She didn't feel the floor as she hit it.

CHAPTER TWO

Pam shivered in the backseat of the limousine. She was nervous, scared. Laura was coming home to Ann Arbor. In a casket. The thought made her shiver all over again.

Through the car's heavily tinted windows, she watched the large airliner crawl to a stop on the tarmac of Detroit's Metro Airport. A plain black hearse inched toward it, followed by a nondescript van with government plates. Surely any minute the plane's door would open and Laura would be standing there, waving and smiling, looking trim and fit and anxious to set her feet on American soil again. As hard as Pam struggled to accept reality, she wasn't ready to concede that she would never see Laura again. Perhaps if she envisioned a different outcome, she could will it to happen. It was one of the mind games she'd been playing over the last couple of days—a defense against the shock.

Eight soldiers in army dress uniforms exited the van one by one and moved into rigid formation next to the plane's cargo door. It was like watching a movie where everyone had a part to play, including herself. She could do this. Unscripted, unrehearsed though it was, she knew how to do grief. She'd played the part of grieving daughter before, and while grieving sister was a new and even more heart-wrenching role, she had no choice but to go through the motions. She clutched the dry tissue in her hand, unsure when or even if tears would fall today. She'd cried so much already that she didn't know how much was left.

The door beside her opened abruptly. A white-gloved hand reached in.

"Pamela Wright? Hello, I'm Lieutenant Camille Chavez."

The gloved hand shook Pam's, guided her out of the limo.

"I'm so sorry, Pamela. I know the words aren't nearly enough, but I want you to know how very deeply saddened I am about Laura. What she meant to me, to all of her colleagues and the people she served with. Her friendship was an incredible honor, one I'll never forget. I miss her so much already."

Camille Chavez's face spoke of her grief. There were dark circles beneath her eyes, exhaustion in her movements the well-trained military bearing failed to conceal.

"Thank you," Pam said shakily. "She mentioned you a few times in her emails. I understand you were good friends."

The lieutenant nodded gravely. "We met at Fort Benning two years ago when I was beginning my nursing career. We both deployed to Afghanistan at the same time last fall."

"You're the one who brought her home, aren't you?" It hurt to say *home*, because Laura was never truly coming home again. One thing was for sure. Laura was never leaving American soil again.

"Yes. I haven't left her side for the last twenty-four hours."

Pam was glad Laura wasn't alone and that the army cared enough to make sure she wasn't. Camille must have cared a great deal for Laura, and Pam wondered fleetingly if they'd been lovers at some point. Since joining the army, Laura had quietly made her way through quite a long line of women. All those years, she'd not been one to be tied down by a lover. Or by anything, for that matter. It was the main reason, Pam supposed, that army life seemed to suit her so perfectly. Except…what the army giveth, it taketh away. Pam felt the threat of tears.

Camille squeezed her hand. "Come with me. We'll do this together, okay?"

Pam nodded as the tears began to fall. They moved to the foot of the conveyer belt that had been shoved up against the cargo bay. It began to whir mechanically as the large door retracted. Pam gasped as the flag-draped coffin came into view.

"I know," Camille whispered.

It was a shocking sight. The flag was crisp and stark against the sunshine, wound snugly around the coffin like a tight blanket. The red in the flag made Pam think of blood. Laura had been killed when the helicopter she was a passenger in crashed in a dust storm while trying to land at a forward operating base. The others had been badly injured but survived; Laura was the only fatality. Pam hadn't yet asked for more details about Laura's death. In time she would, but she wasn't ready for that yet.

The soldiers, lined like perfectly straight fence posts along the conveyer belt, saluted as the coffin whirred its way down. Camille's chin quivered, but she held her own salute and stood as rigidly as the others. Pam's shoulders slumped as the soldiers hoisted the coffin up and slowly but perfectly in step carried it to the hearse. The slamming of the hearse's rear door caused Pam to jump, the finality of it jarring. And just like that, Laura was gone again.

Camille touched her elbow. "Okay if I ride in the limo with you to the funeral home?"

"Of course, but if you want to ride with Lau–"

"No. I'd prefer that you weren't alone right now. And we'll be right behind her."

Wordlessly they climbed into the back of the limo for the twenty-minute drive along I-94 to Ann Arbor, to the same funeral home where Pam and Laura's mother had rested six years ago. So much death in Pam's life. Too much. Could she possibly bear this one? Or was this the one that would break her, she wondered numbly.

The hearse was ahead of them, and through the tinted glass, Pam could see Laura's coffin and the flag shrouding it.

It was almost beautiful, except that it signified the ugliest thing imaginable—death.

Pam stared numbly straight ahead. "I can't believe Laura's in there."

"The army's recommending a closed casket. Her injuries…"

Pam shook her head firmly. "I don't want to know."

"Do you want to view her privately?"

"Do you?" Pam snapped, not meaning to.

"No," Camille said. "I want to remember her the way she was the last time I saw her." Her smile was faint, private. "It was over a month ago. She was envious that I was being sent to Takhar for a while to work at a clinic there. She didn't like being stuck at the Bagram base for a long period of time. She liked getting out to clinics in the villages, the forward operating bases. She got her fair share of getting off base, but she'd never been to Takhar. She was putting on this huge pout, cussing out the army, cussing out the colonel who was in charge of the base hospital. She even threatened to go over his head. Of course, she'd never risk that kind of insubordination. She was just venting."

"She was a good soldier, wasn't she?"

"The best, Pamela. Absolutely the best."

It'd been six months since she'd last seen her sister. It was last October. Laura had had a week off—her last leave before November's deployment to Afghanistan. She'd visited Pam in Chicago for a couple of days, then drove to Ann Arbor in a rental car to tour around. She later emailed Pam that she'd stopped at their old family home, which was up for sale for the second or third time since their mother's death, and visited old friends. A little trip down memory lane, and Pam was glad Laura had done it. Laura had wanted her to come too, but Pam couldn't get the time off work. She wished now that she'd done it anyway, even if it'd meant calling in sick. The Wright sisters were far too rule-oriented, far too worried about fulfilling their obligations to do something like call in sick when they were perfectly healthy.

Oh, Laura, why hadn't you quit that damned army by now? You more than paid them back for putting you through medical school—

you gave them thirteen years, served tours in war zones. Wasn't that more than enough?

Who was she kidding? Laura hadn't been anywhere close to leaving the army. She had loved the army. Loved the camaraderie, the sense of purpose and duty, the risks, the honor. And she looked damned spectacular in that uniform of hers, all proud and a little bit cocky, had the swagger of authority down to a tee.

Pamela cleared her throat to pry her thoughts loose. "What happens next?"

"We'll get everything ready for the viewing tomorrow. Four soldiers will guard her every minute. Day after tomorrow, we'll fly her to Arlington National Cemetery for a full honors burial, as per her wishes."

The army required its soldiers to set out their final wishes ahead of time. They were nothing if not prepared for the worst.

"There's a letter," Camille said gently. "Before every deployment, soldiers write a final letter to next of kin and it's kept on file. I have it with me. You can…"

"I can't. Not right now." Pam refused to handle more than one thing at a time. Later, she would read the letter, would go through Laura's things. It would be so much easier—though easier wasn't the right word—if she had someone to help her through this. She tried to think of the appropriate word instead of easier: Manageable? Tolerable? Smoother? Less damn frightening, for sure, but no one on this earth could help make Laura's death *easier*. She had friends, but none of them had known Laura. There were no other family members of much consequence, no lovers of much consequence for either one of them. Pam's last serious girlfriend had been a fellow med school student. They'd lasted eight months, their relationship more of a competition than a partnership. As for Laura, she hadn't brought anyone home in years, hadn't mentioned anyone of significance in some time. She seemed to either play the field or go for long bouts of celibacy. Their inconsistent love lives caused them to joke about living together after Laura retired from the army. How they'd be two elderly sisters sharing a rambling old house with their yellowed medical diplomas hanging crooked on the wall, their three dogs and two cats curled at their feet, a recycling bin full of wine bottles at the curb each week.

Wanting to smile at the vision but yielding to her anger instead, Pam said, "I thought she would be safe there. She was *supposed* to be safer than the others because she was a doctor."

"It's true, medical staff aren't on the front lines the same, but there's always danger. Even if she'd never left the base, it's still dangerous. The base is attacked occasionally. And we're expected to go outside the wire sometimes—giving clinics in the community, treating soldiers at forward operating bases, even escorting helicopter medevacs sometimes."

In their emails, phone calls and discussions, Laura had always downplayed the danger. Even during her two tours in Iraq, when things were still hotter than hell there, she never said much about the risks. Still, her death didn't make a lot of sense. The odds were so slim and yet…it had happened.

She couldn't think of that now, couldn't play the game of what-ifs. Pamela turned her face to the window. They were in Ann Arbor now, the city she and Laura had spent most of their lives in. The familiar University of Michigan flags and signs were everywhere, giving Pam a soft pang of nostalgia. Students strolled the streets, many of them wearing the customary navy blue and gold school colors, most of them looking carefree and unburdened. It was good to be in familiar territory, the reminders of her and Laura's alma mater wrapping her in a blanket of consolation.

As the procession neared downtown, Pam noticed people clustered on the sidewalk in small groups, some holding small American flags, some with their hands over their hearts. With each block, more people stood on the curb, silently facing them. "Is this what I think it is?" she whispered in awe.

Camille nodded, looking awed herself. "I've heard of this happening in communities. People spontaneously paying their respects." Her voice began to break. "It makes me feel so proud, you know?"

No, Pam didn't know, but she was beginning to understand. People did care, especially about one of their own, and it brought fresh tears to the surface again. Maybe she wasn't so alone after all. She scanned the passing faces. One of them stood out, and Pam pressed her face to the glass. It was Trish Tomlinson, standing on the sidewalk, staring at the hearse, looking stricken.

Pam put her hand against the glass to wave before realizing the tinting was too dark for Trish to see her. *Trish. Thank God.* If anyone would understand, would be able to grieve with her, it would be Trish. She hoped, though she had no right, that Trish would come to the funeral home later and seek her out. *Please, Trish.*

CHAPTER THREE

As the hearse and its flag-draped contents passed slowly by, Trish felt the finality of Laura's death like a steel door slamming shut on her heart. She didn't know what she'd expected, joining strangers on the street to watch the grim procession. Maybe she'd expected someone to say it was just a prank, and Laura would pop out of a sunroof from one of the passing cars, grinning and looking magnificent with her sun-streaked blond hair and gray-green eyes that twinkled with delightful mischief and the *joie de vivre* possessed only by someone who regularly faced danger. Or perhaps someone would announce it had all been a case of mistaken identity and Laura was still in Afghanistan. But neither scenario played out, and it was all Trish could do to keep from sobbing in public.

"What an awful shame," an elderly woman beside her muttered into the air. "How many more will it take?"

Trish didn't care, because it had taken the life of the only soldier who'd ever mattered to her. Intellectually, she'd always understood the risks. They'd talked about them at length when

Laura stopped by the school during a brief visit to town last fall, right before her deployment. They chatted on the school lawn for a few moments, moved on to dinner and a couple of glasses of wine. Like a salesclerk giving her best pitch, Laura explained the benefits of what she would be doing over there, how those benefits outweighed the risks, that her work there was far more important than fear—hers or anyone else's. They'd had the identical conversation seventeen years ago, when Laura joined the army as a way of defraying the costs of medical school. Even then, before she'd experienced the harsh reality of war, Laura had downplayed the danger. But it wasn't enough to convince Trish to stick it out. Neither of them could give what the other needed, and to Trish, the unforgivable bottom line was that Laura had chosen the army over her. She'd chosen a way of life that simply could not include a partner back home.

Trish's fear that Laura would be killed was the biggest reason she'd bailed on the relationship all those years ago. She had not wanted to end up a young widow. Except she wouldn't have been a widow in any official sense, not in Michigan and not with Don't Ask Don't Tell in effect for most of Laura's career. Now, Trish was simply an old friend. A long departed lover. Okay, more than just a lover. Her first love. And first loves you only have once, Trish knew. She and Laura had been forever bound in that heady alliance of unrestrained discovery, of innocent hope, of a magical future they had yet to map out. And while that special union was a long time ago, it had left a permanent imprint on Trish's soul. She'd never been able to wipe the slate clean of Laura.

What now? Trish wondered, her heart heavy as a boulder. She lingered on the sidewalk as the people around her resumed their missions and moved on, their daily lives taking shape again. Should she go home? Finally get on with her life now that the torch she'd been carrying for so many years had been so cruelly and permanently snuffed out? If she went home, she'd only wallow in her misery and stare—again—at the framed 5x7 photo from Laura's medical school graduation thirteen years ago. It was the last time they'd been happy together, right before everything changed. Right before Laura gave herself to the army.

What she'd really like to do is to get good and drunk, but the idea of drinking alone held no appeal.

She stumbled forward, in the direction of the funeral home. She'd read in the paper that the visitation would happen tomorrow, and after that, Laura's body would be taken to the national cemetery in Arlington, Virginia, for a ceremonial burial. But she didn't want to wait for tomorrow's visitation, and it occurred to her that she was acting like the loyal old dog who continued to sit at its master's doorstep even after the master was long gone. Pathetic, but her broken heart would allow no alternative.

A few soldiers milled around outside, talking quietly among themselves, barely glancing her way as the smoke from a couple of cigarettes momentarily assailed her. The front doors were unlocked and Trish marched through them with the air of purpose.

"Can I help you?" A funeral director, far too young to look so dour and serious, asked her with officious politeness.

"I, ah, am a friend of Major Laura Wright."

"I'm sorry but visitation for Major Wright is tomorrow afternoon. Perhaps…"

"Trish! Oh, I'm so glad you came."

Pamela Wright rushed past the young funeral director and into Trish's arms. She was tall, a bit taller than Laura, and built just like her—all wiry strength. She clung tightly to Trish, as though Trish were a lifeline.

"I wanted to be here, but I wasn't sure…" Trish felt awkward, out of place.

When Pam finally broke away, Trish quietly gasped. Pam looked so much like Laura—the short blond hair that mussed easily, the perfectly straight nose, the killer dimples. And those eyes—gray-green and identical to Laura's. How come she hadn't really noticed the uncanny resemblance before? Pam was a younger carbon copy of Laura, seven years younger to be exact, and instantly Trish was transported back to another time, to a time when Pam was a sun-kissed, gangly girl on the cusp of adolescence.

"Of course you should be here," Pam said softly. "I was hoping you would. There's no one else…"

"I know," Trish choked out. She needed to pull herself together, for Pam's sake if nothing else. With effort she cleared her throat. "Whatever you need."

"Will you come in the viewing room with me?"

Trish hesitated. She didn't know if she could handle seeing Laura in a casket.

"It's closed," Pam said, as if reading her mind.

"Okay." Trish followed her through the large double doors of the inner sanctum. The flag-draped casket stood on a dais, a soldier standing perfectly erect at each of the four corners. The room was eerily silent, not even a cough or the clearing of a throat. The flag was brightly illuminated by ceiling lights, the casket clearly the star of this macabre show. Adrenaline and emotion sent Trish's heart galloping. Beside her, Pamela clutched her hand, squeezed it, and it occurred to Trish that *she* should be the one doing the comforting.

"Oh, Pam." Her voice was sandpaper. Unidentifiable emotions tumbled through her, crashing into one another. She was drowning in them.

A large photo of Laura in her dress uniform, poster sized, rested on an easel beside the casket. It was all so unreal, so unfathomable. *Is this really happening?* It could be a movie set, Trish thought.

"I hate that that's the only picture of Laura," Pam ground out, and Trish knew exactly what she meant—that it was an army picture of Laura, as if that's all Laura was, all she had ever been. "I forgot to bring pictures from home. Damn, I…"

"It's okay. I have some."

Pam's shoulders relaxed, but her face remained a mask of anguish. "Trish, I don't think I can do this alone."

"You don't have to. Have you eaten yet?"

It was dinner hour, and although food was about the last thing on Trish's mind, she didn't want Pam to collapse out of hunger and exhaustion.

Pam glanced at her watch, shook her head.

"Come home with me."

Pam looked at her questioningly.

"Unless you want to stay here all evening," she quickly amended. "I can do that too."

"No. I don't think I can stay here any longer."

Then let me take care of you, Trish wanted to say. *I can't take care of Laura, but I can take care of you.* "I'll fix us something to eat. We can choose the photos." *You won't have to be alone and neither will I.*

Pam nodded. In silence they stared at the casket for a few minutes longer until Trish gently guided her away.

CHAPTER FOUR

As Pam followed Trish up the brick path to Trish's house, she was reminded of her childhood home—a two-story, wood-sided Victorian from the late 1800s, with a brick fireplace in the living room, a long porch at the front of the house, a small backyard that hadn't been nearly big enough for the two sisters to play in. But they'd loved that house, their mom especially, and she'd worked hard to hang on to it after their father's death when she and Laura were kids.

Trish's home was very tidy inside, ordered but pleasant and warm. Dark hardwood floors gleamed and were partially covered by brightly colored area rugs. Bold abstracts hung from the walls, professionally framed photos too. A floor-to-ceiling bookshelf was crammed full of hardcovers and paperbacks. A home well lived in and appreciated was what came to Pam's mind. As she took in her surroundings, she noticed the evidence that Trish lived alone. The shoes all looked the same size, identical-sized jackets hung on the coat rack, and there was simply not enough clutter for two people. But she asked anyway.

"Yup, just me," Trish replied with a smile that was hard to read. "And I'm between dogs. My last one died five months ago."

"I'm sorry."

Trish led them to the kitchen table that looked out on to a deck and a handsomely gardened backyard. "I'll get another dog some day, when I'm ready. Do you have any pets?"

"With my work schedule, I don't think I'd have time for a pet rock."

Trish busily rummaged through the cupboards, and it occurred to Pam that she was the kind of person who liked to keep busy, who didn't keep still for long.

"You don't have to go to any trouble, Trish. I'm really not hungry."

"Me either, but I'm going to grill us up some cheese sandwiches and throw together a caesar salad. *And* I'm going to sit here and make sure you eat."

Pam laughed a little, the first time in days. "I'm not the kid sister anymore that you and Laura had to babysit."

Trish smiled, thunked a cast-iron frying pan on the stove. "All those nights your mom worked, Laura and I having to babysit you. We couldn't wait until you went to bed. Remember how we used to bribe you?"

"I sure do. I had quite the drawer full of candy bars, thanks to you guys. I used to sneak down the stairs and peek at you making out on the couch. Amazing you and Laura never caught me."

A faint blush worked its way up Trish's cheeks. "I suspected as much. I suppose Laura and I can be credited for you turning out gay as well, hmm? Being such, *ahem*, visible role models?"

Butter sizzled in the frying pan as Pam thought back to when she was a precocious ten-year-old with a mammoth crush on her big sister's girlfriend. She would dream of Trish kissing her like that, of her sweeping those liquid brown eyes so lovingly over her and looking at her the way she looked at Laura. She used to tag along as much they allowed her, and she'd clandestinely inhale the faint fragrance of Trish's floral soap and shampoo and close her eyes and listen to that honey-smooth voice. It was intoxicating being around the pretty seventeen-year-old Trish, who had the softest touch and the kindest smile and who never treated her like the annoying little sister of her girlfriend. Pam had never divulged her youthful crush on Trish for fear she might have been mocked. Or worse, pitied.

"Well," Pam joked, "I had to get the idea from somewhere."

Trish placed the cheese sandwiches in the hot butter, pulled two glasses from the cupboard and filled them with iced tea. "I guess I'm still waiting for my toaster oven on that one."

"Funny, that's exactly what Laura said the day I came out to her. I was in first year med school. She laughed and said, 'Do you have to copy me in everything?' She was joking of course, because she knew the one thing I'd never copy her in was joining the army."

Exasperation fell across Trish's face in hard lines. "I tried so hard to talk her out of joining that damned army. Threatened to break up with her, promised to follow her anywhere as long as it wasn't to an army base. I tried everything. Even said I'd put off my own schooling and get a job to help her pay for medical school, since tuition was her big excuse for joining."

"I know. I remember some of that tension between you two back then."

Trish poured a premixed bag of salad into a bowl. "That was the start of all the trouble between us," she said on a long sigh. "It only got worse and we couldn't get past it once I realized she would have joined the army anyway, school fees or not. She loved that damned army."

"I hated it when you guys broke up," Pam blurted out. She was devastated when Trish stopped coming around, hated that her sister was so unhappy for months afterward, hated that there was nothing she could do to reverse the situation. "Laura was miserable for a long time afterward. I guess I was too."

"Makes three of us." Trish plated the sandwiches, added a couple of dill pickles on the side. "Sorry this is such a lame dinner."

"No, this is wonderful. If it wasn't for this, I probably wouldn't be eating at all today."

"Oh, Pam." Trish reached across and touched her hand briefly. The gesture nearly reduced Pam to tears.

To avert a burst of emotion, Pam plowed into her sandwich. "You and Laura stayed in touch over the years, so I'm glad about that." *But you never stayed in touch with me. You never even really said goodbye once you and Laura went your separate ways.*

"We didn't for a long time, but the last four or five years, we'd talk on the phone once or twice a year, same with email. I saw her when she came to town last fall. We had dinner. I'm so glad we did."

Laura hadn't much mentioned Trish to her in recent years, but Pam could read between the lines. She knew they still cared for one another on a level that was far beyond their everyday lives. They seemed to have a bond that remained strong between them. "How come," Pam said in a wavering voice, "you and I never stayed in touch?" At one time, she'd thought they might. Or at least, she'd hoped that she and Trish were friends too.

"I don't know. I guess I lost track of you after your mom died and you moved to Chicago. I knew you were busy with medical school and all that, but I do wish we'd stayed friends. I'm sorry." The brown eyes were so genuine, so understanding. Exactly the same as Pam remembered from all those years ago.

"Me too. I'm sorry I didn't track you down. You're right, I was busy. Am busy. But it's a poor excuse." She looked at Trish and hoped her desperation didn't show. "I could really use a friend now."

"So could I. Where are you staying?"

"At the Marriott."

"Why don't you stay here with me instead? Until it's time to take Laura to Arlington? I hate the idea of either of us being alone right now."

The knots in Pam's shoulders immediately dissolved. Yes, she answered, she'd like that. Being with Trish felt strangely familiar and decidedly comforting. Trish was the only tether she had now to this city, was the only person she could talk to about growing up here, about Laura, about her mom, about all the memories. Trish was practically family, and she grounded Pam in a way no one else could right now.

The sun was setting quickly, and Trish switched on a lamp as they moved to the living room. Another switch and the gas fireplace came to life—there was still a chill to the April evening air and a dampness to the old house. Pam picked up the framed photo of the three of them from the mantel. It was Laura's medical school graduation, and she looked absolutely thrilled and totally excited for the future. Pam, who was about to graduate from high school, was staring in awe at her big sister, while Trish stared guardedly into the camera.

"Did you know when this picture was taken that it was pretty much over between you and Laura?"

"Yes. We held on for a few weeks after her graduation, but we both knew our lives were moving apart. I was already teaching here. I didn't want to leave. Laura knew she would never come back here to stay, would probably not settle in any one place for a long, long time. We couldn't find common ground any more."

Pam set the photo back down and moved to the sofa. "You didn't want to be an army wife."

Trish laughed bitterly and took a seat beside Pam. "You mean I didn't want to be Laura's dirty little secret. No, the army didn't exactly put out the welcome mat to same-sex partners, and I couldn't stand the thought of living that way. Besides, I was starting my career here, Laura was embarking on hers. I wanted to invest in my community. Laura was happy bobbing along to wherever the army sent her. It didn't exactly make us compatible."

"True. But you two loved each other so much. I was young and naive, I know that, but I thought you guys would always be together." She remembered how they were in high school—always laughing, always holding hands, always so damned happy, like they were meant to be together forever. "I could hardly believe it when suddenly you weren't a couple. To me it was like, I don't know, what the breakup of the Beatles must have felt like to our parents' generation."

That got a smile from Trish. "Well, like the Beatles, I guess even good things have to end eventually. Life gets harder and it seemed like it got hard pretty fast for Laura and me."

"Would you still be together if Laura had never joined the army?"

"Laura was never *not* going to join the army. She needed that adventure in her life, needed to feel she was doing some good in the world, serving others in a way she couldn't have done working at some stateside hospital or clinic." Trish's face flushed. "Sorry. I don't mean to suggest that what you do…"

"No, I know what you mean." Hell, lots of days, she felt she wasn't doing much good at the hospital either, but in her heart she knew she was doing something useful with her life. Not on a global scale like Laura, but still, she was doing some good; she was helping people. "Laura had a certain hero mentality about her. She was born to it. It was not something I could ever emulate, even if I'd tried."

"I'm glad you didn't, or you might have…"

"Died too?" Pam supplied, her thoughts turning somber. Death was the reason they were here, chatting in Trish's living room, reunited again. How strange it felt that it was just the two of them together, that the third and most important link in their triumvirate, Laura, was absent. A tricycle without one of its wheels.

Trish leaned forward, her elbows on her knees. "Dammit. Why couldn't she have chosen a safer path? I mean, she could have done noble work and not had to risk her life on the other side of the world. This…this…what's happened, it's something I always feared would happen. I can't say I expected it, but I feared it."

Pam's throat tightened. She'd had those same thoughts, knew Laura would be in harm's way as long as she stayed in the army, but she'd convinced herself Laura would skate through it. "There was no way we could have talked her out of it. I tried, I know you tried too. She was going to live her life the way she wanted, no matter what the people who loved her had to say about it. She was her own woman. I accepted that a long time ago."

"I know. You're right." Trish clamped her arms around herself as if warding off a chill. "I guess I could never truly accept that stubborn insistence of hers, which is why I let her go. I had to let her go so it wouldn't hurt so much if something happened to her. And now…"

"Now she's gone," Pam muttered softly around the lump in her throat.

Trish shook her head, her mouth a bitter line. Pam knew she too would grow angry, that she'd go through this same stage at some point. But right now she missed Laura, terribly. Couldn't fathom what the future would look like without her. It was so damned sad, a hollowness that was so gut-wrenchingly awful. She buried her face in her hands and let the sobs rack her body in turbulent waves.

"Oh, Pammy."

If Pam could have smiled, she would have. It was the pet name Trish had called her when she was little, and it transported her back to that time and made her feel loved for a tiny moment. Made her feel sheltered in a way she hadn't felt since those days.

Trish crouched down beside her, pulled her into an embrace, held her tightly, as tightly as a mother would hold a small child crying out in pain. Pam buried her face against Trish's shoulder, felt the warmth of her hand rubbing gentle circles on her back. There was no one else who could hold her like this, who could understand her loss, who could empathize with her aloneness in the world. With Laura gone, Trish was now her only real link to her past.

"Trish, please don't leave me," she choked out.

"I won't, Pammy. I promise I won't."

CHAPTER FIVE

Hundreds of people—possibly as many as a thousand— shuffled past the flag-draped casket to pay their respects. Most of them Trish didn't recognize, though she did notice some former teachers, a few childhood friends, former neighbors of the Wrights, some of her colleagues at the school. Local politicians showed up too, of course, to do their duty. Trish found herself wishing her parents, who'd retired to Hawaii more than a decade ago, had made the trip back. But they were remote, physically and emotionally, as usual. It was just her and Pam, and she marveled at how Pam heroically managed to stay on her feet for the four hours it took to greet everyone personally. Camille stayed close at hand.

The toughest part for Trish was listening to the speeches. An army major spoke first, though he'd only barely known Laura. He talked a lot about the mission, about the army, like it was some higher calling that mere mortals wouldn't understand. It mildly offended Trish. Right now she had only condemning thoughts about the mission and its horrendous human toll.

If she had the power, God knew she'd bring all the men and women in uniform home right this second.

How had it all come to this, Laura in a casket? How had the years slipped by in the blink of an eye? Had it really been seventeen years ago that Laura announced she was joining the army so that she could go to medical school? Followed by thirteen dangerous years of service, starting right before 9/11? With the same sick feeling in her stomach, she remembered the day Laura announced she was joining up. It was a day that closed one chapter in Trish's life and began a new and involuntary one. It was the day she had to begin letting go of the dream of the two of them moving through life together, because the army would become Laura's lifemate, her first priority. The army would take the best of Laura and leave Trish with only the dregs, and that simply wasn't good enough. She deserved more from Laura, and it somehow seemed easier back then to pull away, to start planning for a future without her. *Lines could be drawn so easily, so definitively, when you thought you still had your whole life ahead of you*, Trish mused.

"If you love me, you won't do it."

"If you do it, I'll leave you."

"I won't wait for you, Laura. I won't play second fiddle."

"I won't sacrifice my career for yours."

"I won't live a lie for the army."

Yes, she'd said all of those things and more, using her words like clubs. She'd forced Laura to make a choice between her and the army. And she'd lost.

Camille began speaking, her words giving the service a more personal touch. She described how she looked up to Laura for her professionalism, her talents as a doctor and a soldier, her selfless commitment to the army and her country, her bravery. Always her bravery, Camille said through a tearful smile. She described how Laura once ignored a rocket attack on base to finish the surgical procedure she was in the middle of. How she once went out in an armored vehicle down a road riddled with IEDs (improvised explosive devices) to get to a soldier trapped under a wrecked truck in a ditch. How she would stop at nothing to help someone, friend or foe. The army was lucky to have had Laura, Camille concluded, but not as lucky as she was to have called Laura a friend.

Trish involuntarily held her breath as Pam moved to the lectern, her shoulders rounded with the invisible weight of grief. She looked tired, fragile, so damn alone. She was a beautiful young woman, thirty or thirty-one years old now. Her hair was still naturally blond, her face not yet lined, but her eyes were old beyond their years. Pam had seen much suffering in her young life. Her dad had perished in a plane crash when Pam was barely a preschooler. Her mom, a hardworking janitor at the university who sometimes had to moonlight at a second job to make ends meet, had died more than six years ago of cancer. With Laura off somewhere across the globe, Pam had put off her medical career to be her mother's primary caregiver in her final months. Pam had undoubtedly seen much sickness and suffering in her chosen profession as well, and Trish longed to see Pam in happier times. A smile would be a start, even for a few seconds—a smile that said she hadn't a care in the world. A smile to wipe away all the sadness.

"Thank you all for coming," Pam announced softly. "I know that if Laura could, she would thank you too for not only honoring her life, but for honoring the life she chose as well. Joining the army..." Pam's voice broke and she took a moment to compose herself. "Joining the army is not for everyone. Certainly it's not for me. And as much as Laura's chosen life scared me, it was what she wanted." Pam glanced softly at Trish, and Trish knew Pam's words were meant for her.

"In fact, Laura talked about little else besides the army for the last thirteen years. I know that she truly felt a part of something much bigger than herself, and really, what better sense of purpose can a person have than to be a part of something much grander?"

There were nods of agreement in the crowd, smiles of understanding. Pam took a long moment before she began again. It had to be so hard to say nice things about the army right now. If it'd been Trish up there, there was no way she could do it. She'd tell them to stick the mission right up their asses!

"Laura never talked about the dangers, she only talked about the good things, about the progress being made, about what it was like to help the Afghan people. She told me how humble they were, how thankful. That was what she and I talked about a lot, the helping part, the medical part, and not the fighting. I never wanted to think about that part, and I think Laura knew that. You know, she never forgot about her hometown. She came back here for a few days before her deployment last fall."

Trish remembered how Laura had looked then. Confident and cocky, like the deployment was nothing. But there was a nervous energy about her too. They drove by the old Wright family home on their way to dinner, and Laura was uncharacteristically full of chatter and nostalgia about old times. All through dinner too, she couldn't stop talking about the old days—that championship year she had on the basketball team, her mother's vegetable garden that never seemed to grow anything but weeds, the first time she took her mom's car out alone, the time the two of them had soaped the windows of the home of their most hated teacher. Other, more intimate memories too.

"Jesus, Trish, remember that afternoon we played hooky from school and my mom walked in on us in bed?"

"How could I forget! Oh my God, that had to be my most embarrassing moment in my life ever. Still is! I could never look her in the eye for a long time after that."

Laura laughed so hard there were tears in her eyes. *"Kinda hard to go back in the closet after that. Good thing we didn't even try."*

"Your mom knew all along we were more than just friends."

"Yeah, she probably did. She was pretty cool about it. Much cooler about that than she was about me joining the army. Man. Ever notice she never kept a picture of me in my uniform?"

Laura had grown quiet then. Sad maybe, or just reflective. The conversation moved on to another topic, but Trish sensed that Laura had a bad feeling, a premonition perhaps or maybe some regrets. In any case, she didn't want to talk about it, and neither did Trish. Now she wished they had discussed it, even if it wouldn't have changed the outcome.

"Maybe," Pam was saying, her voice trembling again. "Maybe it was her way of saying goodbye to the place. I guess we'll never know, but I'm glad she had a chance to visit the city one last time, to see some old friends, to think about the old days. Sometimes…memories are the only thing we have left." Pam sniffled, wiped a tear from her cheek. "I'll always have my memories of Laura. She'll always be in my heart." She paused again, closed her eyes, wiped another tear. She was being so damned brave. "She was the best big sister anyone could ever have. I love you, Laura. Thank you."

With that Pam dissolved into a cascade of tears. Instantly Camille sprang to her side, helped guide her down the stage's few steps. Trish rose too, helped Camille escort Pam to a chair in the front row. Pam continued to cry into her wad of Kleenex and Trish slipped her arm around her trembling shoulders. "She loved you too, Pammy. So much."

* * *

It'd been the hardest day of her life, greeting the hundreds of people who'd come to pay their respects, then the speech, then thanking people again at the late lunch. Up to now, she'd thought her mother's funeral had been the toughest day of her life, but that paled in comparison to this. Parents were supposed to die first; sisters weren't, at least not yet. And she hadn't been alone for her mother's funeral. She looked at Trish, lingering as the final group of people prepared to leave. How could she have contemplated doing this without Trish's help? She wanted to ask Trish to accompany her to Arlington for the burial because she couldn't bear the thought of having to sit alone through "Taps," the folding of the flag, watching Laura slip away forever. Her medical training had taught her that when you needed help, when you were struggling, it was important to ask for help.

"You doing okay?" Trish asked quietly.

Pam shrugged and swallowed the words she wanted to say. She knew Trish would come to Arlington if she asked, but it was too much to ask, especially of someone who hadn't been a part of her life and Laura's for such a long time. She didn't want Trish to do it out of pity or guilt.

Camille materialized by their side. A couple of dozen soldiers wanted to head over to the private bar at the American Legion Hall down the street for a drink and an impromptu wake, she informed them. Did she and Trish want to come along? It would mean a lot to the soldiers to have Laura's family there.

Pam felt duty-bound to go, to show solidarity with the soldiers and to thank them for coming. She could also use a drink, but she wouldn't stay past one glass of wine. She wasn't one of them, and she didn't want to be around them if they became rowdy or maudlin. She told Trish she could cab it back to her house if she didn't feel like joining her.

Trish nodded tersely, said she'd see her back at the house. Pam knew that Trish was too angry at the army to sit in a room full of soldiers and socialize with them. Trish's anger and bitterness, the depth of the feelings she still obviously had for Laura, surprised Pam a little. She assumed Trish had moved on a long time ago, but now she wondered if she ever had. She seemed not only single, but completely unattached, completely devoted to her job. She was still young, not even forty. *Too young to be stuck in the past.* The thought saddened her.

Beer flowed like a rampaging river, and so did the stories. The soldiers laughed and cried, talked about Laura and the other comrades they'd lost. Funny stories mostly. Like the time Laura won an impromptu dance contest to a Lady Gaga song, showing moves that even the youngest soldiers didn't have. There'd been a food fight once too, and Laura had gotten them all to stop by suggesting that anyone who didn't leave the dining hall in thirty seconds was going to be signed up to donate blood—that she'd personally drag them off to the lab. (And she would have, they agreed.) They told more serious stories too about how she'd patched them up, made them feel instantly better with her flawless doctoring skills. She could give a needle that felt like little more than a mosquito bite, could stitch a cut without leaving a scar.

Pam sipped her wine, her head reeling. It was good to hear the stories, to see how much Laura was loved and respected. The army was a family, she could see that plainly. But the uniforms, the obvious world she wasn't a part of, reminded her of how drastically Laura's path had diverged from her own. They were both doctors, both gay, shared the same DNA, but really, they'd not had much else in common over the last few years. Their personalities were vastly different. Where Laura was adventurous, Pam was cautious. Where Laura was happy to go wherever the wind blew her, Pam was a planner, a planter of roots. And yet there'd been a strong sisterly bond between them—one they didn't have to talk about or nourish. It was just there.

"I should have known. I should have felt something," Pam said despairingly to Camille, who was sitting next to her, nursing a warm glass of beer.

"Should have known what?"

"That something had happened to her. You know, when she died. I should have *felt* it."

"It's okay," Camille soothed. "She wasn't alone, and that was the main thing."

"Did she…" Pam took a deep breath to calm herself. She hadn't wanted to know the details before, but now she did. Some of them, at least. When she was first given the news, part of the denial was to block out the details of Laura's death. That it would be less real if she didn't know the details. But it was real, and she couldn't accept it until she knew what had happened. "Did she suffer?"

"No, she didn't. A broken neck. But there was other damage. From the impact. A lot of broken bones. It was instant."

Okay, so it'd been fast. She probably hadn't known what hit her, though she'd have known the helicopter was going down. She wondered what Laura's last thoughts had been, what had been playing through her mind as the chopper scissored to the earth. Probably she just hoped to survive and for the others to survive as well. Or maybe there'd been a moment of resignation, of quiet acceptance that it probably wasn't going to turn out well.

Gently, Camille told her more about the crash, about the attempts to resuscitate Laura and then the careful transport of her body in all the stages of bringing her home. She told her how, the next morning after the crash, an Afghan family Laura had once helped showed up at the gates of the base, mourning Laura.

"They gave me something, something they wanted the family to have." From her pocket she pulled out a beaded bracelet in colors of orange and red and gold. "They said that because of her, their daughter would live to see many more sunsets."

"It's beautiful!" Pam slipped it over her left wrist and held it toward the dim ceiling lights. This was better than a medal because this was from someone Laura had helped and meant something to. Yes, it was much more personal than a medal and much more rewarding. Tears brimmed over. "Thank you, Camille. And if you ever see them again…"

"I probably won't, but I understand."

"I wish I knew more about what Laura was doing over there. She didn't say a lot about it, but I want to try to understand." *I need to understand*, she added to herself, *because if I don't, I will always resent her sacrifice.*

"She was keeping a journal over there. Said she'd always meant to keep a journal the other times she was deployed, but she hadn't until this time."

"Do you think she knew it might be the last time? That she wouldn't be coming home?"

"She never said anything like that to me. If any of us ever feels that way—and we do—we don't talk about it. It's like a disease you don't want to spread to others. You don't want to show your fear or any negativity. You don't want anything to become a self-fulfilling prophesy."

"This journal. Where is it?"

"It's with her possessions. It will be shipped to you from the base. It'll probably take a month or so."

Just as well, Pam thought. Maybe by then she'd be strong enough to read it.

"I have her letter," Camille said softly, reaching into her pocket but not removing it until Pam nodded.

Pam accepted the plain white, sealed envelope, its corners curled, and stuffed it in her coat pocket. She didn't want to think about it right now and she certainly didn't want to read it in front of these strangers. She suddenly needed to get out of here, away from the laughter and the crisp uniforms and the eyes that had seen far too much in their young lives.

Camille said she understood and told her a car would be around to pick her up first thing in the morning for the trip to the airport.

On the cab ride to Trish's, Pam considered the news that Laura had been keeping a journal. What had she written about the mission? Did she only list the things she was doing on a daily basis or did she write down her thoughts? Her opinions? Did the journal explain what drove her to live such a nomadic but extremely risky lifestyle? There was something lonely about the idea of never setting down roots, yet Pam was lonely too, and she wasn't living a nomadic life.

She had never meant for her life to be this solitary, had always been quick to blame her aloneness on her busy life as a medical student and now a resident. She'd assumed Laura lived a fairly solitary life too, but what did she know? Laura probably had lots of friends, lots of lovers, people and an existence Pam knew nothing about. A rich and full life, perhaps, and one that was so different from Pam's that Laura had decided not to share much of it with her all these years.

"I didn't know her," Pam whispered into the hug Trish gave her at the door upon her arrival. "And I can't stand that thought."

"Nonsense. You knew her better than anyone." Trish settled her on the sofa and retrieved two glasses of wine, bringing the bottle with her and setting it on the coffee table.

"No. You knew her better than I ever did. Better than anyone, probably."

Trish snorted. "Sleeping with someone doesn't necessarily mean you know them."

That was true. Pam had slept with a total of four people in her life, none of whom she could say she knew very well.

"I remember thinking," Trish continued after a long sip of her wine, "a long time ago, that Laura wanted a life with me.

That the army was just a means to an end. But I was wrong. When she chose the army over me, I realized I hadn't known her as well as I thought."

"Maybe it wasn't that simple. Maybe Laura hoped she could have both you and a life in the army."

"If she did, she was naive. I could never have lived with the don't-ask-don't-tell mentality—keeping our relationship a secret. It would have been impossible to go back to the closet after being out in our senior year in high school, then college." Trish stared at her glass for the longest time. The gravity of their shared sadness was heavy and ominous, like the loud ticking of the antique clock on the mantel.

"You never got over her, did you?"

Trish shook her head. She began to cry softly, and the fact that she didn't try to stop her tears honored Pam. *When everyone else is gone, give me your tears*, Pam thought, remembering fragments of a poem. Their tears were safe with one another.

It was obvious Trish still loved Laura, had never stopped being in love with her. "Oh God, I'm sorry," was all Pam could say. She'd been so overwhelmed by her own grief that she hadn't realized the extent of Trish's pain until now. She put her arms around Trish and pressed her against her, absorbing her sobs, letting her tears stain her blouse. She'd never known that kind of love before, but Trish obviously had, and she was suffering for it now.

She stroked Trish's head, the soft brown waves of her hair silky between her fingers. Trish always did have the nicest hair, naturally wavy, just below her collar these days, still so soft and luxurious. Pam couldn't help but inhale the lemon and mint scent of her shampoo, remembering a time when she'd been a kid, sick in bed with strep throat, and Trish had rubbed her back and read her a bedtime story. She remembered at the time how Trish smelled like all things good and comforting. Like love. Like home. She still smelled of those things.

"I'm sorry," Trish finally said, pulling away and refilling their glasses. "You must think I'm incredibly emotionally stunted. Stuck in time or something. How pathetic."

"No, not pathetic. I'm jealous."

"You are?"

Oops. She hadn't quite meant to say it like that. She knew her face was growing warm and not just from the wine. "Who wouldn't be jealous of that kind of love? I mean, to be able to love someone so deeply."

"So you haven't?"

"Nope." The fact that she'd never been in love had never much bothered her before, but it did now.

"Come on, be serious."

"I am, unfortunately."

Trish seemed to contemplate this. At least the change in topic had put an end to her tears. "But surely you must have had plenty of girlfriends over the years."

Pam laughed bitterly. "Yeah, right. What makes you think that?"

"Like, duh, Pam, you're only gorgeous and smart and successful. Women must be tripping over themselves to get to you."

"Well, if they are, they're not being very obvious about it."

Trish sipped more wine, her eyes sparking. "More like you're not noticing, would be my guess."

Pam could play this little game. "If anyone should have women lined up around the block, it should be you, babe." Okay, so she was getting a little drunk, but it felt good to speak her mind.

"Well, now *that* is some little fantasy. I haven't even had a date in almost two years."

"What?" Trish had to be kidding. Hell, if Trish had been her teacher back in high school, she'd have gotten into *big* trouble. "Now you're just messing with me."

"No, sadly I'm not."

Pam finished her glass of wine and grew bolder. "Is it because of Laura? Because you never got over her?"

Trish shrugged, refilled their glasses. "Maybe, I don't know. That's what Rosa says."

"Who's Rosa?"

"My best friend. Actually, she's the last woman I dated."

"You're best friends with the last woman you dated?"

"Yup. Tried dating for over a year, but she swore I just wasn't into her, and she was right, I guess. We stayed friends. She swears I just won't give anyone else the chance to even compare to Laura. Pretty pathetic, don't you think?"

"Hell no. I'll tell you what pathetic is. Pathetic is never having a relationship that lasts more than a few months. Never finding anyone that even *remotely* stirs my heart. I kind of got to the point where I figure there's no point in even trying anymore."

"Oh, Pam, you have to at least try. Love visits all of us eventually. I just happened to have had it early on in my life. The bitch of it is knowing what love can be like and then never finding it again. Guess Laura kind of ruined me."

Okay, now she was really getting drunk, but what the hell. She'd never have a moment like this with Trish again. She grinned, mischief and bravery bubbling up in her blood. "Well, Laura may have ruined you, but *you* ruined me, Trish Tomlinson."

Trish, glassy-eyed from her own inebriation, eyed Pam speculatively. "What?"

"Yup. Ruined this young teenaged heart. From the time I was ten until..." *Crap*. Okay maybe there was no end date, no shelf life to this silly childhood crush, but she couldn't tell Trish that. And the crush truly was silly. Completely baseless. And juvenile. "God, I don't know, until you and Laura broke up, I had the biggest killer crush on you."

"You did?"

"Yup. I would have jumped off cliffs for you. Got kicked out of math class once for doodling your name in my notebook. Don't tell me you never figured it out."

Trish looked pleased—*thank goodness*—and not all condemning or grossed out. "Okay, I sort of figured you did. You *were* a bit puppy-like around me."

"A bit! Jesus. You were so sweet, you didn't even try to swat me away. I mean, how did you ever stand it?"

"It was cute, actually. I was flattered. I'm even more flattered now to know I could have been your Mrs. Robinson." Trish giggled and waggled her eyebrows.

Pam laughed too, picturing the scene from *The Graduate* where Mrs. Robinson bares her breasts to the young Benjamin and propositions him. "You're not going to take me upstairs and whip your shirt off, are you?" She cringed a little after the words were out, her boldness shocking her a little.

There was a twinkle in Trish's eyes as she said, "I suppose you would have liked that fifteen years ago, hmm?"

No, that's where you're wrong. I would have liked it a lot more recently than that. "Yes, I definitely would have liked that very much."

As quickly as they'd risen, Pam's spirits began to plummet. Trish belonged to Laura—always had, always would, even in death. She'd learned long ago never to compete with Laura beyond following her to medical school. Laura bested her at everything, including with women. She sighed heavily. "So here we are, our hearts forever engraved by someone we can never have."

"Oh, Pam." Trish reached out and cupped her cheek. Her touch was so tender, so full of understanding and kindness. Pam nuzzled into it, closed her eyes, wanted to cry, wanted to kiss those lovely fingers.

Trish was so close that Pam could feel her breath on her cheek. She was afraid to open her eyes, afraid of what she might see in Trish's eyes. She wasn't sure what would be worse, seeing rejection or seeing mutual attraction. No, she decided. No good could come of either scenario. She told herself it was only their emotions getting the best of them, their grief and nostalgia uniting them.

"Trish," Pam whispered, knowing if she didn't ask now, she never would. "Will you do something for me?"

"Of course. Anything."

Pam opened her eyes. *Oh God.* Trish looked at her with so much affection, so much kindness and generosity...all the things that had always cemented her little crush on her. She swallowed hard and pressed on before she lost her courage. "Will you come to Arlington with me? For Laura's funeral?"

Trish's eyes slammed shut, her face a mask of anguish.

Oh shit, I shouldn't have asked. It's too much.

"Y-yes," Trish answered haltingly. "I-I would be happy to go with you."

"You sure?"

"Yes." Trish tried to smile, but the effort fell flat. "We'll say goodbye to her together. It feels like the right thing to do."

"Thank you," Pam replied, knowing Laura would like the idea of them saying goodbye together.

Suddenly, Pam was exhausted. It was as though every part of her body craved sleep, and she could no longer keep her eyes open.

Wordlessly, she slid down and rested her head in Trish's lap. She'd just lie down for a moment, doze for a bit. She closed her eyes and felt Trish's hand smoothing the hair from her forehead, stroking her softly. She knew sleep was imminent.

CHAPTER SIX

Camille looked exactly like the kind of woman Laura might be interested in sexually, and as the three of them were driven in a limousine to the airport, Trish wondered if Camille and Laura had ever been lovers. The thought hurt a little. It wasn't the sex part that felt hurtful. Laura had undoubtedly had many lovers since they'd parted, and Trish had had a few herself. It was Laura's time, Laura's nearness, Laura's heart that she'd missed the most, that she remained jealous of. In what quantity had Camille shared those things with her? How much time had they shared? How much a part of Laura's life had she been? Had they shared laughter, tears, memories?

Camille wasn't giving anything away. She was clearly emotional and upset about Laura's death, but she was stoic too. She was young, closer to Pam's age.

Trish found her voice and interrupted the brooding silence. "What was she like over there? In Afghanistan?"

Camille's dark eyes snapped to her, serious and slightly suspicious. "Laura? How do you mean?"

"I mean…" Trish continued, not really sure at all what she meant. "I don't know. Did she like being there? What was her mood? Was she anxious to finish her tour?" She had imagined all kinds of things about Laura there—that she hated it and couldn't wait to leave, that she loved it and wanted to stay forever. She had no idea.

Camille paused, her eyes softening. "All of us have moments of loving it *and* hating it there. It's complicated. It can be frustrating and rewarding, all in a matter of minutes. You kind of get to a place where you appreciate the roller coaster or at least learn to live with it. But mostly, you come to live in the moment. Take things an hour, a day at a time. Sometimes a minute at a time."

"She wrote a journal over there," Pam said to Trish. "I'm not sure if I'll be able to read it."

"I understand," Trish replied. She'd read it in a flash if given the chance. She wanted to know the things that had gone through Laura's mind, because maybe then she could *finally* understand what drove Laura to stay in the army all these years. Maybe it would tell her why Laura had chosen that life over a life with her.

"You…would you like to read it?" Pam said, a streak of surprise in her voice.

"Yes, I would."

"But it'd be so hard…"

"I know. But I feel like I don't really know the person Laura became these last few years."

Pam blinked her understanding. "Yes. Laura wasn't the person she used to be when you two…you know. I'm not even sure how well I knew her over the last while."

Trish expelled a long held breath. She had no confidence now that she'd ever really known Laura. And maybe if she could understand, could come to know the woman Laura had become, she could let go of those juvenile notions that a part of Laura had always stayed with her. That they both had remained those two teenagers in love.

"The journal," Pam continued. "When it comes, I'd like you to read it."

"Thank you. I'd like that."

Pam turned away to peer through the dark glass, lost in her own thoughts. Trish wanted to ask Camille more, like had Laura ever talked about returning to civilian life, had she ever talked about her dreams, her desires? But both Camille and Pam were being quiet, distant, and she didn't want to intrude.

She looked at Pam's silhouette and thought how vulnerability did not suit her. She had a piercingly confident gaze, a determined set to her jaw, a physical strength in her long, tight body. Her hands looked and felt strong and capable—they were hands that healed people. Yet grief had peeled those strengths away to reveal her vulnerability, her fear, her aloneness. Her skin and eyes were dull. Her body, thin and a bit too angular, slumped in weariness. Her handshake, her hugs, were half-hearted, as though her body had surrendered itself to being crushed, bulldozed, overpowered.

As difficult as all this was for Trish, it had to be much harder for Pam, she decided. She reached for Pam's hand on the seat between them and squeezed it lightly. "Okay?"

"Okay," Pam whispered, still gazing out the window.

They would be okay again, wouldn't they? Trish wondered.

* * *

Arlington, Virginia, was bursting with fragrant apple and cherry blossoms of pink and white and grass that seemed greener and lusher than any Pam had ever seen. The season was at least a month or two ahead of Chicago's or Ann Arbor's. If only she were here for a different reason, she could enjoy it, she thought. But there were reminders everywhere of the grim reason for their presence. Flags were at half-mast everywhere she looked, as though death were a constant, daily occurrence. Soldiers in uniform walked the streets of D.C. There was a war on, and the signs of it were everywhere.

Trish had understood her need for space last night, as Pam secluded herself in her hotel room, ordered room service, took a long bath and then downed a lorazepam with orange juice to help her sleep. She wasn't one of those purist doctors who believed in natural remedies at the expense of pharmaceuticals, nor by contrast was she a pill pusher. Pills of any kind were rare for her to take, but she needed sleep or she would never be able to get through the emotional grind of Laura's funeral.

Now as she and Trish were driven to Arlington National Cemetery, she noticed for the first time that they were dressed nearly identically—black knee-length dresses, plain black pumps, a lilac-colored silk scarf around Trish's throat, a dove gray sweater over Pam's shoulders. Trish looked the part of the grieving wife, Pam the mourning family.

She clutched the small black purse to her stomach in the backseat as the limo approached the gates to the park. The letter—Laura's official goodbye letter—was in the purse, the envelope still sealed, its corners slightly mangled from the trip. She'd not had the courage to open it yet. Hell, maybe she'd never open it. Maybe she'd fling it into the hole with the casket.

"You doing okay?" Trish whispered.

No, she wasn't, but what was she supposed to say? "I'm okay. You?"

Trish sighed. "I don't know, but I'm here, and we'll get through this, okay?"

The meandering drive around manicured, hilly lawns and perfectly shaped trees seemed to go on forever, and around each curve, Pam's insides knotted tighter. She caught glimpses of rows upon rows of white tombstones, all perfectly symmetrical. One of those headstones would soon bear Laura's name. She'd never given any thought to the national military cemetery before, where the dead from all five branches of the armed services were buried. Of course, the Kennedy brothers were buried here, and she'd seen the eternal flame on television before. It never occurred to her that she would one day have a reason to visit this place.

The limo coasted to a stop. *This is it*, she thought, as the door opened and she and Trish stepped out into the air fragrant with blossoms. Her knees weakened for a moment as she caught sight of a four-man color guard standing at attention. Her gaze swung to the escort platoon across the road in front of them, waiting stiffly, their arms like rods at their sides.

"You can stand just over there," Camille said, pointing a short distance away. "I'll stand with you, okay?"

"What happens next?" Trish asked in an uncertain voice. They'd gone over everything earlier, but in her nervousness, she had tuned it out.

"The caisson will bring the casket," Camille said matter-of-factly. "The escort platoon will move out shortly and pick up the caisson, escort it here. The honor guard will carry the casket over there." She pointed to a roped off area where a couple of dozen people milled about, standing in front of chairs. "There will be the flag folding, the rifle volley, the last salute."

Jesus, Pam thought, nervous suddenly. It was all happening so fast. An order was barked, echoing like a rifle shot into the vast sky. The platoon, in their dress blues, marched smartly down the road, their polished shoes tapping the pavement in sync with each step. And then they were coming toward them, marching a funereal march that reminded Pam of how one walked up the wedding aisle, methodically and slowly, a slight dragging motion. As they drew nearer, she spotted the two beautiful white horses behind them bearing a black-shrouded caisson topped with Laura's flag-draped casket. The wheels creaked, the horses snorted in what was otherwise near silence.

It was beautiful, she thought on an intake of breath. Absolutely beautiful.

She gasped again as the riderless horse, boots backward, followed the casket. It reared its head a little, clearly not enjoying the absence of a rider. A calm soldier with sergeant's stripes handled the horse's bridle, never breaking his stride.

They're so damned good at this, Pam thought. *Too good. Too many damned funerals like this one.*

More orders were barked as the procession crisply halted in front of them.

"I'll take you to your seats now," Camille said, inserting herself between the two women and giving them each her arm.

The rest of the funeral was a blur. An army padre spoke, then a colonel. Pam sat stoically in the hard chair, staring straight ahead, her gloved hands folded neatly in her lap. She managed to keep the tears at bay by trying to distance herself a little, by trying to stay a little outside of herself. It was the same tactic she used in particularly gory cases in her trauma room at the hospital. Crushed heads, beaten bodies, an accidental leg amputation from an equipment malfunction at a meat factory. She dealt with them by shifting to a different place in her mind, a place that was almost unreal—where anything that happened while she was in that place wasn't really real.

She felt Trish flinch beside her as the seven firing squad soldiers fired their twenty-one volleys. Eight soldiers stood erectly beside the casket, facing one another, as the flag was lifted from it and folded in rapid, exaggerated movements. She didn't cry as it was presented to her, but Trish was furiously wiping away tears. Not even the playing of "Taps" got to her... she'd somehow managed to steel herself against that. It was the last salute that broke down her final barrier. The dozens of soldiers raised their hands all at the same time in that slow salute of mourning she'd also seen them do at the funeral home. Three seconds up, three seconds hold, three seconds down. It was the last time anyone would ever salute Major Laura Wright again, and it broke her heart.

Pam cried, didn't try to hold the tide of emotions back. She felt Trish's arm tighten around her waist as they stood. Someone had pressed a rose into each woman's hands. Trish stepped away, stood alone at Laura's casket for a moment, then carefully placed the red rose on top of it. Pam did the same, whispering to herself, *I wish I'd known you better, big sister. I wish you were still here. I will miss you for the rest of my life.* She placed the rose on the casket, felt herself shrink and wilt until Camille clutched her elbow to prop her up.

"Pamela Wright?"

A woman in army blues, crutches beneath her arms and a cast on her right leg, hobbled up to Pam.

"Yes?"

"Lynn Stonewick. May I have a word?"

She'd leaned on her crutch so that she could stick out her hand. There was something pleading in her eyes. Clearly, she didn't want to be hurried.

"Sure," Pam replied, leading them a few feet away for privacy.

Trish hovered, never more than an arm's length away. It occurred to Pam that she didn't mind Trish's protectiveness, which came as a surprise. Fiercely independent, she typically liked to handle her issues alone. But this...this was too much for one person. She knew with certainty she would be buckling under the weight of Laura's death right now if not for Trish.

"Your sister. Major Wright. I...I was in the helicopter with her when it crashed."

"Oh God." She hadn't meant to say the words out loud.

"I'm sorry," the young woman muttered, and Pam wondered if she meant she was sorry she survived, sorry Laura died or sorry for bringing up the crash.

"Why?" Pam whispered, her thoughts racing feverishly. "Why did it crash?" What she really meant was, why hadn't Laura survived? Why had Lynn survived and not Laura?

"I don't know," the woman uttered, gulping uncomfortably. "There was a sand storm. We couldn't see the ground. We couldn't see anything. It just happened so quickly. But I wanted you to know she wasn't alone. You know, when it happened. We tried to help her."

From her peripheral vision, Pam caught Trish shooting daggers at the soldier.

"Come on," Trish urged gently, her hand slipping into Pam's to steer her away.

Pam let herself be guided back to the limo, all the while cognizant of the young soldier leaning on her crutches, silently, sadly, watching them.

"You know," Camille said pointedly to Trish beside the car. "Laura and I, we weren't...you know."

"Okay," Trish answered. "But you didn't have to..."

"Yes, I did. You're still in love with her, aren't you?"

"Does it show that much?"

"Yes, and it's okay. Everyone deserves to be loved that much."

"Did she, you know, ever mention me?"

Camille looked puzzled. "She mentioned you all the time, but she would never really *talk* about you. Do you know what I mean?"

Pam nodded, knowing exactly what Camille meant. It was Laura to a tee. She'd often mention Trish's name to Pam over the years, talk about some of the things they had done when they were together, but she never talked about her heart, about how she felt about Trish then or maybe still felt. Whether she regretted how things had turned out between them.

Too bad, Pam thought as she and Trish climbed into the back of the limo. If Laura had opened her heart to Trish these last few years, told her how she really felt, maybe things would have been different. Maybe they'd have reunited, maybe Trish would have been able to talk Laura into leaving the army. She felt her chest clench at the thought, because she knew in her heart that the army would always have been a contentious issue between the two of them, that Laura would never have quit the army for Trish.

"Driver," Pam said, not thinking about Laura's final letter until this very moment. "Please take us to a quiet part of the cemetery for a moment."

Again they drove past the endless rows of white tombstones, beneath the silence and the shade of the massive trees. At the top of a knoll overlooking the city, Pam asked the driver to let them out. She waited for Trish to join her on a white stone bench.

"I never thought I'd say this," Trish said, "but it's beautiful here. And so peaceful. I'm glad Laura wanted to be buried here."

Pam opened her purse and pulled out the sealed letter before she changed her mind. "I don't want to do this alone. It's her final letter."

"Oh, Pam, I'm so sorry."

Laura's handwriting had always been so neat, so undoctor-like—the opposite of her own illegible hieroglyphs. Her heart pounded, producing a tremble in her hand as she began to read.

Dear Pam,

If you are reading this, I am so very sorry. You have to believe I never meant to hurt you or cause you grief.

Please understand why I chose the path I did. It's what I needed to do, Pam. It was what I was meant to do. Maybe it will never be worth it—that is not for me to judge anymore. It is not for anyone to judge. It is what it is. I know I have done a lot of good with my life, and really, what else is there when all is said and done? To say that is not to diminish my sacrifices or anyone else's in this life I chose. I know what I gave up. I know what my heart is missing because of my choices.

Pam, out of everyone else in the whole world, I would still have chosen you as my sister. You are the best! You're a wonderful, talented, smart woman—smarter than I could ever be. I know you will have a happy life. Or at least you'd better, or I will never forgive you! My wish for you is that you be happy, and that you find someone to be happy with. Don't go through this life without the love of a good woman, okay?

I know we will see each other again. Until then…

Love you always,

Laura

It still didn't explain anything. Didn't explain why she chose work over love, why the army had been enough for her. Or had it? There was a hint of regret, wasn't there? And why couldn't she say Trish's name? Why could she never honestly talk about Trish, what they had and what they'd thrown away for the sake of her joining the army? Was it a failure so profound that she could never speak of it again? *And why is it so important to you that I not go through life alone, huh? No, Laura, it doesn't work that way. You can't wish for me the things you didn't have the courage and commitment to do yourself.*

She folded the sheet of paper in clipped movements and wordlessly handed it to Trish. *It doesn't explain anything*, she kept thinking. *It doesn't explain a damned thing.*

Trish read the letter with pursed lips before silently handing it back to Pam.

"We couldn't have saved her from the army, Pam. I'm not sure I really understood that before now."

"She never wanted to be saved from anything."

Abruptly Pam stood and took one last look at the distant city below. She felt anger rising like a slow, steady geyser inside. How could you save someone who had never wanted to be saved?

CHAPTER SEVEN

Trish swam until her quivering arms could no longer propel her forward.

Her friend and one-time lover, Rosa Moran, urged her on from the lane beside her. "Come on. One more, my friend. You said yourself you were in for a little self-flagellation today."

Trish smiled and clung to the edge of the pool. Rosa's vocabulary was so much richer than her own. "I said I was feeling a little masochistic today. I didn't say anything about self-flagellation."

"You're not going to wimp out on me now, are you?"

"God, yes. I'm going to drown if I don't stop."

Rosa, a fitness buff addicted to triathlons, followed Trish out of the pool. She'd probably have stayed and swum another dozen lengths if only Trish weren't pooped, but trying to match Rosa in the fitness department was one of those things, like suddenly becoming a world traveler or spontaneously moving to one of the coasts, that was never going to happen to Trish. She was in decent shape, loved to swim and walk and bike, but she had no intention of killing herself with exercise or doing something as outrageous as entering a triathlon. *Talk about self-flagellation!*

They wrapped themselves in plush towels and padded to the locker room. Rosa had stuck close to Trish the last three weeks. Ever since Laura's funeral. Today was the first time Rosa had been able to get her out of the house for a reason other than work.

"That was a very commendable twenty-five laps," Rosa said as they changed into their clothes.

"Please." Trish hated to be babied, and Rosa was babying her big-time. "It was a crap attempt and you know it."

Rosa smirked. "You're an English teacher. Surely you can do better than 'crap.'"

That produced a chuckle from Trish. "It sucked. How's that?"

Rosa shook her head. "All right. Fine. But cut yourself a little slack, would you? It's okay, you know."

She placed her hand meaningfully on Trish's arm, and the gesture nearly brought Trish to tears. Rosa and, of course, Pam were the only people who understood the depth of what Laura had meant to her, how desolate and carved out Laura's death now made her feel.

Later, at a table for two at the nearby Starbucks, Trish looked frankly at her friend, and said, "I feel so…so…*excavated*."

"Excavated. I like that word."

Rosa was a fiction writer and a creative writing professor at the U of M. She loved it when people presented unusual words to describe the way they were feeling. Or to describe anything, for that matter. In fact, it was a weird hobby of hers to walk down the street or sit in a restaurant with a piece of paper in her hand, a pen in the other, and write down all the words she could think of to describe what she was seeing around her. Thankfully, she wasn't doing that now.

"I shouldn't, I know…"

Many times, during the eighteen months they'd been lovers, Rosa had scolded Trish for the intensity of her feelings toward Laura. Not only were those feelings getting in the way of their relationship—hell, they were a relationship of three, Rosa told her numerous times—but they were getting in the way of Trish living her life. Of Trish being happy. "You can't spend the rest of your life wishing for something you can't have," Rosa often lectured her in frustration, with Trish readily replying in anger, "I can if I want—it's my life." Things went quickly downhill for them after a couple of those epic battles.

"*Shouldn't* doesn't mean you don't feel like shit about what happened."

Trish raised her eyebrows at the word "shit."

"Oh, all right. 'Bereft,' then. 'Aggrieved.' 'Disconsolate.'"

"I was thinking more like 'wounded.'"

Yes, that was it exactly. She had a gaping wound in her heart that would not heal. Okay, she'd had a bruised heart over Laura for longer than she could remember. But now it was a gaping, mortal wound, as though her heart had been flayed open. This was a much deeper and, of course, permanent form of losing Laura.

"I'm sorry, Trish. I was so jealous of her when you and I were together. I think I almost hated her. And I'm sorry for that. And I'm sorry she died. And I'm so sorry you're going through this."

"Thank you for saying that." Trish took a swallow of the too-hot coffee to melt the lump in her throat. She knew Rosa meant it, but Trish couldn't be sure Rosa was capable of truly understanding what she'd lost. "Sometimes I'm sorry I ever loved someone so much, because I feel like I'll never be able to love anyone else that much again. I always suspected as much, but now it feels like a truth."

"It's not a truth, it's an assumption, and a poor one. I think you will love again, and the only reason you haven't is because of the great big roadblock you always unceremoniously deposit into the middle of a new relationship. The one complete with signs. 'Rough Road Ahead,' or, 'Be Prepared To Stop.'"

They'd had this argument many times since their dates and lovemaking detoured to friendship. She knew intellectually that Rosa was right, that she'd never get past Laura if she never really tried. That it was entirely up to her whether she allowed herself to move on or not. Now, however, while the pain of Laura's loss was so fresh, she didn't want to think about what getting past Laura might mean. She didn't want to get past her, not right now. No. Right now she wanted to feel every inch of the razor-sharp pain, because that meant that in some way Laura still existed. At least in her heart if nowhere else.

Trish sighed. "Part of me knows you're right, but right now I can't even consider not loving Laura. It would feel disrespectful, disloyal."

"Oh, you'll always love her. Trust me on that one. But the human heart has an infinite capacity for love. You have a lot more room in there than for just Laura. And really, honey, is it fair to Laura, to what you two had together, to let it paralyze you forever? Especially now?"

Tears hovered below the surface, like distant storm clouds that threatened to dump their torrent. Trish couldn't talk about letting go, not yet. She'd held on to Laura for so long, it was as though she were a permanent part of her now.

Rosa seemed to sense Trish's silent objection and changed the subject. "How's the sister doing? Pam? Have you heard from her since the funeral?"

She'd heard from Pam a few times. They'd fallen into a loose habit of checking in with one another every couple of days, either by text or email. "I think she's trying to put one foot in front of the other, get through the days. It's hard. She's the only one left in her family now."

"What's she like?" Rosa's blue eyes were piercing, like those of an eagle. It was disconcerting sometimes, as though she could read a person's thoughts through that mind-stripping gaze of hers. "You've never said much about her."

True. She'd hardly ever mentioned Pam in the handful of years Trish and Rosa had known one another. There'd never really been a reason to until now. She'd not often thought about Pam, other than during her mother's illness and death six years ago and in the occasional polite inquiry she'd pose to Laura the few times they'd emailed or talked on the phone. How things had changed. Now she thought about Pam constantly, about how she was doing, about what she was doing, about whether she was okay.

"She's nice. She's a good kid," Trish said with a shrug.

"Kid?" Those eyes lasered her over the rim of a tall latte. "Surely she's not a child *now*."

"No, of course not. She's thirty or so. She's a trauma physician in Chicago. And yes, she's gay, since I'm sure that was going to be your next question."

"Chip off big sister's block, eh?" Rosa was Canadian.

"Yes and no. She's never had any desire to join the armed forces or to go save the world." She knew she sounded bitter about Laura's career, was belittling Laura's choices. And Rosa was smart enough to realize it too.

"Ah, so Laura got to keep her title as saint of the family, eh?"

"Do you always have to be so blunt?" She wasn't criticizing. Sometimes bluntness was a good thing.

"I'm a writer. I don't have time for evasiveness or avoidance tactics."

"Anyway, I'm not sure I'd agree about the saint part. Pam put her career on hold to look after their mother while she was dying of cancer a few years ago." Laura did a good job of looking the hero in that splendid uniform of hers, but Pam was no less valiant. *I should tell her that some time.*

Rosa held up her cup in salute. "Well, well. No wonder those Wright women are so easy to fall for."

Trish puzzled at Rosa's words. *Fall for?* Yes, she'd fallen for Laura a long time ago, but not Pam. To her, Pam would always be that cute, adorable kid who trailed after them, all wide-eyed and in search of her own identity.

"Oh, Rosa, you're always trying to incite some kind of reaction from me, aren't you?"

"Nothing doing. Just keeping you honest, my dear."

"Whatever."

Rosa, she realized, was one of the few people in her life who'd ever given her complete honesty, even if it sometimes pissed her off. Pam, too, had given her nothing but honesty. Trish recalled their recent and somewhat inebriated conversation about Pam's lifelong crush on her—a crush she'd not necessarily outgrown, if Trish had read between the lines correctly. It was flattering that such a beautiful woman was attracted to her, but it wasn't real, wasn't substantial in any way. It was simply an extension of affectionate, youthful feelings brought to the surface by shared grief. Emotions had been running through them both like stock cars on a NASCAR track since Laura's death.

Trish's cell phone rang its text alarm from inside her knapsack.

"Go ahead. Answer it." Rosa smiled, cat-like, as though daring her.

"I don't want to be rude."

"No worries. I need to go to the washroom anyway."

Trish pulled out her phone. It was Pam.

Should I do it?

Do what? she texted back.

Go on a date with Connie. She's been bugging me 4evr. I have her on hold.

Trish laughed to herself. It was as though she were Pam's big sister now.

Yes, she texted back. *Go for it, lol.*

There, she told herself as she tucked her phone away. *I hope Pam has a glorious date with this woman. See, Rosa? You're being ridiculous. I am not falling for Pam. Or anyone else!*

* * *

Pam sipped her wine with as much enthusiasm as a fly and wondered if she was doing the right thing. She was still numb, had trouble concentrating, forgot things easily. Had barely the energy to get out the door each day. She'd only been back to work a week, although she could hardly call it "work," since they were giving her only easy cases in the ER, cases that a fourth-year medical student could more than handle—sprained wrists, sore throats, cuts to suture. Even those took all her mental and physical energy. She'd burst into tears the other day reviewing a simple blood test because the patient had the same blood type—B positive—as Laura.

She kept revisiting the day the two army notification officers had shown up at her door, how their horrible message had changed her life forever. It had instantly vaulted her into this new and strange reality of life without Laura that she could not adjust to. She didn't know how to do so, or if it was even possible. Intellectually, she knew she had to try, if for no other reason than she hated living this way, as though she were a ghost moving invisibly, unable to feel.

Two days ago she'd gathered her courage—or perhaps it was more like ignoring her head—and finally acquiesced to the persistent Connie. If nothing else, it would be a diversion, she figured. Now they were on a date, and Pam couldn't decide whether it was a terrible mistake or if there was still a sliver of hope of salvaging the evening.

"My last girlfriend, Dawn. She drank the same Valpolicella as you."

"Oh," Pam said dumbly. What was she supposed to say to a statement like that? *Sorry I remind you of someone you're no longer with?*

"Yeah, she liked it a little too much. Not as much as Ginny liked her gin and tonics though." Connie laughed in a shrill voice that reminded Pam of nails on a chalkboard. "Guess her name suited her, huh?"

Be nice, Pam told herself. She bit her bottom lip and tried. Really tried. But she couldn't quite pull it off. "So you're telling me you only date alcoholics?"

Connie's face reddened, and Pam instantly regretted her sarcasm.

"Sorry," Pam muttered. "I didn't mean that the way it sounded."

Actually I did, but I shouldn't have said it.

The nails on a chalkboard screeched again. "No, that was pretty funny, actually. You're not one, are you?"

"What?"

"An alcoholic?"

No, but I might become one if I stayed with you for any length of time.

"Ah, no. And I don't smoke or do drugs. And I don't leave my dirty clothes on the floor, but I do sometimes skip washing the dishes for a couple of days."

"You're funny, I like that. And you sound like a keeper to me," Connie slipped her a flirtatious wink. "What do you like for breakfast?"

"Huh? Oh." Pam knew she was blushing furiously as she finally grasped the underlying meaning of Connie's question.

Connie popped an olive in her mouth and began sucking on it in a way that Pam guessed was supposed to be sexy. The truth was, it made her want to throw up.

"You know," Connie said around the olive she was now munching, "we could skip dinner and make our breakfast plans. For tomorrow morning."

Oh God, what am I doing here? Pam asked herself for about the ninth time tonight. Connie was cute with her twinkling blue eyes and trim little figure and her come-on smile. But Pam didn't want to sleep with her. Didn't want to keep making benign conversation with her that should have been easy but was as hard as pulling roots from dry ground. *This is painful,* Pam thought. She did not want to be here.

Reflexively Pam began rubbing her temple. "I hate to do this, Connie, but I feel a terrible headache coming on."

"Oh, no. Look, our food will be here any minute. I'm sure that's all it is."

"No, I don't think so. It feels more like a migraine starting."

"I'm sorry. I hope it's not anything I said?"

"No, no, not at all," Pam lied. "I just…don't think I can do this right now."

Connie reached across the table and lightly touched Pam's fingers, and Pam resisted the urge to pull her hand away. "Is it because of your sister's death?"

Oh, God, Pam thought. *Not this again.* Connie had been trying to engage her in conversation about Laura for days, either on the phone or by email. Trying to do her social worker bit on her. The only person Pam wanted to talk with about Laura was Trish.

"Look, I'm sorry," Pam said impatiently, rising so quickly from her chair that it wobbled precariously. "I think I need to go."

"Let me walk you to your car."

Thankfully they'd driven their own cars to the restaurant, since Connie had been coming directly from work while Pam had had the day off.

Connie deftly maneuvered herself between Pam and her car. "Please give me a chance, Pam. We could be good together. Or at least have a good time together." Her eyes left no question about her intentions.

"Connie, really, it's not you, okay? I'm just...I'm still having a hard time, you know?"

"I know. And I want to help."

You can help by letting me get in my car, Pam wanted to say.

"Maybe..." Connie continued, suddenly flinging her arms around Pam's neck and clutching her in a death grip. "Maybe we could talk sometime at my place. Do some hug therapy. What do you think?"

Now that's a new one! Hug therapy? Seriously? She almost laughed out loud. "I'm not really the huggy type."

"Then how about this." Connie pressed her hot mouth against Pam's and kissed her thoroughly, mashing her hard little body into Pam's.

For the briefest of moments, Pam's defenses began to loosen. A tiny flare of uncontrolled excitement rose through the pit of her stomach before her common sense prevailed. If she slept with Connie, it would only be sex, nothing more. And she was not that kind of woman.

Pam wrenched herself away. "Sorry, but I need to get home and get something cold on my head."

"Okay, bunny. I'll call you tomorrow to make sure you're okay."

Bunny? Is she for real? Oh my God, wait until I tell Trish about this!

Pam was only a few dozen yards down the street before she used her car's Bluetooth to dial Trish. She was laughing so hard, she could barely talk.

"Trish? You won't believe the date I've just had! Oh my God, are you sitting down?"

CHAPTER EIGHT

Pam sat in her Subaru longer than she knew was polite. She could see Connie peeking through the blinds, waiting for her to come up the walk and knock on the door. But her legs felt leaden and her hands wouldn't open the car door. It was as though she were paralyzed suddenly.

Damn it, she thought, hating this sudden case of indecisiveness, of cowardice. Last night's date with Connie had been a disaster, one of her worst dates ever. She and Trish had laughed about it over the phone, and she'd gone to bed swearing that she'd never see Connie again. Or certainly would never go on a date with her again.

Yet here she was twenty-four hours later, sitting outside Connie's neat little bungalow after spontaneously calling her and asking if the invitation to come over for a drink—and more—was still good. She was lonely. Ridiculously lonely. She didn't want to be, she tried to convince herself it didn't matter, but she finally decided that one more night of sitting at home alone with her tears and her grief and her unbearable sadness was going to send her over the edge. Human contact, even in this less-than-ideal form, was preferable.

All right, she thought, gazing through the dusty windshield. She tried to steel herself. *I am going to do this. I am going to spend an evening with someone and not think about Laura and not think about the fact that I'm so alone in this world.* It was desperate behavior. Of course it was. *She* was desperate. Desperate to be with someone who desired her. Desperate to be with someone who would make her—or at least her body—feel alive for a couple of hours. It was pure escapism, but so what? She and Connie were both adults.

Before she could change her mind, she pushed open the car door and jumped out. Her long, confident strides up the brick walk gave no indication of her hesitation only moments ago. Connie opened the door before she even had a chance to knock.

"Hi, sugar."

Sugar. Ugh! Pam bit her lower lip and swallowed a smart-ass retort. "Hi, Connie. Sure this is okay? Such last-minute notice and all?"

Connie's smile was predatory. "It's more than okay. I'm so glad you called. I didn't think…"

Pam simply shrugged and refused to discuss her about-face.

Connie led her into the candlelit living room, where two glasses of wine waited for them on the low table in front of the sofa. Wordlessly they sat down, Connie immediately scooting closer. *Okay*, Pam thought, *any closer and you'll be in my lap!* But wasn't that what she wanted? Wasn't that why she was here?

Pam reached for her glass of wine, knocked back half of it.

"It's okay," Connie soothed. "Relax."

God, how she hated when people said that. Who could relax on command? Didn't Connie know that saying it only made it worse?

Connie's hand crept on to her knee and began drawing soft circles. "I've always been so attracted to you. I'm so glad you finally agreed to see me."

I'm not seeing *you*, Pam wanted to say. *I'm here to fuck you because it's what we both want, nothing more.*

"I don't really want to talk," Pam whispered, not looking at Connie.

"Okay, we don't have to talk. Why don't we kiss?"

Jesus, now they were negotiating. Pam set her jaw and turned to look at Connie. "I don't want to kiss either."

Before Connie could utter a response, Pam pressed her body into Connie's until she yielded against the sofa, then she climbed on top of her. Hastily, she unfastened the buttons on Connie's blouse, simultaneously squeezing soft breasts through cotton until Connie began to moan. Oh yes, this was going to be easy, she thought, as Connie pushed her breasts toward Pam's mouth and began demanding softly, over and over, that Pam fuck her. Pam took each breast into her mouth, sucked taut nipples, drove a hand between Connie's legs. She could feel Connie's wetness through her thin cotton slacks.

Pam silently marveled at how easy mindless sex was. And it truly was mindless. Not a single, composed thought formed in her mind as she gave in to raw, physical yearnings. Her body's hunger surprised her. She consumed Connie—tasted her, stroked her, grinded into her, clutched her, groped her, all at a furious, greedy pace. And in turn, she let Connie pleasure her with her hands, her mouth, until nothing mattered but release. Afterward, in orgasm's receding tide, when thoughts began to slither back into her mind—thoughts of Laura, thoughts of her empty home, even thoughts of Trish—Pam reached for Connie and began the process of emptying her mind all over again. It seemed, for the moment, the only way to divorce herself from her overwhelming grief and loneliness.

The sex wasn't especially enjoyable, she could admit that easily enough, because Lord knew not all orgasms were created equal. Sex with Connie was simply a release, a distraction, a function she needed to do for herself with a more-than-willing participant. Of course she would regret it in the morning, she knew that, but hadn't one of the lessons from Laura's death been to live in the moment? *Yeah, that's what I'm doing. Living in the goddamned moment.*

* * *

Trish glanced quickly at the Michigan wall calendar magnetically attached to the fridge and happily stroked off another day. Well, the day was only beginning, but what the hell. Fourteen more working days before school was out for the summer. *Thank God*, she thought, as she reached inside the fridge for her lunch bag. She needed the break more than she ever had in her nearly fifteen years of teaching. Laura's death left her struggling to get through work each day. Her colleagues knew she'd once been lovers with the luckless soldier who'd been killed, but she hid her deepest emotions from everyone but Rosa and Pam, because grieving so deeply over the death of a long-ago lost love wasn't something most people would understand. They'd look at her with pity, or confusion, and wonder what was wrong with her that she'd never moved on from Laura, she imagined. And they wouldn't be wrong. But in Trish's mind, love didn't always follow common sense and protocol. Love was the most beautiful and most confusing damn thing in the world.

Her phone rang. She almost let it go to the answering machine, then thought better of it in case it was the school calling, warning her about some problem awaiting her.

"Trish here," she answered quickly, before she could change her mind.

"Hi." It was Pam, talking so quietly that she was hard to hear.

"Hey you. This is a nice surprise."

"Sorry, you're getting ready for work, aren't you?"

Something in Pam's voice instantly alarmed Trish. "Are you okay?"

"Yes. No...I don't know."

Trish took the cordless phone to the kitchen table and sat down. Work could wait. "What's going on?"

"I just got a registered letter delivered to me. From the army. Laura's personal belongings should be here by the end of the week."

Crap. She knew the day was approaching, and that seeing Laura's things would be difficult for Pam. Dog tags, Laura's journal, whatever personal effects she'd had with her in Afghanistan. "Would you like some company on the weekend?"

"God, yes. I hated to ask."

"You didn't. I offered. I can drive to Chicago after work Friday." It was a four-hour drive. Since it was June, she could easily get to Pam's before it got dark.

"That would be great. Are you sure you don't mind? I really don't want…"

"Look, I totally understand. You know I want to be there for this part, right?"

There was silence on the other end, and Trish wondered if Pam was still there. "Pam? Are you still there?"

"Yeah, still here."

"Is there something else you're upset about?"

"Am I that easy to read?" She didn't sound pleased.

The truth? She found Pam incredibly easy to read, even after all the years they'd not seen one another and in spite of their seven-year age difference. Maybe it was their shared bond over Laura, all the memories they had in common. In any case, Trish already felt more connected to Pam than she'd felt to anyone in a very long time.

"Yes, you are," Trish answered simply.

Pam sighed miserably. "I slept with Connie last night."

The words took a moment to register, and when they did, Trish swallowed against an impossibly dry throat. "Connie? But I thought…"

"I know. I thought so too."

"Then why?" Her voice was tight, full of unrestrained disappointment. She hated herself for it. She wasn't Pam's mother or lover or big sister. It was none of her business, and, yet, Pam's admission had hit her like a punch to her gut.

"Shit, I don't know. I guess I just needed to be with someone last night. I needed to *feel* something, you know? Something besides numbness, sadness. I just, I don't know."

Trish did understand that brand of loneliness, but she wasn't about to fall into bed with the first woman who happened along, and she resented Pam for doing so. For being so weak.

"Christ, Pam. You're only going to complicate things for yourself and for this Connie woman." She couldn't say the woman's name without sounding hostile. Jesus, why was she being so childish about this? She tried to lighten her voice. "Sleeping with someone isn't going to make you feel better, okay? It's only going to make things worse."

"I know, I know. You're right. I just…It was stupid, I agree. It's not going to happen again."

Pam sounded chastened, which only made Trish feel worse. She hadn't meant to scold her, to make her feel worse than she probably already did. "I'm sorry, Pam. I didn't mean to sound so rude. Or judgmental."

"No, you're absolutely right in what you said. I need you as my compass right now. I feel so damned lost. So…alone."

"I know, sweetie, I know." If she could take Pam into her arms right now, she would, but it would have to wait a few days. "Look, I have to go to work, but I'll see you in a few days, okay? And if you need anything in the meantime, if you need to talk, call me. Any time of the day or night. I mean that, okay?"

Pam's voice was thick with emotion, and Trish imagined tears welling in those gray-green eyes. "I don't know what I'd do without you right now."

Trish tried hard to sound upbeat. They'd have to brace each other up right now as best they could. "Well, you won't have to worry about that. I'm not going anywhere, and I'll be seeing you real soon, okay? Maybe we can even try to do something fun."

"Okay," Pam answered faintly.

As Trish hung up, she tried to ignore the jumble of emotions the call had sent spiraling through her. She hated knowing how upset, how lost, Pam felt, and how helpless she felt in turn. What she couldn't reconcile was the unexpected jealousy that had risen in her like a serpent when Pam told her she'd slept with Connie. She had no right to be jealous of who Pam spent her time with or how she spent her time with them. And yet she undeniably was.

Her stomach felt rock heavy with the unsettling realization. What the hell was *that* all about?

CHAPTER NINE

Trish's presence calmed Pam and gave her an instant feeling of peace. It made her stronger too, like she just might be able to handle sorting through Laura's coffee table-sized box of personal belongings, including the journal she knew would be inside. They'd agreed to wait until tomorrow to do it, when they'd both have more energy. The box stood in the living room, an ominous reminder of the grim task ahead.

Pam had whipped together a vegetarian dish of penne and cauliflower in a parmesan and bechamel sauce, with fresh basil sprinkled on top. Italian was the one thing Pam could cook well and loved eating, and Trish appeared grateful for a home-cooked meal after the long drive.

She knew Trish was tired, but she suggested a drink at the famous Drake Hotel. It was nine o'clock, the perfect time for a Friday night drink on the town, and Pam wanted to show Trish the historic landmark that had welcomed such notables through its doors as the Kennedys, President Obama, Frank Sinatra, Princess Diana, Elizabeth Taylor and countless other celebrities. Mostly, though, she didn't want them sitting around her townhouse staring at that big box, contemplating its contents. They could save it for tomorrow.

Trish had gamely agreed, and now they sat in the hotel's upscale bar drinking eight-dollar Cuba Libres, an autographed glossy of Judy Garland peering down at them.

"Makes me feel like somebody important," Trish said with a smile.

"It does have that feel to it, like only important people come here. I love the history of the place. Can't you can almost feel it oozing out of the walls?"

"You're right. If I close my eyes, I can picture Frank Sinatra and Marilyn Monroe sitting here drinking martinis, the place blue with cigarette smoke."

"I'll bet some pretty big deals were brokered right here in this bar. Probably even guys like Capone. And politicians like Mayor Richard Daley, the Kennedys."

"You love Chicago, don't you?"

"I love its history, its architecture. The characters and the character of the place. But I don't know that I'll stay here forever. There's something about the peace and nostalgia of Ann Arbor that's got a special place in my heart. Even more so now."

"Think you'd ever come back to stay?"

Pam shrugged, not yet fully committed to the idea. She didn't want to move all over the country, change addresses all the time the way Laura had. Staying in one place was important to her. "Maybe. I haven't decided yet. My residency's up in another month."

Trish's eyebrows lifted in surprise. "What are you going to do?"

Before Laura's death, she'd planned to sign on again with the same hospital. Now it was hard to feel the ground under her feet, and decisions no longer came easily. Some days, simply choosing what to eat or what to wear was a monumental decision. "I don't know. I can't seem to make up my mind about anything anymore. Even the simplest decisions are difficult."

"I know. I'm done in two weeks for the summer, and I've never needed a break as badly as I need one now."

"That's what I'm leaning toward, taking a long break. I haven't had one in years. And I feel like if I don't, I'm going to make some big mistake at work that's going to cost someone their life." Pam hadn't confided her secret fear—a fear that had kept her awake at night lately—to anyone before now. "I feel like a menace at work because I'm so distracted, so...not myself. It's only a matter of time before I make a serious mistake if I can't get my head together again."

"I'm so sorry," Trish said, reaching across the table and placing her hand on top of Pam's. The gesture touched Pam inside, almost made her want to cry. She was full of barely controlled emotion these days, and it scared her. What if she lost it in front of a patient? Or a patient's family?

"Well, it just figures, Pamela Wright!"

Both women snapped their heads toward the bitchy voice. Connie Mayfield stood beside their table, hands on her hips, her lipsticked mouth a slash of blood-red anger.

"No wonder you haven't called me all week. You could have just told me you were seeing someone else," she hissed at Pam.

Pam saw that Trish looked exactly as she felt—mortified. She wanted to crawl under the table, but found her voice instead. "I'm sorry, Connie. I didn't mean to hurt you. Trish is a friend and..."

"Yeah, right." She scowled at Trish's hand over Pam's on the table. "You could have at least been honest with me."

"I am being honest."

"I mean honest about what happened between us the other night. Honest about not wanting to see me again."

Pam squirmed in her seat, hating the fact that Connie was forcing a public scene. Dyke drama was *so* not her thing. She tried to keep her voice level. "Look, I didn't mean to treat you badly in any way. I'm just not looking to get involved with anyone right now, okay? And I'm sorry I didn't communicate that very well."

"You sure didn't mind getting *involved* with me the other night."

Pam flinched, her face burning with embarrassment. She needed to put out this fire with Connie once and for all. "I had a nice time with you, I really did. I just don't want it to continue. I'm sorry."

Connie's expression alternated between disappointment and anger. Her gaze fixed on Trish. "She's a player, you know. I'd watch out if I were you."

She twisted around on her heel and stormed off, much to Pam's relief. They both giggled a little, muffled by their hands, in case Connie was listening.

"Thank God," Pam muttered. "I feel like I just got caught cheating or something."

Trish winked teasingly. "On me or her?"

That was a sobering question and one Pam didn't want to answer.

On the drive back to Pam's, they laughed about the scene with Connie, with Pam interspersing apologies. "I'm really not a player, you know."

"I know, sweetie. I know."

She swallowed against fresh emotion at the endearing term. If Trish kept calling her "sweetie," she was going to cry, dammit.

"Have you ever done anything like that?"

"Like what?" Trish asked.

"Had a one-night stand."

"Once. After Laura and I broke up for good. I was angry, so hurt. I don't really remember what I thought it would accomplish."

"Did it help?"

"Hell no."

"That's what I thought. Believe it or not, Connie is the first time I've ever done that. I'm not proud of it."

"You don't have to explain, honey. I know who you are."

Honey? Okay, you're going to have to stop calling me "sweetie" and "honey" unless you really mean it. Because I am not a little kid anymore that needs her hand patted.

Pam could not figure Trish out sometimes. There were moments when she seemed clearly nothing more to Trish than Laura's little sister. A child. A cute little nuisance to be tolerated. But there were other moments where it almost felt like they were intimate friends, perhaps even on the brink of more. It was damned confusing.

Back at her townhouse, she showed Trish to the guest room, choosing to wait in the living room with the Nora Roberts novel she was too embarrassed to let anyone else see.

When Trish called out that she was ready to say goodnight, Pam stashed the book under the sofa and went to Trish's open door and hovered. Her eyes immediately dropped to the low-cut cotton V-necked T-shirt and baggy boxers Trish wore. She couldn't seem to pull her eyes away from her breasts, the way they jutted out from the shirt like firm hills that needed climbing, her nipples like mountain peaks.

She spoke before she allowed herself any more time to think. Or any more time to stare. "Trish? Can I ask you something?"

"Of course." Trish took a step toward her, smiling innocently, her head tilted invitingly.

Damn, that soft skin needs caressing, kissing. "Do you think you would ever…" Pam's courage deserted her suddenly. *Shit.*

"Yes?" Another step closer.

"That you could ever…"

Trish was only a half step away now. She smelled faintly of lime and mint. "Ever what?"

"Ever…" Pam's heart was in her throat. "Ever think of me as someone other than Laura's little sister?"

Confusion bloomed on Trish's face. "But you *are* Laura's little sister."

"I know. I mean… Jeez." She hadn't felt this flustered since the first day of med school.

Trish reached out and gently took her hands. "Take a deep breath and tell me what you mean, okay?" Like her touch, her voice was warm, comforting, bolstering. "Whatever it is, it's okay, I promise."

Yes. It *would* be okay if Trish said it would be. She trusted her implicitly, knew she could never make a fool of herself with her, because Trish truly cared about her.

"Do you think…" Pam said slowly, starting over. She wanted to be clear. "Someday. That you could ever love me?"

"Oh, Pam." Trish stepped closer, dropping Pam's hands and pulling her into a hug. "I do love you, don't you know that? I've always loved you, and I always will."

"No." Pam pulled back enough to look into Trish's eyes. They were dark, unreadable. "That's not what I meant. I mean, *really* love me." Her hands slid down to Trish's hips, saying what her words could not.

At the intimate gesture, Trish's eyes widened in recognition. Yes, now she was getting it, Pam thought with satisfaction. *She knows exactly what I mean.*

"Oh, Pam," she rasped, her eyes rapidly blinking.

"Shhh. Don't say anything."

Gently, Pam tugged Trish's hips toward her, then bent her head to kiss Trish's neck. Her skin was so soft, so smooth against her lips. Exactly as she had imagined. She closed her eyes, planted small kisses just beneath Trish's jaw. There was no resistance. She ached to place her hands on Trish's thick glossy hair. *Then do it*, she commanded herself. And she did. Soft, silky waves filled her hands, spilled through her fingers like a waterfall. Trish moaned a little. Pam's hand reached down to her chin, lifted it toward her. She'd wanted to kiss those full, shapely lips since…God, how long? Since she was eleven, twelve? And now it was going to happen.

Her stomach tightened at the first brush of her lips against Trish's. So soft. So sexy. So perfect. God, how she wanted her. Had always wanted her. Had dreamed of this moment for as long as she could remember. It was a stupid, childish crush, way back then. A fantasy. But not now. Never again would this moment be a fantasy, because it was really happening. It was real. They were grown women, attracted to one another, expressing that attraction for one another. And no matter what else happened or didn't happen, she would always have this moment. *They* would always have this moment.

The kiss intensified, their lips moving together so perfectly—too perfect for a first kiss, Pam thought with wonderment. *We fit so beautifully. Not only our mouths, but our bodies too.* And then all thought evaporated from her mind as she held Trish and kissed her long and sensuously, with all the years of pent-up attraction and lust. Trish kissed her back just as ferociously, as much full of need, until Pam's knees nearly buckled. Never had she experienced a first kiss with someone that was as full of magic as this.

It could have been minutes, maybe even an hour, when Trish finally halted the kiss to look deeply into her eyes. Oh no, Pam thought. *What have I done?* There was fear there, confusion, maybe regret too. Perhaps a hundred different things battling it out behind Trish's eyes, and Pam could see that she'd shaken her to her core. But there was unmistakable desire too. Desire and thrill, and Pam wanted to do a little dance.

"Pam," Trish said hoarsely, shaking her head slightly. "I don't think…"

"I know, I know. I'm really sorry."

"No, it wasn't you. I mean, it was me too. I just think…"

"I know." *God, please let's not dissect this right now*, Pam thought. She wanted to enjoy the moment, the memory, a little longer. "Look, let's just go to bed…"

"W-What?" Trish's eyes widened dramatically. It was almost comical.

Pam laughed. "That's not what I meant." Well, she did mean it. Sort of. Didn't she? As much as she desired Trish, found her sexy and alluring—hell, she'd been in love with her for years— she didn't want to risk going to bed with her now and ruining everything.

With her thumb, she caressed Trish's cheek one last time. "Goodnight, Trish. Sleep well."

* * *

Trish slept fitfully, at one point dreaming that it was Laura she'd been kissing. She woke to the thought, sad and a little shocked, that it was Pam she'd kissed. Little towheaded Pamela, the gangly kid with the toothy smile who'd trailed after them for years, wanting their approval, their attention, wanting to be just like them. All that time wanting, it seemed, *her*. She smiled at the thought of Pam in class doodling her name in her notebooks, of Pam always searching for her in the stands whenever she and Laura would watch her at school track or her basketball games. Pam wanting to join them on their dates.

Yes, she'd known then that young Pam had had the hots for her. But this, this was something entirely different. This was no schoolgirl crush. This was a mature woman, a strong, independent, beautiful and smart woman who'd kissed her last night. Kissed her like she was the first and last woman she ever wanted to kiss. Trish sucked in her breath, felt a shot of electricity zap her stomach. And her crotch. She'd kissed Pam right back, desired her right back. Her body had responded in all the right places, and if things were different—if her brain hadn't clicked in and thrown up all sorts of stop signs—she'd have gone to bed with Pam in a flash. Because Pam was everything she could ever want in a woman, if she were to make a list. Sexy, smart, adorable, loving, fun.

Oh God, she thought. When had all *this* started? When had she started thinking of Pam that way? When had she started being attracted to her? Christ, she'd not seen her in years up until three weeks ago. Until Laura's death. *Oh God, oh God.* Panic rose and began to consume her like flames in a haystack. How could she possibly kiss Laura's little sister, have even *considered* going to bed with her, at a time like this? What the hell was wrong with her? It was Laura she'd loved, still loved. What kind of respect were they showing to Laura's memory, fooling around like this? Playing with something so dangerous, so wrong. *Damned wrong.*

She swung her legs over the side of the bed. It was still early, not quite seven, but she'd get some coffee going. Think this through some more. She'd tell Pam what they'd done was wrong, that they needed to shake off whatever spell had come over them both. They needed to be sensible, responsible. They needed to get a grip.

She found ground coffee in a canister, dumped some into the basket, then filled the water receptacle. The gurgling must have awakened Pam or maybe the aroma. She stumbled in, rubbing her eyes, wearing an adorable scrub shirt with teddy bears on it and purple silk boxers.

"Good morning," Trish said, trying to rid her head of the vision of snuggling in bed with Pam, of touching those silk boxers. *Jesus!*

"Morning. Oh good, you found the coffee." Pam yawned, opened the cupboard, retrieved two Le Creuset mugs, filled them both with coffee. "Sugar? Cream?"

"Just a bit of cream please."

Pam took hers black, the way Laura did, Trish noticed. She carried both mugs to the small eat-in kitchen table, pushed one toward Trish. "I make a killer French toast. You hungry?"

She was starving, actually. "Sounds great. But can we talk first?"

"Okay."

Pam looked apprehensive suddenly, and Trish was secretly glad she wasn't the only one sweating about last night.

"I think maybe I've been giving you some signals you've misinterpreted. And I'm sorry for that."

"Meaning what?"

Okay, so Pam was direct. Not that it surprised her. "I've led you to believe that I'm attracted to you, that…"

"So you're saying you're not?"

Trish couldn't lie to her. She did feel attracted to her, even if it felt somehow wrong or misplaced. "That's not the point."

Pam's eyes darkened, narrowed. "It sure as hell felt like the point when we were kissing last night."

Trish took a sip of her coffee, closed her eyes for a moment. Images of their kiss intruded behind her eyelids. A kiss that was both sweet and needy, comforting and demanding. A kiss that—there was no denying it—had rocked her to her toes. Damn, this wasn't going to be easy. "Look, I don't want to get into why we kissed, what we…"

"But I do want to get into it."

"No. The point is, we can't go around kissing each other, acting like we're dating. Because we're not. And we can't. We're not ourselves right now."

Trish watched Pam take a long, contemplative sip of her coffee. She was so much like Laura. The eyes, the smile, those killer dimples, the direct way about her. But she was more laid-back than Laura, more quietly self-assured, more grounded perhaps. Certainly much less of a daredevil. Yes, she was a version of Laura but with both feet on the ground. *Dammit.* If Pam had been the older one…if Pam had been Laura, how differently things might have turned out for them both. For all three of them.

"Look," Pam said on a sigh. "I get it, okay? You're still stuck on my sister. And because of that, you can't give me a chance. It'd be, I don't know, immoral or something. Incestuous."

Pam was both right and wrong. Yes, she still loved Laura. Had continued to love her over the years, to her own detriment. But it wasn't only Pam she wouldn't take a chance on, it was any woman. Rosa had found that out the hard way.

"Pam, I just don't want us to get sidetracked here. I don't want to confuse the issues. We're here because of Laura. To help each other through that."

Pam rose, her shoulders stiffening. "I know. You're right. I'll start on breakfast, and then we should start on that big box in the living room."

Trish cradled her mug in both hands. She'd not handled this little talk very well. In fact, she was pretty sure she'd made things worse, more confusing. And she'd hurt Pam. But how could they have a reasonable discussion about their feelings when she didn't even know what it was she felt? And if she were honest with herself, she was afraid. Afraid to question if she really was feeling something sexual, something deep, for Pam. And if she was, if they both were, what the hell were they supposed to do about it?

CHAPTER TEN

Pam used a knife from the kitchen to slice away the packaging tape from the huge box, so plain and unobtrusive-looking in contrast to its very personal contents. She both dreaded and anticipated what was inside. Trish stood behind her, peering over her shoulder before kneeling down beside her as Pam peeled the lid off the box.

If nothing else, Pam thought as she plunged into the task, it would take her mind off last night's kiss and this morning's awkward conversation. Clearly Trish wanted to brush the whole thing off, pretend it never happened. She'd made her point that nothing more would ever happen romantically between them. Surprisingly, Pam found herself accepting the situation. Or maybe it was more like giving up. *Whatever*. It was time to grow up and put her childhood crush on Trish where it belonged—in the past. Trish was never going to be the fantasy that came true. And besides, they were both in too much pain to see clearly through their emotions. They hadn't even begun to complete their grieving over Laura.

Neatly folded inside were two sets of camo battle dress uniforms. Carefully, Pam unfolded the blouse, thumbed the name patch on the chest that said L. Wright, the insignia of a major in the center of the chest. She fingered the material, slightly scratchy yet also soft. The clothing momentarily brought Laura close again, and she clutched it briefly to her chest like an empty hug. Laura's medals hadn't been included in the box. The army had notified Pam that they would come separately—an Iraq campaign medal, an Afghanistan campaign medal, a commendation medal and, of course, a Purple Heart.

Near the bottom of the box were a couple of scrub shirts, still with Laura's scent on them. Pam would cycle them into her own scrub shirts she used for work. She pulled out Laura's personalized stethoscope, the one Pam and their mom had jointly given her upon graduation from medical school, inscribed with her name. Pam had her own inscribed stethoscope, but she would keep Laura's forever. Her hand shook as she held on to it.

"You were so proud of her, weren't you," Trish said quietly.

"She was a good role model. The best."

"Did you ever consider doing anything other than becoming a doctor yourself?"

Pam shook her head. For about two minutes she'd entertained the idea of becoming an engineer, but once Laura graduated from medical school and promised to help her with her medical school bills, Pam jumped at the chance. "I never would have been able to do it if she hadn't helped pay my way."

"I guess, in a way, the army got two doctors for the price of one."

"You mean *paid* for two doctors. They were never going to *have* me."

"No, of course not. Did Laura ever give you any grief for not joining the army or try to pressure you?"

"Not at all. She understood we were different that way. She told me she was glad I didn't, so she wouldn't have to worry about me outranking her one day." Laura had a habit of joking about serious topics, a defense mechanism.

In a small jewelry box was a white gold necklace, along with Laura's University of Michigan medical school ring. Pam had an identical ring. She held Laura's and the necklace out to Trish. "You should have these."

"Oh, Pam, I couldn't possibly."

"Yes, you can. You need something of Laura's. I want you to have them. Laura would have wanted you to."

Trish took the jewelry, threaded the necklace through the ring, then clasped it around her neck. She immediately caressed the ring against her chest like a worry stone. "Thank you so much. I'll wear it always."

"I'm glad you loved her so much." Pam's voice wavered a little. "Everyone deserves to be loved as much as you loved her." She meant it, even though she was a little jealous of the love Trish and Laura had shared. No one had ever loved her like that, and it wasn't fair that Laura had taken Trish's love and thrown it away so easily. Had Laura truly understood what she'd given up? Pam knew with certainty that she would never have discarded Trish's love that way.

There were a few more things inside the box, but Pam needed a break. Going through Laura's things was every bit as difficult as she imagined it was going to be.

"Why don't I put some tea on," Trish suggested, rising from her place on the floor.

When she returned with two mugs, Pam was fingering Laura's worn, leather-bound journal, which had also been stuffed with snapshots. Camille was in one of them. The others in the photos with Laura were all strangers, all wearing uniforms, their arms slung loosely around one another in smiling companionship. The images brought home the fact that she hadn't known any of the people in Laura's life the last few years. She hadn't really known the grown-up Laura.

"Shall we start?" Pam said to Trish, who sat beside her on the sofa.

"How about we take turns reading?"

"Okay. I'll start."

Pam opened it to the first page.

I've never kept a journal during a mission before. Actually, I've never kept any kind of journal. I always thought they were sort of juvenile. Or kind of a romantic thing to do. But then it occurred to me that when I'm old and I can't remember stuff, or if I start talking about the War on Terror one day and people look at me like what's the big deal, it couldn't have been too bad—I can read to them from this journal. Through my words, I can show people exactly what it was like. And so it's going to be the best damned war journal anyone's ever written.

Pam smiled at that, looked at Trish. "Laura always liked to be the best, didn't she?"

Trish laughed, her eyes bright with memories. "Do you remember in high school, when she played on that girls hockey team?"

"Of course. I went to all her games. I never could figure out why she suddenly quit after two years."

"Oh, I know exactly why she quit. If she didn't score at least a goal a game, she figured she'd had a bad game. She quit because she couldn't be as good at it as she wanted to be. Basketball was her first love. And of course, she was starting to get serious about her schoolwork at this point. Hockey was taking a backseat, and she didn't want to do something she couldn't give her all to."

That made sense to Pam. Laura never went halfway with anything she set her mind to. "Well, then, I expect she's right about this journal being the best."

Pam continued reading out loud.

"Nov. 9, 2012:

The first day of the next fifteen months in Afghanistan. I am now boots on the ground, in theatre, in the 'Ghan, for my second tour here. I arrived in a US C-17, which is basically a huge cargo transport plane. Landing at Bagram Air Field is an adventure. Outside a war zone, travelers are used to the gentle descent, cheerful announcements, a soft landing and sometimes applause for the pilots. In Afghanistan, a slow and direct approach leaves a plane vulnerable to missile attacks, so the plane stays high and at the last possible moment drops into a steep spiral dive. Even if you know what's coming, it is no fun. Makes you want to vomit, to be honest. G-force pushes and pulls on your body as the pilot aims the plane toward the ground like a dart. At the last minute the plane levels out, then it hits the runway.

"It's hot, dusty here, and the bright morning sun hits me hard as though I had been struck blind. I'd forgotten my sunglasses on the plane, and there was no time to go back for them, so I marched on, tears streaming down my face as I tried to adjust to the light. I know some people might think I'm upset to be posted in this country again, but I'm not. I'm ecstatic. This is exactly where I want to be, doing what I was trained to do. And it feels damned good to be around people who don't look at you like you're crazy for wanting to be in the middle of the war, the way they do back home. I've always hated sitting on the bench during a really big game, watching everybody else play. I want to play, need to play and now I get to play."

"But it's not a game," Trish interrupted, her voice growing tense. "How can she compare war to a game? You don't lose your goddamned life in a game."

"No, you don't. But the way she wrote it, I can understand how she felt when she wasn't over there. Can't you?"

Trish sighed, sipped her tea. "I guess."

"I don't think she was trying to trivialize war. And she wasn't a novice. She'd been to Afghanistan before. And Iraq."

"Exactly. Which is exactly why she should have known the danger. It's exactly why she shouldn't have wanted to go there."

Gently, Pam closed the journal. "I know you're angry, but…"

"Aren't you?" Trish demanded, her face flushed.

"Of course I'm angry that my sister is dead. And I'm angry that my parents are gone too. But being angry isn't going to change anything. It's not going to make my life better. And it's not going to help me understand why Laura's work was so important to her."

Trish rose in a flurry, her anger making her brittle. "I'm sorry. I need to take a walk or something."

"We don't have to do this journal together if it's too hard."

"No. I want to. I just need to take a breather."

She watched Trish stalk out the door and wondered why she didn't feel the same kind of anger. She was sad—sad to the core—and full of an empty kind of loneliness. It left her listless some days, confused, not herself. The episode with Connie was evidence of that. But who was there to be angry at? The army? Laura had willingly joined, knowing and even embracing all the risks. The army never tried to sugarcoat what it was about. She could be angry at the Taliban, but they were a faceless, evil enemy that was easy to hate in an abstract way. She wasn't particularly religious, so blaming God wasn't an option either. Anger was a wasted emotion, she told herself.

When Trish returned a short while later, she looked far more at ease. She apologized, said she wanted them to read more of the journal together. Trish's anger, Pam decided, was her own, and was not something she would allow herself to be sucked into. She could only control her own emotions and not someone else's.

They read more about Laura's chaotic surroundings at the base. The cement air-raid shelters every few dozen yards, the large dining hall, the bunkhouses, the boardwalk with its café, restaurant and general store, the noisy trucks kicking up dust everywhere, the loud jet engines of planes and helicopters coming and going every few minutes. She described the hospital too, which was actually quite state-of-the-art, all things considered. There was a blood lab, ultrasound machines, a new CT scanner. Laura noted how much it'd improved in the three years since she was last there.

Over take-out pizza for dinner, Pam confessed that reading Laura's own words, reading about her daily life over there, almost made it seem like she wasn't gone. Like she was still there in the desert, dodging trouble.

"I know," Trish agreed, staring blankly past Pam. "What's going to happen when we come to the end of it?"

Pam didn't have an answer to that.

"Nov. 20:
We tried to practically kill each other in a game of road hockey tonight. Probably it's because an entire artillery company is heading outside the wire tomorrow on a long convoy. It's a way to blow off steam, to pretend there is no fear of what might happen. IED

and suicide attacks have been increasing lately in this part of the region, and tomorrow's mission is damned dangerous.

"Neil Jackman's a twenty-two-year-old corporal heading out on the mission. He's a reservist on his first tour. He tries to act tough, but I can see he's the nervous type when people aren't looking, always checking and double-checking his equipment, taking apart his weapon and cleaning it constantly. Earlier today he came into the hospital and sought me out. I'd taken some blood from him a week ago because I suspected he was a little anemic. We were going over the results (he isn't anemic, so his symptoms are probably from stress). He seemed really tense and uptight, so I came straight out and asked him if he was scared about tomorrow. He looked around to make sure nobody was listening. Then he broke down in tears. Sobbed like a little boy.

I can't tell him everything's going to be fine, because I don't know that. One thing about the soldiers serving here, they want the truth. Doesn't matter what it's about, whether it's about enemy activity, the extent of an injury, or if your mate back home is screwing around. There's no time here for sugarcoating anything. It's too real here for lies. The sun is brighter, pain hurts more, laughter is deeper, and so is sadness. Everything cuts twice as deep here. So I let Neil cry for a few minutes, then I asked him what was really bothering him. He told me he'd had a bad dream that he wasn't coming back. Ever since, he just can't shake that nagging feeling that he is going to get killed, he confessed. Who am I to tell him it's just a load of crap? I asked if he wanted to talk to a padre or a social worker. He said no. I even asked him if he wanted me to try to get him out of it for medical reasons. Again he said no, that he didn't want to be a coward, that he had to man up. He thanked me for the talk and I watched him leave a few minutes later. It's hard to walk toward what might be your own death. I told him to keep moving forward, that it's what we do as human beings, even when we don't know what lies ahead. I hope he's okay."

Pam and Trish quickly paged ahead to Laura's entry two days later. It was a simple one-liner.

Cpl. Neil Jackman, KIA today.

* * *

They spent a couple more hours on the journal Sunday before Trish said she'd better start the drive back to Ann Arbor. Pam agreed she wouldn't read any more of the journal in Trish's absence, which made Trish happy because it would be too much to bear reading alone for either of them. It was hard not only because Laura was gone, but because it was written in such a way that it felt like they were right there with her, as though everything she wrote about was still happening. It'd been heartbreaking to read about the young soldier who'd had a premonition about his death, and Trish wondered what Laura had felt when she was told the news. She hadn't commented in the journal, perhaps because the soldiers didn't allow themselves to grieve too long, to show too much emotion. She wondered too if Laura had had a premonition about her own death.

"I have to work next weekend," Pam announced. "But what about getting together the weekend after that?"

"I'll be done teaching for the summer by then. I can come here again."

"Or I could come to your place?"

"All right. Come to my place."

Trish hated the awkwardness between them since the kiss. She was hesitant now to hug Pam or to even touch her, fearing it might be misconstrued. They needed to talk about it, but not now.

After much hesitation Trish said, "Are we okay?"

Pam leaned against the front doorframe. A smile spread slowly, mellifluously, across her face. "We'll always be okay."

Trish's instant relief weakened her knees. Whatever they needed to clear up between them didn't matter right now. What mattered was that they were still here for each other. They were still friends.

Trish found a 1980s station on the radio and cranked it up for the drive home. She smiled as she listened to the Culture Club, Tina Turner, George Michael. Songs from her and Laura's youth. She felt numb, but almost pleasantly so, wrapped in adolescent memories of innocent joy.

CHAPTER ELEVEN

Trish and Rosa followed their usual Saturday tradition—an early morning swim and then breakfast at The Broken Egg downtown. They'd had to miss last weekend when Trish was in Chicago, and just as she'd expected, Rosa had spent most of the morning grilling her about her visit with Pam.

Trish told her about the journal and the other items in the box that belonged to Laura. Not one to miss anything, Rosa had noticed right away Laura's ring dangling from a necklace around her neck. She frowned at it, kept making disapproving faces, but said nothing. It wasn't long before the dam burst.

"How come she never gave you a ring when she was alive?"

Trish's fork stalled just before she was about to shove it in her mouth. It teetered in her suddenly shaky hand, bits of scrambled egg spilling over. She gave up and set the fork back on her plate. "What are you talking about?" she asked on a long sigh.

Rosa screwed up her face. There was no mistaking her feelings. "She never gave you a ring while she was alive. Why would you wear her ring now?"

"Because I loved her. You know that. It's the only thing I have of hers."

"But Trish, a ring is something special, don't you think?"

Trish rolled her eyes. She knew where this was going and didn't like it one bit. Rosa and her goddamned self-righteous moralizing. "Of course a ring is special. What Laura and I had was special. Jesus, Rosa, you know our whole history, chapter and verse."

"Yes, but this ring thing is new. And I don't like it."

Trish pushed her plate aside, her appetite gone. If Rosa was trying to provoke her, well, she was damned well succeeding. "You never liked anything about Laura, admit it."

"No, you're wrong. What I didn't like was that Laura still had a hold on you all these years. Years you could have been making a life with someone else."

"Look, Rosa, it was never going to work out between you and me in the long run, Laura or no Laura."

"Fine, maybe not." Rosa's eyes were misting over. She'd been hurt by their breakup, but Trish thought she was long over it. Perhaps she'd been mistaken. "But we were never going to know, because Laura was a constant albatross around our necks. She was always with us."

"Do we really have to go over all this again? God, Rosa, I can't believe you are still so consumed by jealousy for Laura. It's getting old!"

"Fine. I'm jealous, okay? Always have been, always will."

Wow, that was a first, Trish thought wryly. Rosa admitting a fault. If they weren't discussing such a sensitive topic, she might savor it.

"But you still don't get it," Rosa continued.

Oh, Christ. She really did not want to fight with Rosa right now. She needed a friend, someone who understood what she was going through, and a little sympathy too. She didn't need this condemnation, and she certainly didn't need to rehash their breakup.

"Don't you see?" Rosa continued, her voice full of barely suppressed rage. "She was never coming back for you, she was never going to change. And yet you held on and held on, blind to anything else but that one single-minded fantasy."

Hastily Trish took money out of her wallet for her share of the check. She didn't need this crap, and she would not listen to it any longer. Clearly, Rosa was pissed at her and was letting her have it with both barrels. It was totally unfair.

"She's dead," Rosa continued. "And now you're holding on to a dead woman. A ghost."

"Stop it," Trish hissed, on the brink of tears.

"No, I won't stop it because you need to hear this. If you don't let her go, you're going to die right along with her. Life is for the living, Trish. And that means *you*. If you want to remember Laura and your time with her, fine. But take off the rose-colored glasses and see her and your relationship with her for what it really was. And then get on with your life."

Trish tossed a ten-dollar bill on the table. Without a word, she stalked out. Tears streamed down her face as she began to run down the sidewalk, away from Rosa and her stupid petty jealousy. Rosa didn't understand. Nobody did. Well, Pam probably did, but Trish was afraid to rely too much on her because she didn't want her emotions and her neediness misinterpreted. Christ, could she not do anything right these days? She'd led Pam to think she wanted to sleep with her, and now her best friend was pissed at her.

As she reached her car, she fingered Laura's ring. It was strong, solid, like Laura. It felt as though Laura were here with her now, or at least a piece of Laura, and it was reassuring. Why couldn't Rosa understand that? She missed Laura, was grieving for the only true love of her life. Why did Rosa have to be such a fucking bitch about it?

She slumped against the steering wheel, gathering her thoughts. If she wanted to hold on to Laura, it was nobody's business but her own. She'd hold on to her for as long as she damned well wanted.

* * *

Pam took the elevator to the hospital's third floor, where the ICU units were located. She had an hour or so of break time and wanted to check on the status of a woman who'd been rushed to the ER yesterday by ambulance.

The thirty-four-year-old single mother of two had arrived unconscious; she'd collapsed suddenly in her kitchen in front of her kids. Pam accurately suspected a brain aneurysm, which had been confirmed by an emergency CT scan. She'd called in neuro, and the patient was rushed into surgery. She'd survived the surgery, but her recovery and survival remained uncertain.

Pam was greeted by neurology resident Nancy Watters, who was checking the computers supplying oxygen and nutrients to her patient. Pam and Nancy had done their one-year general internships at the same time.

"How's she doing?"

"Still too soon to tell. It's out of our hands now, if you know what I mean, but Pearson did a wonderful job last night."

Dick Pearson was the best neurosurgeon in the city. He would have given her the best possible chance, for whatever that was worth. The odds of her surviving were less than twenty percent, but so far she was holding her own.

Pam cast her eyes in the direction of the room across the hall, where a man with second- and third-degree burns lay unconscious. He hadn't come into the ER on her shift, thank goodness, but she'd heard all about him. Three days ago he'd shot his wife and teenaged daughter to death, then set the house on fire, hoping to kill himself in the process. So far, he'd survived.

"What about him?" Pam asked with a jerk of her thumb.

Nancy made a face of undisguised contempt. "Looks like he's going to pull through."

"Figures, doesn't it? It's so goddamned unfair."

Nancy placed a friendly hand on her shoulder. "Don't try to figure out what's fair and what's not fair in this place. Fair is a place where you ride Ferris wheels and buy cotton candy, as my grandma used to say."

Pam smiled, even though she felt like crying in frustration. "I know, you're right, it's just…"

"I know. Hey, how are you doing by the way?"

Pam shrugged casually, but inside, panic was squeezing her chest like a vice. She needed to get out of here. "I'm doing okay," she managed, failing to fight the urge to flee. "Sorry, Nance, I gotta run."

She pounded down the stairs, which ended right next to the chapel. She was not religious and had only ever poked her head inside once, just after she first started at the hospital, to see what it looked like inside. Now she felt an unusual pull to sit quietly in a pew. Not because she sought the comfort of God or religion or whatever it was, but because it was a quiet place where she could perhaps be alone with her thoughts. Maybe she could even find some peace and get out of this dark place she felt trapped in.

Pam sat down and stared, unblinking, at the flickering candles on the faux wood altar. She thought about the single mother upstairs fighting for her life, how she needed to pull through for her kids' sakes. She thought of the killer who deserved to die but probably wouldn't. And then there was Laura, who was only trying to help people, and yet she'd been rewarded for her good deeds by getting killed in a helicopter crash. What fucking sense did any of it make? she wondered bleakly. *What's the point of trying to do anything good, when there is no justice, no fair God or Goddess, no heaven, no ultimate reward?*

"You look like you're angry at the world."

She turned her head toward the soft voice of the man standing behind her. It was the chaplain—an older, balding man who smiled kindly with his eyes and his mouth.

Pam saw no reason to be evasive. He'd brought the subject up, after all. "No, I'm not angry at the world. Just at God, if there is one."

"May I sit with you?"

Pam gave a perfunctory nod, preferring to be alone but not wanting to be rude. She'd sit for a few minutes with him, then make her excuses.

"You're a doctor here," he said, staring straight ahead, like Pam.

"Yes."

"Did you lose a patient today?"

She supposed that was why doctors appeared in the chapel now and again. She shook her head.

"You know, God doesn't mind if you get angry with Him. He has big shoulders."

Oh, please. She hated it when people talked like God was a real person. "I'm sorry, but I should get back to work."

She started to rise from her seat when the man's hand on her arm gently tugged her back down. "No, I'm sorry. We can leave God out of this, you know. Will you tell me more about why you're angry?"

For a long moment Pam stared at her intertwined hands in her lap, wondering if confiding in the pastor was worth the effort. Finally, she decided she had little to lose and, who knows, maybe even something to gain. If nothing else, this man of the cloth seemed a safe place to deposit her anger.

"Why is death so…so random? So *unfair*."

"How do you mean?"

"Why do good people sometimes die young or tragically, and wicked people seem to get off scot-free? Why does it not make any sense?"

"Ah, but you see, death is not punishment and living is not always a reward. They're simply a part of the circle of life."

Pam's anger bubbled to the surface again. "Tell that to the two kids whose mom is clinging to life upstairs in the ICU. I'm sure they're not feeling so philosophical about death right now. Nor am I."

The pastor scrutinized her with intense dark eyes, but his voice was soft and gentle. "Someone you love has died recently."

Pam caught her breath. "Yes."

"Someone who didn't *deserve* to die?"

"Yes. My sister. She was an army doctor serving in Afghanistan when she was killed recently. A helicopter crash."

"Ah, I see. I'm very sorry for your loss."

"Thank you."

They sat in silence for a few minutes until the pastor spoke again. "My dear, to think of death as punitive is the same kind of thinking that is behind capital punishment. An eye for an eye. That sort of thing. Have you ever considered that sometimes living is the real punishment and death the reward?"

Pam supposed he was right. Some people had to live with excruciating pain, or poverty, or abuse, or any number of diseases and life-sucking conditions. In cases like those, death probably was deliverance.

"In my sister's case, death was not a reward."

"But who are we to judge? Sometimes God's plan is…"

"I don't want to hear about God's plan," Pam erupted. "A loving God wouldn't allow or plan for ninety percent of the shitty things that happen in this world."

"All right. I'm sorry. I said I would leave God out of this, didn't I?"

Pam shook her head and wiped at a tear before it could spill over. "I just don't understand any of it."

"You know something, Doctor? I must confess, I don't understand most of it either."

"You don't?"

Wincing, he shook his head. "Nope. But we're only human. We're not capable of understanding everything that happens in life. That's the way it's meant to be."

"But you believe in the power of God, even when you don't understand his plan, as you call it. You believe in a God that can't save good people or who can't always help the deserving."

"That's true, but you believe in medicine even when you can't save every patient, no?"

Pam conceded his point. "So I'm just supposed to accept these things?"

"Can you change the outcome if you choose not to accept death?"

"I can try to fight it when it's within my power to do so. That's why I'm in medicine."

"And when it's not in your power?"

"No, then of course not. I can't change the fact that my sister is dead."

"Precisely. Your anger and sense of helplessness will not bring her back."

Nothing was going to bring Laura back. She knew that. Still. "I'm not the kind of person who can accept that these things just happen. That when your number's up, it's up. Or that God has a plan and all that. You know what I think?" She didn't wait for him to answer. "I think sometimes shit just happens, and that innocent people sometimes die. That's what I think. What I can't accept is the unfairness of it all."

The chaplain sighed in resignation. "You're a doctor. It's good that you fight for your patients, that you don't accept death easily. But what makes you a good doctor doesn't necessarily make you someone who is at peace in her life."

Pam didn't like where this conversation was going. It was getting too personal, too judgmental, too uncomfortable.

"Look," the man said, resting his hand on her arm again, as if sensing she was about to bolt. "I've seen a lot of people die. And I've tried to help a lot of people through the grieving process."

"Then you must have formed some opinions."

"What I do know for certain is that death teaches us more about life than it does anything else. That life is meant to be lived and to be lived fully. To love and to do good in this world. Be true to yourself and follow your dreams. That's what I've learned about death, because those are the very things that are important about life."

So Laura's death was meant to teach her and others these great lessons about living? No. She refused to believe that. Laura didn't need to die so that she could figure out how to live more fully, how to be happier.

"Thank you, Pastor." She stood.

"I hope it helped." His smile was hopeful.

Pam nodded politely and left, stopping in the stairwell to lean against the cool solidity of the cinder block wall. Nothing much helped right now. She had an urge to call Trish and tell her about the conversation with the pastor. She wondered if Trish would agree with the part about learning to live more fully, to go for the brass ring while you could. Pam had gone for her dreams, and yet, admittedly, there was an emptiness in her life that her medical career hadn't been able to fill. Even before Laura's death, she had begun to question her purpose.

She pulled out her phone, called up the contact list, stared at Trish's number. She hesitated. Things had become awkward after the kiss, and now she didn't know where they stood. Trish had reassured her they were still friends, and yet the kiss had undeniably put up a wall between them. *Stupid, stupid kiss! Why the hell did I do something so stupid?*

She leaned against the wall, would have punched it out of frustration if it weren't cinder block. Her sister was dead, and the woman who had become her closest friend, her saving grace, was emotionally inaccessible to her now. She'd be seeing Trish in a few days. She hoped they could navigate their way around this, so that she could breathe again.

CHAPTER TWELVE

Dressed in nearly identical shorts, tank tops and running shoes, Trish and Pam ran the circumference of the high school's track once, then walked it. They decided to try to do ten laps this way, alternating between running and walking, because Trish had put her foot down about jogging the entire ten laps. She wasn't the athlete Pam was. For the sake of nostalgia, Pam had wanted to visit her old school and run the track again.

"I bet this track brings back a lot of memories for you," Trish said, still catching her breath from the run. Pam, like Laura, had excelled at sports.

"It does. Especially the bleachers." Pam pointed to the north side of the track.

"The bleachers?"

Pam laughed. "My first kiss with a girl was underneath those."

Trish laughed too. "Wow. And I thought your most exciting memory here would be the time you broke Laura's school record in the two hundred meters. I thought *that* was pretty exciting."

"Next to kissing a girl? Not even close!"

Trish lightly punched Pam in the bicep as they walked side by side. It was a relief to laugh together. Any awkwardness between them since the kiss had evaporated on the grounds of their alma mater in the late June sunshine. There were so many memories here, the air was practically electrified with them. They were like a cloak giving Trish instant safety, sureness, confidence. Those warm feelings had propelled her to a teaching career at the same school—she'd never considered teaching somewhere else. It occurred to her now how little her life had changed over the last twenty years, other than the fact that she earned a paycheck and paid a mortgage. Trish Tomlinson, the girl who never left Huron High.

Trish halted, light-headed with this revelation.

"You okay?" Pam asked in alarm, her fingers immediately engulfing Trish's wrist to take her pulse. "Do you feel faint?"

"No, I'm fine." She wasn't really, but she could pretend she was and try to change the subject. Except Pam was looking at her so earnestly, so full of worry. A fat, wobbly tear splashed suddenly on to Trish's cheek. She couldn't lie to Pam.

"Oh, Trish, I know. I know." Pam's hand slipped into Trish's and held it tightly as they resumed walking, but slower now.

"No," Trish mumbled. Pam didn't understand. She wasn't, for once, crying for Laura; she was crying for herself and her pathetic life. "No, it's…Never mind, okay?"

"No, I won't 'never mind.' What is it? What's wrong?"

"I'm so ridiculous, Pam. All this time…"

"All this time what?"

They walked on, and Trish didn't speak for a long time. When she did, her tears had stopped, and in her mouth was the bitter taste of self-recrimination. "I'm such an idiot. I never even gave myself a chance to move on."

"What are you talking about?"

"I never moved on from Laura because I never even left high school. Isn't that pathetic? I willingly put myself in this huge rut and called it a life."

"No, that's not true. And what's wrong with staying here? Lots of people teach at their alma maters. It doesn't matter that you never left Ann Arbor. It's a great city, Trish. I love it here. I always have. I *envy* you!"

Trish shook her head. "You got outta here, started a life, just like Laura did. But me, it's like I was afraid to try anything new, go anyplace different, start over. Maybe I stupidly thought if I stayed here, Laura would come back home. That everything would be as it once was."

Pam squeezed her hand. "Believe me, moving away and starting over somewhere else doesn't solve all your problems. If anything, it's harder to set down roots, to feel a part of anything when you go someplace else. You felt rooted to this community, invested yourself in it, and there's nothing wrong with that."

"That's true, as long as it's not a way of trying to hold on to the past."

"Is that what you were doing? *Are* doing?"

"I didn't think so at the time. I mean, I never articulated it like this before. But now I'm not so sure."

"I think you're reading too much into it. It's Laura's death that's made us doubt things, question our lives this way."

"Maybe, but the truth is the truth, regardless of what makes you come to the realization." Trish stopped walking, looked hard into Pam's eyes. "I can't move on if I don't examine my motives for the things I've done, for the way I've lived my life. If I don't come to terms with those things."

"Are you saying you want to move on?"

"I think so, yes. I mean, I need to. If I can't, I'll..." *Die just like Laura*, she wanted to say.

Pam seemed to understand because she nodded grimly. "Moving on from Laura doesn't mean you loved her any less. You know that, right?"

Trish nodded through fresh tears. "I know."

They walked again, Pam's hand still in hers. It felt nice.

Tentatively, Pam said, "Can I ask you something personal?"

"Of course."

"When was the last time you slept with my sister?"

That was easy to answer, but Trish found herself balking. She wondered why Pam wanted to know, but asking her would make it seem like she was evading the question. "When she was here for your mother's funeral. It just sort of happened."

"Not when she was here last November?"

"No. We had dinner together, but that was it. You seem surprised."

"That you slept with her six years ago? Or that you didn't sleep with her last fall?"

There was an edge of accusation in Pam's tone. Why should it matter to her when she last slept with Laura? She studied Pam's profile, the angry jaw, the pulsing vein in her neck. "Have I upset you in some way?"

"No. Look, forget it."

"Are you angry at me or at Laura?"

Pam dropped her hand. "Come on, let's run again."

Pam took off like a shot, her long legs pumping. She was fast and Trish couldn't quite catch her. After after a lap, Pam stopped and waited.

Trish jogged up to her. "Will you answer the question?"

"I'm not angry, I'm just…I don't know, okay?"

They walked some more in silence. Then Pam stopped and faced her, her expression pained, her hands on her hips. "Here's my problem. I don't understand why Laura never went back to you, when clearly you were the only woman who'd ever captured her heart. And I don't understand why you continued to be in love with someone who didn't want to commit to you. I'm confused, Trish. I don't understand, and I want to understand."

Trish instinctively fingered Laura's ring on the chain around her neck. "You think I'm stupid, don't you? Or weak? For carrying a torch like that for so long."

"No. I don't. But I don't understand…"

"About carrying a torch for someone?"

Pam's face colored. Her collapsed expression said she knew exactly what Trish alluded to.

"I'm sorry." Trish reached out and touched her arm. "I didn't mean to be such a bitch."

"No, I deserved it. And you're right. I do understand that part. I just hadn't thought of it that way."

"So what are we going to do about it?"

Pam grinned, her eyes sharpening with mischief. "We both need to find some hot, spectacular woman who completely blows us away and makes us forget about anyone else."

Trish smiled back. "And if we can't?"

"Then I'll have to keep trying to convince you that I'm worth taking a chance on." Pam continued grinning, but her eyes were dead serious.

Trish tilted her head, smiled back. "You're a lovely woman. And I have no doubt you're worth taking a chance on."

"As long as it's someone else taking a chance on me?"

Trish's breath caught in her throat. Memories of their kiss flooded her mind. Memories so intense that a twinge of arousal rushed back into her belly, her thighs. *What's wrong with me?* she wondered with no small amount of shock. This gorgeous, smart, successful, lovely woman is interested in me, and all I can do is think about the past and all the reasons why I shouldn't give her a chance.

Pam laughed lightly. "You look like you're having an anxiety attack. I was only teasing, you know."

Trish playfully bumped her shoulder, happy to have dodged a serious discussion about the two of them. She needed time and distance to give her a little perspective about Pam. Laura too, and the shifting balance of dynamics. "I'm starving. How about we go grab lunch, then get back to Laura's journal?"

"You read my mind. How about the Red Hawk Bar and Grill on campus?"

"Perfect. I think I've earned a giant cheeseburger and fries."

* * *

Pam ravenously tucked into her battered fish and fries and watched Trish do the same with her burger. From tall glasses, they sipped microbeer that had been brewed at a distillery nearby. It was a companionable silence, but Pam remained embarrassed by her earlier comment. The one about how she was worth taking a chance on. She'd known as soon as she opened her mouth that she sounded like an egotistical jerk. Trish was never going to give her a chance, and the more she dwelled on it, the more she didn't want to be like Trish anyway—stuck on someone you could never have, to the point of not allowing yourself to love anyone else. No. The sooner she could let go of this useless teenaged crush, the better. *If only there wasn't that little smudge of mustard I'd love to lick off her lips*, Pam thought helplessly.

"Should we?" Pam said, forcing a change in direction. She removed Laura's journal from her backpack on the seat beside her.

Trish nodded her approval, and Pam opened to where they had left off.

"Dec. 28:

I'm lonely today. I guess because it's the holidays, though things look the same around here, except for the little piece of mistletoe some optimistic person hung up in our staff lounge area. I miss Pam. I miss home, wherever the hell that is. More like the idea of home. But I'll get over it. I always do. In the meantime, I'll let this loneliness keep its grip on me for a day, and I know I'll spend it thinking about regrets, playing the what-if game in my mind. Like what if I'd quit the army by now. Where I'd be and what I'd be doing. And who I'd be doing it with. I suppose Trish would still take me back after all these years—"

Pam stole a glance at Trish, who seemed to have stopped breathing for a moment, but she nodded for Pam to go on.

"—if I went back to Ann Arbor as a civilian. I could practice medicine there probably. Or start a practice with Pam like we've talked about. And days like today, I dream of those things—having a home with someone, going to work every day, taking nice drives on the weekends, maybe a Saturday picnic somewhere, a jog along the river, going to a game at the Big House. It feels good to dream about those things on a day like this. But tomorrow, I'll wake up glad I'm here in the middle of a war zone. Glad to see my colleagues, to joke with them, to bug the colonel to let me go to one of the FOBs. Glad for that one big chest that holds all of my earthly belongings. Glad to know there's really only one person in the world who needs to worry about me, but she's my sister, and so it comes with the territory. The only thing that encumbers me is duty, and I wouldn't have it any other way. It's enough for me, and it's enough (usually) to erase any regrets and smother any ridiculous dreams. Duty is my religion. My wife."

Pam closed the journal and slipped it into her backpack before finishing her beer. "Wow. I think that's enough to digest for now."

Trish nodded, stared into her glass for a long time. Her eyes looked full, as though tears might spill over at any moment. But they didn't.

"You okay?" Pam asked quietly.

"Yes. I'm okay. I guess it drives it home, doesn't it?"

"Yes. She wouldn't have been happy living any other way. It really was her calling, like a religion."

"I thought medicine was a calling too. Shouldn't that have been enough?"

"Not for her."

"But it is for you, right?"

Pam shrugged. "I thought so. Now, I'm not so sure."

Surprise registered on Trish's face. "What's changed that?"

"Laura dying."

"Yeah, it's changed things for me too."

"Really? Like what?"

The waitress came by, collected their plates and took their order for coffee.

"Wanting to chase my dreams more than I have been," Trish said.

Dreams. Medicine had been Pam's big dream. Graduating, completing her internship, working in a big city hospital's bustling ER. Now that her dreams were reality, she'd stopped dreaming. Stopped wanting, until she'd met Trish again. Now she felt empty without a dream, and she didn't want to die that way. At least Laura had died still dreaming. Hadn't she?

"It's stupid really," Trish was saying, her mouth quirked into a sheepish smile.

"What? Tell me."

"I've never told anyone this before."

Pam leaned forward on her elbows. "Dreams are never stupid. I'm intrigued."

"Don't be. It's not that exciting. It's…I don't know. I guess I've always wanted to write a book of some kind."

"Really?" Pam had never known anyone who wanted to write a book before. Well, besides one of her professors who always talked about the ophthamology textbook he was going to write some day. But that wasn't what Trish was talking about. "What kind of book?"

The waitress swung by with their coffees, momentarily suspending conversation. Trish still looked a little embarrassed, but also invigorated. Like someone caught in a dream. Pam was a little envious.

"I'm not really sure. I've thought about a romance novel. I'm halfway through writing one actually."

"Really? That's so cool. I've never known anyone who's written a romance novel before. Is it girl on girl?"

"Of course, silly."

"And let me guess, girl gets girl at the end?"

"Oh, stop making fun. I knew I shouldn't have told you." But Trish didn't look annoyed. In fact, she looked a little glad for the attention.

"I'm not teasing, honest. I think it's great that you started writing a book. When are you going to finish it?"

"Probably never. I started it three years ago."

"You can't give up, not when you're halfway there."

Trish sighed, took a sip of coffee. "I guess I can't bring myself to write a happy ending. I know the girl is supposed to get the girl, but…"

Pam understood perfectly. "It's fantasy. The girl is *allowed* to get the girl, you know."

"I know. I just don't know what that feels like, you know?" Her voice caught, and Pam reached across the table to touch her hand.

"So write about something else," Pam suggested. "A mystery or a thriller. Maybe even something nonfiction?"

"I know, you're right. I should start something different and forget about this romance nonsense."

"Don't give up on it, Trish." It saddened Pam that for Trish there hadn't been a happy ending. She supposed she should feel encouraged that Trish's heart remained her own and not possessed by someone else, but she wasn't. Trish was a woman of substance and someone who deserved to be loved back.

"What about you?" Trish's eyes probed her. "You're not thinking of quitting medicine, are you?"

Pam looked away. She didn't want to see the concern on Trish's face. "My contract is done in a couple of weeks. I haven't signed on for another term."

"Are you going to?"

"I don't think so. It feels like I need some time to figure things out." That was an understatement.

"Does that mean you don't want to be a doctor anymore?"

Pam didn't exactly know what it meant. She couldn't fathom not being a doctor. It's what she'd dreamed about doing since she was a teenager and watched Laura go off to medical school. Her mother and sister had both made financial sacrifices to help her pay for her education, and she didn't want to dishonor them by abandoning it. She was good at it, too, and yet, she was so lost now, so numb, so full of doubts. She could not find it in herself to care much about anything. Continuing her work felt passionless, an act of simply going through the motions. She didn't want that, and her patients certainly didn't deserve that.

"I guess I want to feel the way Laura did about her work," she said, emotion strangling her voice. "Like it's a religion. Or a wife."

"Oh, honey, I'm sorry. I know Laura's death has made you feel like you're at a crossroads. For what it's worth, I think you're too good at what you do and you enjoy helping people too much to give it up."

She hoped Trish was right and that her passion for medicine would return. But what if it didn't? Her stomach clenched at the thought. There was no guarantee she would want to go back to it, but hell, there was no guarantee with anything, as Laura's death was so painfully reminding her.

"I need to be sure it's what I want to do," Pam said. Sure that it was what she really wanted for herself, that she wasn't Laura's shadow, copying Laura in everything she did—from medicine to wanting Trish. With quiet desperation, she wondered now if that's what she'd been doing all these years, playing the role of little sister mindlessly following in big sister's footsteps. If that was true, then it was time to find her own path. Time to be the leader instead of the follower. Of course, it wasn't like she had a choice anyway, because her leader was dead.

She looked at Trish and tried not to let the panic show on her face. She didn't want to give up everything she'd worked at for so long, every dream, every ounce of her love for Trish, simply because they weren't original ideas.

"Pam? What's wrong?"

"Nothing, I…"

"Trish darling!" A large African American woman, about six feet tall and with the wide girth of a middle-aged ex-athlete, slapped Trish on the shoulder. "Girl, what a treat running into you here."

"Bev, how are you? Oh, sorry, this is my friend Pam. Pam, this is Bev Jermaine. Coaches the women's basketball team at our school."

Pam half stood and shook the woman's meaty hand. Yup, definitely basketball mitts. "Pleasure to meet you, Bev."

"Oh, the pleasure is all mine." Bev's dark eyes swept appreciatively over Pam before returning to Trish. Her teeth gleamed in the widest grin Pam had ever seen. "Please tell me you're bringing this lovely woman to the party tonight."

"Oh, I, ah…"

Trish's face began to flush. A party was news to Pam.

"Don't tell me you were going to weasel out of it." Bev pretended to be angry, but was soon grinning again. "'Cuz you know I'll come find you and drag y'all there."

Trish cleared her throat. "I, ah, wasn't sure we were up for a party. Pam is Laura's sister. She's visiting me this weekend."

"Oh. Shit." Bev clasped a heavy arm around Pam's shoulder. "I'm really sorry about your sister, Pam. My condolences. And I totally I understand about the party."

"Thanks."

Bev's scrutiny of her took on a patina of awe. "I've heard a lot about the Wright sisters at the school over the years. Your athletic accomplishments are legendary."

"Please. I only wish it were true."

"You still play basketball?"

"Once or twice a week with the guys at work."

Bev frowned. "Then for sure I'm not going to ask you for a little one-on-one while you're visiting. You'd kick my ass. Anyway, seriously. If you ladies feel like a nice distraction tonight or a drink, then come on out, okay? We'd love to have you both. A happy crowd always makes things better."

"Thanks, Bev. We'll think about it." Trish rose and hugged Bev.

"You know fun is never in short supply at our place." Her laugh was so deep, it resonated in Pam's toes.

"I sure do know that. Thanks. And tell Jean I said hello."

Bev winked. "You can tell her yourself tonight. Pam, again, great to meet you."

"Thanks. Great to meet you too, Bev."

As soon as Bev moved along, Trish began apologizing. "I should have mentioned the party to you. I just didn't think…"

"Hey, it's okay. I'd have done the same if I were you. But I don't mind going. Honestly. It might even be nice."

"Really? You sure?"

Pam shrugged. "Why not? It'll be mostly gay people, I take it?"

"Mostly, yes. Every year around this time, we have a party to celebrate the end of the school season. Most of us are teachers or connected to the school in some way, but not everyone. And some are straight, but they're all very gay friendly. Nobody's afraid to let their hair down."

"Sounds like fun." Trish looked like she was holding something back. Pam pressed her. "Something you're not telling me about this party?"

"No, not really. I just need to figure out how to kiss and make up with Rosa, because I'm pretty sure she'll be there."

"You had a fight?" Pam asked in alarm.

"Sort of. Not really. I don't know. Things didn't end well when we got together last week."

The waitress dropped their bill on the table, asked if there was anything else. Pam pocketed the bill, ignoring Trish's protestations.

"Well?" Pam said as they walked to Trish's car. "Is your falling out so bad that you need to avoid her?"

"Oh, hell, I don't know. I guess I need to give myself a slap or something."

"So the falling out is your fault?"

"No, it was both of us. She had some pretty harsh words for me. Words I didn't want to hear, and I was pretty nasty about it. She's texted me and tried to call a few times, and I keep ignoring her."

"Do you think you two can work it out?"

"I guess. Or we should at least try, anyway."

Pam slipped her arm through Trish's. "Good. Then we'll go to this party later. I'd like to meet your friends."

Trish laughed. "You might be sorry."

"I don't think so." Pam enjoyed the thought of experiencing Trish in the company of her friends, relaxing and enjoying herself. They both needed a little fun, some casual conversation for a change. While she enjoyed—*needed*—their deep, cathartic talks, they were also exhausting. "Will there be music? Dancing?"

"Ha, you can count on it. Especially since it's at Bev and Jean's. They love old R and B stuff. And Bev doesn't need an excuse to put on her dancing shoes."

"Sounds perfect."

CHAPTER THIRTEEN

Trish put the party out of her mind as they read more of Laura's journal. Her writing style was pure, honest, with the right mix of emotion and observation. She'd have made a good journalist, it occurred to Trish. She hadn't given a lot of thought to the war the last few years as it shifted from Iraq to Afghanistan, other than wondering what Laura was up to and whether she was safe. She'd never found herself very curious about what went on in a war zone, but now she was. She eagerly absorbed Laura's journal entries, sometimes closing her eyes when it was Pam's turn to read so that she could picture exactly what the words described. She could almost see the dust, feel the heat, hear the thwack of helicopter blades and the thundering scream of jets overhead.

"Jan. 3:
Medevac brought in a Taliban soldier this afternoon. He'd been shot up pretty good by a British soldier during a roadside ambush. His left leg was shredded by bullets, his left hand pretty much shot right off. He was conscious, but he refused to speak

to our interpreter. Wouldn't look any of us in the eye. Kind of had this look of disdain on his face, like he hated our guts, which was mutual. I supposed it really pissed him off having a woman doc, which secretly pleased me. It's true that some of our staff get a little rough with the enemies when they're brought in like this. You know, as in, forgetting to give them a shot of morphine, not being very delicate with the IV, or tying the tourniquet a little too tight. Believe me, I'd have loved to kick this guy to the curb with a few more areas of pain to worry about. He might very well have killed or injured some of my friends over the course of this war and might inflict more damage once we let him go. But it's my job to help anyone who comes through these doors, and, yeah, it fucking kills me to do it sometimes, but I know the day I can't do this, I'll have to stop being a doctor. The Hippocratic Oath doesn't talk about wars and enemies. People are people. They're not born this way, they're made. And so just maybe, when we help save these guys, they'll pause a second or two next time they pull that trigger, and it might be long enough to save a life. Or maybe they'll stop fighting us. I don't know. My cynical side says it won't make a damn bit of difference, but I believe hate just leads to more hate. Sometimes that thought is the only thing that makes me push forward and help a guy like him.

"Anyway, I think we saved his leg, but not his hand. With luck, he was left handed and won't be able to fire a weapon again."

Trish looked at Pam. "I didn't know they had to treat the enemy sometimes. Does that ever happen to you, where you have to treat a killer or a bank robber or something?"

"Sure. Not often, but regularly enough. It's tough, I won't lie about that. In some ways it's easier to do your job when you don't really give a shit if they live or die. But it's definitely not as satisfying to save someone that you can't identify with or feel any positive or empathetic emotions for. Isn't it pretty much the same in teaching? Some kids you feel good about helping, and some you don't?"

She'd had a few students over the years who'd been lost causes and some she thought she could help turn around. She'd spent many of her personal hours one semester trying to help a fifteen-year-old boy who was battling a lot of personal demons—alcoholic parents, bullying issues at school, poor grades. As hard as she tried, whenever the two of them would take a step forward, they'd take another two steps back. A school janitor ultimately found him hanging from the bathroom ceiling one morning. It'd taken her a long time to get over it.

She told Pam the story. "Those times when you give so much, it feels like sometimes you never get those pieces of yourself back."

"I know. And sometimes you need to step away, try to find that part of yourself that made you want to go into that profession. I think that's where I am at right now."

"If you need to take time for yourself, then you should do it. Is there anything I can do? I have tons of space here if you want to come back and stay for a while."

Pam immediately perked up, and for a moment there was that look in her eyes again—the one that temporarily rendered Trish speechless. She could fall into those gray-green pools, lose herself. But no. She couldn't let that happen. She also couldn't backtrack on the offer she'd just made.

Pam's smile faltered. "I'm not sure that would be a good idea."

Desperate to change the subject, Trish glanced at the antique clock on the mantel in her living room. "Crap. If we're going to mooch some food at the party, we'd better get going. I'm sure the barbecue's fired up by now."

Each clutching a bottle of wine as a hostess gift, they walked the seven blocks to Bev and Jean's, having decided it was easier than worrying about a car.

Bev launched herself at them with a bear hug. She was the kind of person who threw formalities out the window and made best friends quickly. Bev then introduced her partner Jean to Pam. The cozy brick bungalow was teeming with people, most of whom Trish knew, and most of them were lesbians. The dress was casual—shorts and polo shirts or sundresses—and there was a palpable sense of summer and freedom in the air. Alcohol, conversation and laughter flowed in great proportions.

The smell of steak on the barbecue wafted through the air, and Trish's stomach growled.

"Come on, kids," Jean said, tugging at them. "Let's fix you up with some supper."

"And wine," Bev added with an indulgent grin, taking the bottles from them.

Soon after, their plates and glasses full, Trish proceeded to introduce Pam to as many people as she could around mouthfuls of food. Some of them shot Trish a knowing smirk, figuring Pam was her date. She wanted to explain, then decided against it. People could think what they wanted. And really, was it the worst thing in the world if people thought she was sleeping with a gorgeous, younger woman who also happened to be a doctor? You incorrigible cougar, she told herself and grinned slyly.

"You sure look like you're in a delightful mood."

Trish looked up at the sound of Rosa's voice and felt her smile involuntarily dissolve. "Hi, Rosa."

Rosa, her mass of gray curls going off in every direction, tried in vain to pat them into submission as she thrust herself toward Pam.

"Oh. Um," Trish said, trying for cool and detached, but she knew she wasn't pulling it off. She was nervous as hell. "Rosa, this is Pamela Wright. Pam, this is my friend, Rosa Moran."

She watched them shake hands, smile politely, pretend they weren't sizing each other up. Rosa gave Trish her trademark raised eyebrow, then a jerk of the head to indicate they should talk. Alone. She told Pam she'd be back in a few minutes.

Inside a guest bedroom, Rosa hugged her, tentatively at first, then more meaningfully. There was nothing sexual to it, and that was the problem. There never *was* anything sexual about their physical contact, at least not for Trish. If there had been, maybe their relationship would have had a fighting chance.

"I'm so sorry about our disagreement," Rosa said. "You're my best friend in the world. You know that, don't you?"

"Of course I do. And I'm sorry too. I got defensive. And I was rude."

"No. I know how sensitive you are about Laura, how private you are about her and your past, and I kept provoking you. I'm sorry, Trish. I wish I could explain myself better, but I think I was feeling a lot of things that day. Most of them not good."

Rosa released her, and Trish saw her eyes drop to the necklace with Laura's ring on it.

She hated when Rosa was right, which was annoyingly often. It was true she'd been holding on to a ghost. And not because Laura was dead. She'd been holding on to that ghost for years. Holding on to something she would never, ever have again. She'd never looked at herself, at her life, with so much brutal honesty before. Laura's death had provided the aperture through which she could see herself more clearly, and for the most part, she didn't like what she saw.

Trembling with emotion, she said, "I don't think I know how to let go anymore."

Rosa's smile was generous, forgiving. "I think you already have started to let go. I think that's the part you're struggling with. It feels foreign to be without something—someone—that's been a part of you for, what, twenty-plus years?"

Trish sank on to the edge of the bed, elbows on her knees, chin propped on her hands. "Jesus, Rosa. I don't know if I can do it. Or how to do it. I feel so lost. So alone. Like I'm standing on the end of a diving board."

Rosa sat down beside her, put her arm around her shoulders. "You're not alone. I'm here for you. And so is that woman out there who looks like she's totally in love with you."

"What? What are you talking about?"

With a smile, Rosa shook her head. "I think you know exactly what I'm talking about."

* * *

Pam chatted with Bev, accepted the glass of wine that was pressed into her hand. She let Bev introduce her to the latecomers and the few people she'd hadn't yet been introduced to, noticing there were several nice-looking women in the mix. Women who gave her a second look and an encouraging smile. She was flattered, thinking she should probably take a few of them, or at least one of them, up on the subtle offers that seemed to be floating her way, but Pam simply smiled back with enough aloofness to suggest she wasn't looking.

Bev clapped a friendly arm around her shoulder. "You're single, aren't you?"

Reluctant to admit it, Pam stalled.

"Well?" She moved closer and whispered, "A few women have asked me."

"I, ah…guess so."

Bev's laughter was meant to scold. "That's some answer. Is that like sort of being a virgin? Oh, never mind. I'm just raising a little hell with you. Sounds to me like you're single but would rather not be. Is that it?"

"No. Maybe. I don't know."

Bev raised her eyebrows but said nothing more. She steered Pam outside to the large patio, where tiny multicolored lights twinkled overhead. A dance area had been constructed out of plywood boards, and Motown music blared from speakers designed to look like rocks tucked up against shrubs. A handful of couples danced: some gay, some straight. It'd been a long time since she'd been to a house party, Pam realized, as she soaked in the music, the dancing, the laughter. Med school graduation was probably the last time she'd attended one.

"Have some fun and don't be shy," Bev advised before disappearing.

Pam sipped her wine, wondering where Trish and Rosa had gone. Probably—hopefully—making up from their spat. She considered Rosa as she watched two women dance close to "The Way You Do the Things You Do." Rosa was older than Trish, maybe by a decade or so. Average looking, but she had sharp, intelligent eyes. She looked like the kind of woman you could have long, insightful, energizing conversations with. She imagined Trish being attracted to Rosa's mind, but she couldn't quite fit them together sexually. There didn't seem to be any sparks between them, any physical chemistry. She wondered how they'd gotten together and guessed they'd started out as friends, probably with Rosa suggesting more, until Trish relented.

You're being harsh, Pamela. There's absolutely nothing wrong with Rosa. Maybe she's exactly the kind of woman who turns Trish's crank…

"Hi."

Pam turned to the pleasant-looking woman who'd silently stepped up beside her. "Hi."

"Stacey Fisk," the woman answered, sticking out her hand.

Pam shook it. "Pam Wright."

"Nice party, huh? You like Motown?"

"Of course. Can't grow up forty-five miles from Detroit and not like Motown music."

"So you're from here?"

"Yup. Originally. You?"

"Indianapolis. Moved here six years ago for the job. Hey, wait a minute. You're the woman whose sister was killed in Afghanistan, right?"

Pam winced, an arrow of pain shooting through her for an instant, silencing her. She wasn't used to strangers bringing up Laura's death and probably never would be. She nodded reluctantly.

"I'm so sorry about that. I'm sorry to bring it up the way I did. I didn't mean to sound insensitive about it."

"It's okay," Pam lied, her palms itchy. Where the hell was Trish, anyway?

"Look, I should've told you. I'm a newspaper reporter. *The Journal*."

"Stacey, I don't want to…"

"It's okay. I'm used to my job being a conversation stopper when I tell people. My paper did a couple of stories on your sister when she died."

Pam had read them. The first was a news story, the second an obituary.

"I'd like to do something more on her some day," Stacey continued, growing animated. "An in-depth feature story about who she really was. What exactly she was doing over there, why she was a career army doctor. What she thought of the war. All that kind of stuff."

"I don't know," Pam said. Her first instinct was to have no part of it.

Stacey's smile was reassuring. Harmless. She was probably well-practiced in the art of softening people up. "Just think about, would you? Sounds to me like she was kind of a pioneer. A woman, a career army doctor, serving several tours in hot zones. Someone like her deserves to have her story told. She was a real hero."

"Yes, but I don't know that she'd have wanted a big story written about her. She wasn't the type who sought the limelight." In fact, Laura always laughed bitterly whenever someone called her a hero. To her, all kinds of people were heroes, from bus drivers to construction workers to stay-at-home moms. A uniform doesn't automatically make you a hero, she'd told Pam on more than one occasion. But Laura was wrong not to consider herself a hero.

"I understand." Stacey fished a business card from her shirt pocket and gave it to Pam. "If you ever think her story should be told, call me, okay? I'm not into sensationalizing stuff or making anyone look bad, if that's what you're worried about." Stacey pushed her long blond bangs around her ears, lowered her voice. "I know what it's like over there."

"You do?"

"I was in Afghanistan three years ago. My boss sent me over for a week to follow the family of another soldier who'd been killed. It was kind of a healing journey for them. They wanted to go over there, see what it was like, see where their son got killed."

Pam's heart began to pound as Stacey's words coagulated in her mind, slowly, like thick sludge. Why hadn't she thought of that before? Laura's journal was one thing, but actually going there, boots on the ground, made stone-cold sense. Seeing where Laura had died, seeing firsthand exactly what she'd been doing over there, who she worked with, the people she helped, how they lived, what the hospital conditions were like. Maybe it was exactly what she needed to do to understand Laura better, to get the closure she hadn't been able to find.

Stacey was still talking, something about an army program for families of KIA soldiers, but Pam tuned her out. She could contact Camille. Camille would know about such arrangements. And then there was Trish. Would Trish want to go too? Or would Trish think she was nuts? Her mind whirled, and Stacey was saying something to her in a much softer voice.

"Pardon?"

Something slow was playing on the stereo. Stacey's mood had clearly transitioned from business to pleasure. "Dance?"

She wasn't bad looking. Kind of cute, as a matter of fact. But Pam wasn't the least bit interested. She had no real reason not to be interested, yet she couldn't bring herself to accept a dance with Stacey. The truth was she didn't want to be in anyone's arms but Trish's, and if that made her a hopeless loser, then so be it. "Sorry," Pam muttered. "There's someone I need to find."

* * *

It was a relief to be on happy terms with Rosa again, Trish decided, and smiled at her friend. She hadn't realized until their little falling-out that she needed Rosa in her life. Being lovers hadn't worked out and never would—they both understood that—but they would always be friends. They could talk about anything, although Laura would probably always be a sensitive topic between them. But that was par for the course.

"Let's seal this with a dance," Rosa suggested, holding her hand out in a grand gesture of deference. Something from Smokey Robinson was playing on the outdoor speakers.

"All right."

The song was "Just to See Her," and it made Trish suddenly think of Pam. She'd seen Pam talking to a blond woman earlier. A pretty heavy discussion by the looks of things.

"That blond woman," Trish said to Rosa as they danced together. "Kind of lanky, sort of androgynous looking. Talking to Pam earlier. Who was that?"

"That was Stacey Fisk."

"The name sounds familiar. Who is she?"

"Newspaper reporter. Friend of Jean's, I think."

"Hmm, wonder what she wanted with Pam?"

Rosa laughed. "Probably trying to pick her up. I mean, who wouldn't?"

Okay, that's not funny, Trish thought. She didn't want to think of someone trying to pick up Pam. Worse, she didn't want to think of Pam saying yes, and not just because she'd shared that heart-stopping kiss with Pam. Nor because Pam was Laura's little sister and Trish felt protective toward her. *Shit.* Maybe it was for exactly those reasons. And more.

She felt eyes on her, turned, and there in the shadows, against the brick wall of the house, leaned Pam. Thumbs hooked through the belt loops of her hip-clinging khaki capri pants, tight shirt clinging to every muscle and curve, breasts tantalizingly pushed forward by the perfectly fitting blouse, long slender neck that looked so smooth, so kissable. And that strong Wright jaw. Pam's eyes were in shadow, but they were gazing at her, Trish knew, and her heart crashed to a halt. Pam quite literally stole her breath.

"She really is a looker," Rosa said, whistling softly.

"What? Who?"

"Laura's little sister. She's attracted to you. And I'd say it's mutual."

Trish didn't want to have this discussion. Not now, not here, and not with Rosa.

"You're blowing things out of proportion," Trish said tersely, hoping her tone might put an end to the subject. "We're old friends."

"Old friends, eh? How come she's looking at me like I'm a lobster she wants to toss in a vat of boiling water? And then carry you off?"

Trish laughed at Rosa's graphic description. "You really do have an imagination, don't you?"

"I'm a writer and a creative writing professor, remember?"

Pam advanced toward them, deftly maneuvering around the other dancing bodies.

"Give her a chance," Rosa whispered as Pam stepped up to them, her eyes serious, her mouth an uncompromising line in the dusky light.

Maybe Rosa was right and Pam really did want to make her disappear at all costs. It hit her that Pam might be jealous that she was dancing with Rosa. A tingle flared in her chest, sank to her stomach, then lower.

"May I have the honor of cutting in?" Pam asked, gallant like Cary Grant playing out a scene in a move. It gave Trish the urge to swoon.

Rosa's smile was almost too eager. Probably a little worried about that vat of boiling water after all, Trish thought with amusement. Rosa backed away, did a little bow, and Pam took her place in Trish's arms.

"Really," Trish said, trying to smother the sexual heat slowly engulfing her body. Sweat prickled her scalp. "You didn't have to come to my rescue."

"That's not why I'm dancing with you. You and Rosa look like you've patched things up just fine."

"We did. And…Wait, is that why you're dancing with me?"

"You busted me. I was afraid you might patch things up a little too good with Rosa. And because I wanted it to be me dancing to this song with you."

Trish looked into Pam's eyes, expecting to see defiance or some kind of possessiveness. Instead, Pam looked satisfied, emboldened.

"I know," Pam continued, "that I'm not supposed to talk like that. We're supposed to forget the kiss. And me, how I feel about you, I know it's off limits. I know…"

"Wait." Gently Trish placed a finger on Pam's full lips. She knew she shouldn't touch her like that, especially when Pam's eyes slid shut at the intimate contact, but she couldn't help herself. Pam was damned alluring, incredibly gorgeous and extremely vulnerable right now. She smelled good and felt so good, so right in her arms as Smokey sang in his silky way. Then Aretha's "Natural Woman" began playing. It was too much, because it nearly moved Trish to tears. She couldn't breathe because of the way Pam filled her, couldn't think past her pulsating senses. But she could share none of this with Pam. "You're getting ahead of yourself. Just slow down, okay?" She was commanding herself as much as Pam.

Pam nodded, remained silent as they swayed together.

God, Trish thought. It was shocking how quickly her burgeoning feelings for Pam were taking over. She'd thought things were under control, other than that momentary slipup when they'd kissed. Everything was tidily in its place, or so she'd believed. Pam had simply maintained that schoolgirl crush on her, and she was only feeling things for Pam because she was grieving and missing Laura. They were both lonely, both in need of the warm embrace of someone who cared. That's all it was, she told herself. *A supportive friendship*.

Yet this, she thought as she inhaled Pam's scent, this bordered on complete irrationality. The mere nearness of Pam was doing things—exciting things—to her body and turning her mind to mush. For once, she wanted to go ahead and feel instead of think. Go with her heart and the lust swelling between her legs. She wanted, at least for this moment, to throw out every excuse that was holding her—them—back.

Another song began playing, something by Gladys Knight, and they continued to dance, not wanting to let go. Their bodies were melded together, their curves and angles fitting perfectly, snugly, softly together. Pam's leg pressed lightly between hers, producing just enough friction to start Trish's clit throbbing as though it had a heartbeat of its own. *Jesus, I'm turned on. If we were home right now I wouldn't be able to say no. Wouldn't want to say no.*

Something bumped hard into her, causing her to miss a step. She felt liquid seeping into the ass of her shorts.

"Shit!" She spun around, stumbled against Rosa on the ground beside her. Rosa was picking herself up from one knee, grinning or grimacing, Trish wasn't sure which. "Rosa, what happened?"

"Oh, damn. I'm so sorry Trish." Rosa examined her empty wineglass, then frowned at Trish's stained shorts. "I lost my footing and…Oh, no, I've ruined your shorts."

Trish craned her neck to try to see how bad the wine stain was. Figured that it had to be red wine. "Look, don't worry about it. If it doesn't wash out, they're only from Kohl's. Nothing expensive." She didn't care about her shorts. What annoyed her was that Rosa had so clumsily interrupted the two of them, but she didn't dare show it. She didn't want Rosa to pick up on the vibes between her and Pam. "Just a suggestion, but maybe you should switch to water, hmm?"

"Speaking of wine," Pam said, disappointment etched on her face. "I think I'll go get us a glass. I'm a little thirsty."

Watching Pam disappear into the crowd, Trish said sternly, "Tell me that was an innocent little accident."

"I'm not jealous, if that's what you think," Rosa replied.

"You're not typically clumsy either. Want to tell me what that was all about?"

"I thought you could use a moment for reflection. For a little perspective. Things looked like they were getting a little fevered between you two."

"Didn't you tell me about an hour ago that I should give her a chance? Weren't you practically ready to throw me into her arms?"

"Yes, I think you should give her a chance. But I know you, Trish, and I know you're not quite ready for what was about to happen."

"What, sex on the dance floor? Is that what you think?"

"Pretty much. Look, if you go too fast with her, you'll beat yourself up. You'll convince yourself that you're using her as a way of getting Laura out of your head. Or something along that vein. And then it'll get ugly."

"But that's not..."

"I know. But I don't want to see you confuse the issue. Pam deserves better than that, and so do you, my friend."

Trish blew out an exasperated breath. "Dammit, Rosa."

"I know, Trish. Just go slow, okay? I care about you, you know."

"Thank you. I know you do."

"That's what friends are for. And you know that I'm okay with that, with not being more than friends, right? I mean, we're clear on that once and for all?"

"Yes." Trish smiled. She was lucky Rosa had stuck by her. "We are."

Pam returned, a glass of wine in each hand. "Here, Rosa, take one. I'll go grab another."

"No, but thank you. I don't want to ruin anyone else's clothes. Except maybe that elegant-looking woman talking with Bev." She winked at Pam. "I wouldn't mind helping *her* into something more comfortable."

"Speaking of ruined clothes, I think we're going to have to go soon," Trish said. "It's not much fun hanging around here with a wet ass."

Pam's eyes flashed mischievously. "I agree, and for the record, I think *you* should change into something more comfortable."

"Bye, kids," Rosa said. "Behave yourselves."

CHAPTER FOURTEEN

The air was warm and humid, the glow of the orange streetlights like small orbs of setting suns, Pam thought.

She wanted to hold Trish's hand on the walk back to the house, but she couldn't think of an excuse that would allow it. It was a romantic thought that wouldn't leave her, though. So was the desire that this was a real date and that there was more of the evening in store, back at the house—a glass of wine together on the two-person glider on the front porch, gazing into each other's eyes and talking about the future. A little making out in the dark too.

Pam didn't like admitting that she was a closet romantic, but in her bones she knew it was true. It was why she read schmaltzy Nora Roberts' and Nicholas Sparks' books and had a healthy collection of lesbian romance novels as well, all of them stashed neatly under the bed. Even an old Barry Manilow tune on the radio could send a shiver of sentiment through her. She'd never been with a woman worthy of unleashing her pent-up romantic zeal on, but with Trish she knew she could. Every romantic song, every vision of a candlelit dinner or a walk on the beach made her think of Trish. With Trish, all of these and more were possibilities, not simply fantasies.

Trish broke the silence. "Can I ask you something?"

"Of course."

"Earlier tonight. What were you talking to that newspaper reporter about?"

"She was talking to me about Laura. She'd like to do a story about Laura sometime. Her life, her sacrifices. You know, what kind of person she was, why she joined the army. Kind of an American hero type of story."

"Tell me you're not considering it."

Pam shrugged one shoulder. "She made some good points. Laura really was a hero. I think maybe, at some point anyway, her story deserves to be told to a wider audience. I think people should understand what our soldiers are doing over there and why they do what they do. I'd like people to know Laura's sacrifice wasn't for nothing."

Trish remained silent, and even in the dark, Pam could see her jaw clenched tightly. Her stride became more staccato, heavier. Angry stomps that reminded Pam of the sound of marching soldiers.

"Trish, you can't stay mad at the army for the rest of your life."

"Why not? They took her away from us forever. And besides, it's not the rest of my life yet. She hasn't even been gone three months. I can damn well stay mad as long as I like."

Pam didn't say more; she didn't want to cause a big fight. But she knew Trish's anger and rage at the army would eventually eat her up from the inside out if she didn't let it go or at least figure out a way to blunt it. The army had been Laura's choice—as much as she and Trish had disagreed with it. And it had been Laura's choice to go to Afghanistan. Hell, if Laura had wanted to play it safe, she could have had her pick of base hospitals, stateside or in Europe. She'd paid her dues, but coasting wasn't in her blood. She'd wanted to be where the action was, doing her part, with her eyes wide open.

Pam had been on the verge of telling Trish about her idea of going to Afghanistan to see where Laura had made her sacrifice, to find some closure to whatever open-ended questions still existed. But Trish was so angry, Pam didn't dare bring it up.

By the time they got back to the house, Trish's body language had noticeably changed. The tide of anger had visibly receded.

"It's such a nice night, will you sit on the porch with me a while?" Trish asked, pulling two wineglasses down from the cupboard.

A warm shiver coursed through Pam. Had Trish read her mind about the porch glider?

"Okay," she answered, turning away so that her face didn't give away her desire. "Sounds good."

Minutes later, Trish beside her on the glider and a glass of wine in her hand, Pam leaned her head back and closed her eyes, enjoying the peace—the sublimity—of the moment. She felt completely at home, completely content. Yes, complete, she realized. It was as though everything had fallen into place as she let her unanswered questions, the unfinished conversations with Trish, fall away like autumn leaves from a tree. Nothing mattered at this very juncture but the two of them and this warm, still night that felt like a loving embrace. She could stay this way forever.

"I'm glad," Pam said after a while, "that you and Rosa are friends again."

"Hmm, yes. I think we always will be, in spite of the occasional rough patch. You never did ask me what our fight was about."

"I had an idea."

"You did? I mean, you do?"

"I figure Laura is probably the predominant theme of your disagreements with Rosa."

Trish quietly sipped her wine, smiling in wonder. "Sometimes I underestimate you."

Pam laughed. "Big mistake."

"Believe me, I've begun to figure that out. You're a smart woman, aren't you?"

"Not always," Pam said wistfully. A smarter woman would have sorted out her feelings for Trish a good many years ago.

A smarter woman would probably have moved on instead of carrying this torch forever.

"Rosa," Trish said, "pretty much told me I was never going to be happy, was never going to *live* again, unless I let go of Laura for good. I got angry with her because I didn't want to hear the truth."

Pam sat up straighter, looked hard into Trish's eyes. "Do you think you can finally do it?"

Her mouth tight, Trish shook her head slowly. "Do I have a choice? I have to do it, Pam. I mean, Christ, she's not coming back. At least I finally get that part."

"That's not what I mean. I mean here." Pam touched the flat of her palm to the center of Trish's chest, above her beating heart. "Can you do it here?" Her own heart beat wildly in anticipation of Trish's answer.

Slowly, Trish placed her hand on top of Pam's, holding it to her chest. "Yes. I think I can. I mean, I want to this time. But it won't happen overnight."

Pam understood. There might be a chance for the two of them after all, but it would take time.

"What made you finally decide you want to move on this time?" Pam asked tentatively.

"You mean besides the fact that Laura is never coming back?"

"Yes, besides that. People sometimes hold on to ghosts for a long, long time." *Please don't be one of those people, Trish.*

Trish moved Pam's hand to her cheek. "I don't," she whispered, "want to miss out anymore on what's right in front of me."

Pam's throat went dry. Her heart pounded so hard, so fast, she feared it sounded like a hundred galloping horses. She swallowed, hoarsely pushing the words out. "And right in front of you is what?"

Trish smiled, turned Pam's hand and slowly kissed the backs of her fingers until Pam felt as though she were melting from the inside out. She swore hot lava was throbbing through her veins as Trish's touch tore her apart in a million different directions.

"Right in front of me," Trish said, her eyes brimming with emotion as she searched Pam's face, "is a beautiful, wonderful woman I've been willfully blind to all this time. A beautiful, wonderful woman I care so very much about and am so attracted to. I don't want to lose you, but I'm scared, Pam."

Pam's heart nearly stopped. They were the words she'd longed to hear, but why was there always a caveat? A "no" where there should have been a "yes"?

"What are you scared of, Trish?"

Trish's eyes snapped shut, her body stiffening. The magic of the moment was quickly slipping away. *She* was quickly slipping away from Pam.

"Tell me," Pam urged.

"I don't...Jesus. Don't you see? I'm scared I might end up thinking of you as some sort of replacement for Laura. Or that you're a rebound thing. I can't do that to either of us."

Pam smiled in spite of the seriousness of the subject. "It's been too many years for this to be a rebound."

"Oh, dammit, you know what I mean. A clone, then." Trish broke into a smile too. "You're right. This definitely isn't a rebound situation."

Pam understood Trish's fears. She had to be sure she was over Laura before she could love Pam. That she wasn't simply transferring her feelings for Laura on to Pam. Or that she wasn't using an affair with Pam as a catalyst to get over Laura.

"I do know what you mean, Trish."

"Good. Then you know I have to—that we have to—go slow. No timetable, no pressure, no expectations."

Pam grinned triumphantly, taking what she could get. Even though Trish was making no promises, at least she was giving her a chance, and that was worth celebrating.

"What about you?" Trish asked with concern. "What pace would work for you?"

"Slow is good. And I agree. No timetable, no pressure, no expectations."

"But how do you feel about that?"

"Honestly?"

"Of course."

"Like I want to make love to you this minute. Like I want to start being your girlfriend right now. I may not have the iron discipline of my soldier sister, but self-control is underrated these days. I can wait for you as long as it takes because I want us to do this right."

"You're sure?"

Pam smiled, equal parts frustrated and satisfied. "I've waited all this time, haven't I?"

"True."

They sipped their wine in silence. The rhythmic chirping of the crickets and the silence of the neighborhood was a stark contrast to the churning inside Pam's stomach. She was ecstatic that Trish was giving her—them—a chance, but what did it really mean? Would it simply be more of the same…a flirtatious friendship? Would they ever really be a couple? Would they ever really be free of the specter of Laura? And would Trish be capable of not comparing her with Laura every time they made love or every time they had a fight? An even bigger question was could *she* stop comparing herself with Laura, stop feeling inferior to her older sister? *Christ, what if I'm making love to Trish and I start worrying that I'm not doing her as good as Laura? That I don't measure up?*

Doubt crept like a hand around her throat, slowly tightening its grip. Sweat began to scratch at her scalp. Her face burned. Maybe she wasn't woman enough to try it with Trish after all. Maybe *she* was really the holdout here, the fearful one. Hope was crashing like a falling meteor and there was nothing she could do to stop it.

Trish watched her with deepening concern. "What's wrong, sweetheart?"

Pam could hardly speak. "I don't know if I can do this, Trish."

She didn't give Trish a chance to answer. Instead, she set her glass down abruptly and jumped to her feet. Shaking off the hand reaching for her, Pam strode into the house and ran upstairs to the guest bedroom, desperate with the need to be alone. As much as she wanted Trish, she couldn't help but feel that trying to be together was a futile exercise. That they were doomed, thanks to Laura. Laura was the one who'd brought them together twenty years ago and again this time. Without Laura there was no Trish and Pam, and three was a crowd in a relationship.

Facedown on the bed, Pam began to sob. Even in death, Laura was ruining her chances of ever being with Trish.

* * *

Trish woke early. Failing to hear any stirrings from the guest room, she decided to whip up an omelet and coffee and take breakfast up to Pam. Quietly she worked in the kitchen, trying not to panic about last night. She'd thought they were making real progress, or at least baby steps, toward some kind of relationship. Of course it was going to be a minefield, and they'd have to take it very slow, and even then, the path was undoubtedly going to be fraught with difficulties. But the way Pam had stormed off, everything was back to square one. Intellectually, she understood Pam's concerns—obstacles more like—but it was frustrating all the same.

Outside Pam's door, Trish set the tray on the floor and rapped softly on the door. After a moment, Pam told her to come in. Trish picked up the tray and opened the door, her eyes needing to adjust to the dim light.

"Oh, hi," Pam replied, sitting up quickly. The sheet slid from her naked body, momentarily exposing her breasts before she could yank the sheet back up.

Trish nearly dropped the tray as her eyes strayed to Pam's covered breasts, sweet visions of what she'd just witnessed resurfacing in her mind. She hoped Pam hadn't noticed that she was practically drooling. Not to mention her sudden clumsiness.

"Hope you're hungry."

Pam smiled, but she looked like she hadn't slept much. "It looks and smells great. Will you have some with me?"

"That's why I brought two forks."

Trish sat down on the edge of the bed and put the tray between them. "I was a little worried about last night."

"Can we not talk about it right now?"

Trish's heart plummeted. She wanted to talk about what was wrong between them before the chasm only deepened, but she didn't want to force a showdown. "Okay."

They ate quietly, talked a little about the party, about nothing of significance. Finally, the omelet gone and their coffees mostly drunk, Trish gently tried again. "I wish you would talk to me about what's wrong. About last night. Please?"

Pam shook her head a little, stared blankly ahead.

Trish set the tray on the dresser, returned and sat down beside Pam. *Jesus.* It was lethal sitting so close to her, knowing only a thin cotton sheet covered that beautiful body. The raw urgency of her need surprised her. She wanted to touch Pam, wanted to be touched by her. She didn't know how things were going to develop between them over the long run, but at this moment, she desperately wanted to make love to Pam. Wanted to be naked next to her, wanted to taste her, to be inside her. Wanted to let their bodies do all the talking. Then maybe things would be clearer between them.

"Pam," Trish whispered, her trembling fingers rising to Pam's shoulder, to the edge of the sheet.

"I'm scared," Pam replied, her eyes flicking to Trish's. "I don't want to be, but I am."

"So am I."

Trish's fingers gently pushed the sheet lower and lower, her eyes never leaving Pam's. There was no resistance as the sheet dropped to Pam's waist. She didn't dare look, didn't want to break the spell. Instead, she moved closer until her lips were a breath away from Pam's.

"Maybe we've been doing too much thinking, too much rationalizing," Trish whispered.

"Maybe."

"I want to kiss you."

She could see Pam's throat bob in a nervous swallow, but her eyes spoke a different language as they looked longingly at Trish. Softly, slowly, Trish began kissing her, gently touching her lips ever so softly to Pam's. Her eyes closed in spite of the temptation to snatch another look at Pam's breasts, just inches away now and so very close to where her fingers lay.

The kiss intensified, their lips hot with unrestrained passion. Pam's fingers moved insistently to Trish's hair, pulling her closer in a sure signal that she wanted more. Pam moaned as Trish's mouth slid down to her throat, which was soft and warm and tense with desire. *Oh yes*, Trish thought as Pam moaned again. How she wanted to make her not only moan, but scream out with exquisite pleasure. She wanted Pam's hands directing her head to other parts of her body too. It'd been a while since she'd made love to a woman, but with Pam, it was as though her body instinctively knew what it wanted and needed to do, with a mind purely its own.

Trish's eyes slid open as she kissed Pam's throat, her neck. She watched her breasts rise and fall with each sharp intake of breath. *God!* They were beautiful. Not exactly small, but efficient and practical—much more so than Trish's larger, fuller breasts. They were shaped perfectly too, the nipples stiff peaks atop the gentle slopes. Rewards after the ascent.

Without further delay, Trish moved her mouth to the closest breast. Softly, she kissed all around the nipple, cupping the breast with her hand like a fragile baby bird. Pam tensed pleasurably, arched her back. *Oh, yes, she wants me to suck it.* The thought turned Trish on even more. Pam's blatant desire intensified the wet throbbing between her own legs. Thinking was the most overrated goddamned thing in the world, it occurred to her now as she began sucking Pam's erect nipple.

Oh, why had she wasted so much time thinking and worrying, instead of doing and enjoying? She'd spent so many years of her life contemplating when there was so much pleasure to be had. And dear, sweet Pam was the most pleasurable gift she'd ever been offered, other than Laura perhaps. But she and Laura had been so young then, so innocent and spontaneous. They had been blank slates with the future yet to be drawn. But this. This was different. This had the rich sweetness of both wisdom and maturity, of a desire nurtured for years.

Whatever this was—all of this—they were both going into it with their eyes wide open, both fully cognizant of the past and the present. Finally, Trish thought with mild surprise, she was ready to give herself to Pam and to accept Pam's gifts.

The sudden relaxing of Pam's body forced Trish to lift her mouth. She recognized the sudden easing of sexual tension, the body exhaling its arousal. With disappointment, she raised her eyes to Pam's, saw that she was quietly crying.

"Oh, baby," Trish said softly, taking Pam into her arms and rocking her. "It's okay."

"No. I don't think it is."

"What? Will you tell me what's wrong?"

The tears abated, but Pam's eyes remained clouded with sadness. "I can't do any of this until I'm confident it's going to work out between us. It would devastate me to make love with you and then for things not to work out between us. I don't want this to be an experiment. To make love and then decide it was a mistake."

Trish lovingly brushed a lock of hair from Pam's forehead. "I want things to work out between us too. I wouldn't be doing this if I didn't think we stood a good chance, don't you know that?" She smiled weakly in an attempt to contain her sadness and disappointment. "I don't exactly go around making love to a different woman every week."

Pam smiled back, and Trish's fears loosened. She didn't want to lose her, not when they were so close to scaling the mountain between them.

"I know that," Pam said. "It's not that. It's not you." She reached up and fingered Laura's class ring on the necklace around Trish's neck.

"But I thought it was me we were waiting on? I was the one who wasn't sure, remember?" Hopelessness tugged at Trish. She knew full well this was about Laura. It always came back to Laura. "Look, I know I'm ready to put Laura in my past now. I'll always love her, and our years together can never be replaced. But I'm ready for a new life, for a chance at happiness again. I won't cast off all my baggage overnight, but I am starting to leave it behind, piece by piece. Don't you believe that?"

"Yes, I do. Oh, Trish." Tenderly, Pam reached up and traced the outline of Trish's mouth with her fingertip.

It was Trish's turn to submit to her frustration. She tried to swallow the tears back, but she didn't entirely succeed. "I'm trying as hard as I can. Won't you give me a chance?"

"Yes," Pam replied. "I will. But not right now."

"Why? What's happened to change things?"

"It's me that can't walk away from Laura. All my life I've wanted to be like her. Wanted the things she had. Now I'm no longer sure who I am. Am I Laura's clone, or am I my own person? It's like she's this giant shadow over me, and I don't know how to get out from under it."

"Oh, Pam. You're not Laura. I wish you could see that."

"That's the point. I need to figure it out for myself. I need to find my own identity before I do anything else. Before I can get on with my life."

Trish swiped at a tear racing down her cheek and watched helplessly as Pam pulled the sheet up to cover her naked chest. She rose from the bed, stood rooted in place as though she were paralyzed. If she turned and walked out the door, she feared she might never see Pam again.

"What if," Trish said shakily, "this really is who you are? This woman who wants to love me, who does love me with all her heart?"

"Then I'd be the happiest woman in the world to take your hand and walk through life together. But I need to be sure, before we complicate things further."

No, Trish thought, the prospect of losing Pam slamming into her. This couldn't be. Just as she'd begun to understand Laura's hold on her and begun, finally, to shed it and to realize she could love Pam, Pam was sending her back into the abyss of confusion, insecurity and doubt.

"I'm only asking for some time," Pam said shakily.

But what, Trish thought with desperation, if Pam decided she'd only wanted her all these years because she'd been Laura's? That she was something to be inherited, passed down from one sister to the other? If Pam believed those things, there was no hope for them, and the thought nearly buckled her knees.

She turned, finding just enough strength to leave.

CHAPTER FIFTEEN

Pushing aside her half-eaten salad, Pam sipped coffee in the hospital cafeteria and considered telling her friend and colleague, Nancy Watters, the monumental decisions she'd made. She hadn't talked to anyone about them yet. The option of talking to Trish was most definitely off the table.

Nancy frowned at Pam's plate. "I know the food in this place sucks, but I always thought their salads weren't half bad. It seems you don't agree."

"I guess it would help if I actually had an appetite."

Nancy set her fork down on her plate. "Okay, my friend. Enough of this. What's been going on with you lately?"

Pam winced. "That obvious, huh?"

"Yes. And look, I have to be honest. I heard through the grapevine yesterday that you're letting your residency expire in a couple of weeks without re-upping. I was waiting for you to tell me about it, but…"

"I'm sorry. I should have told you. And I was going to, honest."

"I know it's been a terrible time for you since your sister died. Why don't you take a leave for a couple of months? You know Langton would be more than happy to grant you one."

Pam smiled helplessly at Nancy. She was one of the good ones, one of the young docs on staff whose general philosophy—about medicine, about life—matched Pam's. Nancy cared about her patients, went the extra mile for them, for her colleagues too, and they respected her for it. She was bluntly honest without being cruel, kind without being condescending, skilled without being egotistical. All of the things she tried to be as well. She was going to miss Nancy.

"I need more than a leave right now," Pam said. "I need time, distance, to figure out where to go from here."

Nancy looked decidedly unhappy with the news. "With your career?"

"Yes. And more."

"I knew there had to be someone you weren't telling me about." She tilted her head inquisitively. "Tell me about her."

The request didn't surprise Pam. Nancy was straight, engaged for about five years to a man she seemed in no hurry to marry, and she was completely understanding and non-judgmental about Pam's sexual orientation. Pam could tell her anything, but she went for a delay tactic instead. "It's a long story."

"Fine by me. We've got fifteen minutes before rounds start."

Nancy wasn't to be dissuaded, and after a moment, Pam relented with a laugh. She gave the abridged version of her and Trish's past—admitting the teenaged crush she'd had on Trish, about Laura and Trish's breakup after Laura finished medical school and entered the army full time, of how she and Trish had become reacquainted after Laura's death, how they'd been spending a lot of time together. And how things had grown complicated between them.

"So let me get this straight," Nancy said.

"Straight?" Pam flashed a grin.

"Er, okay, you know what I mean. So you've loved Trish since forever, but Trish didn't really know you existed in that department until this spring. You've been spending a lot of time together, gotten to know each other as friends and equals, provided emotional support to one another. You kissed, she freaked out, saying she wasn't ready for *that* kind of relationship with you. This weekend, she admitted she might be ready, you kissed again, almost made love, and then *you* freaked out, saying you weren't ready. Sheesh, is this an episode of a soap opera? Or maybe a chapter from one of those schmaltzy books you're always secretly reading?"

Pam's mouth fell open. "You know about my books?"

Nancy waved a hand through the air. "Please. I've seen you stash them away in the staff room before running off to answer a page."

"Okay, fine, you busted me. I like schmaltzy books, straight and gay. They're my weakness."

A spark lit up Nancy's eyes. "I've always wanted to read one of those lesbian romance novels."

"Ah-ha! So that's why you're having the longest engagement in the history of this hospital."

"Don't get your panties in a twist, Wright. I'm not switching teams. It'd be fun to read about it, that's all."

"Dammit. My toaster oven broke the other day, too. I was hoping for a new one."

"Huh?"

"Never mind."

"So, where were we? Oh yes, I believe I just summarized your love life for you."

"Yes, and it's not funny. I really am confused about her, Nance."

"I know, and I'm sorry. I'm not trying to make light of it. Why are you confused? The woman you've secretly loved for decades finally feels the same way. Are you afraid she's going to change her mind?"

Pam hesitated. Putting the intensity of her feelings into words was difficult. "Partly, yes. But my biggest fear is that I'm not really in love with her. That I only thought I wanted to be with her because she belonged to Laura. Now that Laura's gone, I don't have to compete with her. I don't have to try to emulate her any longer. It'd be horrible for Trish if I've only loved her all this time because she was the prize in a game."

"Did you talk to her about it?"

"Yes. I told her I needed to find my own identity. That I needed to be sure of what I wanted." Pam swallowed around the sudden lump in her throat. "Without Laura as my compass, I feel lost."

Nancy pushed her plate aside without finishing her lasagna. "Look, I can't pretend to know what you're going through, having your sister killed over there and how that's turned your world upside down. Maybe taking some time away from Trish and from work is absolutely the right thing for you to do right now."

Okay, so her idea wasn't crazy after all, Pam thought with relief. "But what if I never come back to those things?"

Nancy's eyes narrowed skeptically. "You mean medicine too?"

"Maybe."

There was a long pause while Nancy studied the wall across the crowded cafeteria, as though it might divulge the meaning of life. Thankfully, she didn't jump all over Pam. "I hope that's not true, Pam, because it would be a great loss. In many ways. But it's your life. You need to try and be sure you're doing with it what you want, no matter what direction it leads you in. And that you're sharing it with the person you want to share it with. Don't settle for anything less. And you should take all the time you need, because these are the biggest decisions you'll ever make in your life."

Pam expelled the breath she hadn't realized she'd been holding. "Thank you. I needed to hear that."

"So what are you going to do when you leave here in two weeks?"

Her next plan was a big step and possibly not a very safe one. She'd confided in no one stateside yet, but it was time to tell someone. "I'm going to Afghanistan."

"What?" Nancy was rarely ever rattled, but now she blanched as if she'd seen a ghost. "Tell me you're not serious."

"I am. I'm going in three weeks."

"Why on earth would you do that? It's not safe over there. They're still fighting, and there are random shootings and bombings every day. You could be killed!"

"Yes, but it's highly unlikely. I'd only be going for a few days. It's part of a special program for families of soldiers who've been killed there. They get to see where their loved ones served, visit any memorials, get to know the people they worked with. It's supposed to be a healing journey."

"Therapy under fire, sounds more like."

Pam tried to shrug the comment off. "Let's hope not."

She had been in touch by email all week with Camille setting things up, thanks to the tip she'd been given by that journalist at the party. It had come about quickly, both the plans and her decision to do the trip, and it felt right. Between making the trip and reading Laura's journal, Pam would have a much better understanding of her sister by the end of it all. And a clearer awareness of their differences, she hoped. Ideally, the experience would culminate in a crystallization of her own wants and needs, her own identity. More than healing, she hoped it would be a journey to self-discovery. She was counting on it.

"Is Trish going with you?"

The question startled Pam. She hadn't mentioned Afghanistan to Trish. In fact, they'd not spoken much at all since last weekend. Things were still delicate between them. "I don't think it'd be her cup of tea."

"So you haven't asked her?"

"No, and I'm not going to. Didn't you just agree with me that I need space from her?"

"Yes, but maybe this trip could be a healing one for her too."

Pam shook her head adamantly. Trish would never go for it. She hated everything to do with the army and with war. Not only that, but she'd probably be pissed as hell that Pam was going. "No. She'd just try to talk me out of it."

"Is that why you're afraid to tell her about it?"

"You're good, you know that? You should have been a lawyer."

"What, argue with people all day long? Naw, I'd rather cut into their brains." Her grin was evil.

Pam glanced at her watch and jumped to her feet. "Two minutes to rounds. Better roll."

Nancy sighed loudly, picking up her tray from the table. "Tell her."

"Tell who what?"

"Trish. Tell her you're going to Afghanistan. If you don't, she'll never forgive you."

* * *

Trish opened Laura's journal to the last place she'd read. Pam had left it with her, telling her to keep it for a while, to go ahead and read it on her own. She'd catch up with it later, she promised.

Faithfully, Trish had read a few pages every day, partly in retaliation for Pam distancing herself from her and partly because the journal intrigued and amazed her. Laura was a very good writer, and while the journal didn't diminish Trish's anger at the war, it was helping her understand what it had been like for Laura over there, the trials and tribulations of fighting and helping.

As for Pam, well, she was simply running away from her like a scared child. *Fine.* Let her make her own discoveries, just as Trish was coming to discover how far apart she and Laura had truly grown from one another over the years. How different their lives and their worlds had become. They could never have bridged those differences, Trish now believed. They'd grown into two very different people, with different goals, different personalities, different expectations, different priorities.

Jan. 24:
Eating is comforting, and so is being around others, and I could see that people were lingering in the dining hall, despite having finished their meal. I was happy to sit there too, slowly unwinding, listening to snatches of conversation around me.

Suddenly there was the most awful sound, loud and getting louder by the second. It was deafening, a high-pitched screeching sound that pierced you to your bones. I felt certain it was a rocket landing directly on our heads. Somehow I managed to move and I threw myself from my chair and dove under the table. Others had begun reacting too, some running for the door, others diving on to the ground, one soldier even reaching for his sidearm, though I don't know what good that would have done.

I had crawled up against the structural wall, in the knowledge that if the building came down I would be somewhat safer beside it.

Then someone started laughing, and I thought to myself, "Okay, the noise is gone, and I'm still here, so that has to be a good sign." There was no smoke or fire either. More good signs. As we were scrambling back to our seats, someone came in and said it was only a plane and a bloody Italian one at that. Some pilot hotdogging it.

Sometimes a plane will sweep down out of the sky and fly low and fast, to terrify the enemy or at least demonstrate the awesome technological superiority of the coalition. The idea, of course, is to do it over the attackers' position, not over your allies' base, and frighten the living daylights out of them.

Nevertheless, it's a stark reminder of how your paradigm shifts in wartime, how normal can become completely abnormal in a split second. How a loud noise can make you think your life is about to end. Daily, sometimes hourly here, we're reminded that no one is truly safe and that life can be changed forever in an instant.

Trish set the journal on her lap, thought about how life could be altered in a split second. Her life had permanently changed in the instant she'd found out about Laura's death. Like nothing else, it had made her realize she could never go back. That a big part of her life was over. But Laura's death had also brought her Pam, and that was a gift. *Out of death is born the fertile ground of life. Destruction almost always makes way for rebirth. From hate are planted the seeds of love.* She didn't know where she'd heard those lines, or if she'd just now made them up. The urge to write was overwhelming, and Trish opened her laptop on the coffee table and turned it on.

As she waited for it to boot up, she thought about those lines and how they might relate to her life. From Laura's death, could she begin living her life again? And was Pam part of that equation? How would she know when the time was right to forever slip the bonds of Laura's love, to give herself fully to someone else? Someone who would love her and make her their life's priority. Someone she could build a future with.

The email program on her computer chimed. It was a message from Pam, the first in days, and Trish eagerly opened it.

Hi, T:

I've been busy, starting to wrap things up at work. But I wanted to tell you of some news. I am going to Afghanistan in a couple of weeks. It's a program the army offers for grieving loved ones of soldiers killed in action. I know you are probably hating this idea right now, but I feel it's something I need to do. Please try to understand.

Pam

Trish took deep gulps of air, like a drowning person, and commanded herself to calm down. For a long time—she didn't know how many minutes went by—she stared at the computer screen. Afghanistan? The war zone? Pam was going right into the war that killed Laura? How could that be? Was she crazy?

Feeling sick to her stomach, she pulled the cordless phone from its cradle and stabbed angrily at the keypad. On the third ring, Pam picked up.

Without preamble, Trish said, "What in hell's name do you think you're doing?"

"Wait. Let me explain."

"Explain what? That you're going over there like some ghoul or daredevil to see where Laura died? Jesus, it's dangerous over there, Pam!"

"I know that, but it's only for a few days, and the army will keep me safe."

"Safe?" Trish was incredulous. "Like they kept Laura safe?"

"Look, I'm a civilian. They won't put me in harm's way. And I'm not a daredevil or a ghoul. It's a healing thing, a chance to see where Laura worked and to talk to the people she worked with. And Camille tells me there's some kind of memorial to her at the base, and they're going to do some other kind of dedication to her."

A knot of emotion throbbed in Trish's chest. Dammit, she was *not* going to lose Pam to Afghanistan too. Quietly seething, she said, "Is this also part of your plan to figure out your identity?"

"Yes." Pam blew out an exasperated breath. "I need to do this, Trish. For me."

"Dammit, Pam."

"I know."

No, Pam didn't know, Trish thought. She couldn't have been presented with this gift, this glimpse of how life might be with someone else, only to have it snatched away again. By the goddamned army! Was there no limit to the army's cruelty? To its possessive reach? *Jesus Christ!*

"Then the least you can do is to let me come with you." The words were out in an angry burst before she could stop herself.

"Trish, you don't want to do that."

"Why not? And don't tell me it's dangerous. If it's safe enough for you, it's safe enough for me."

"No, that's not what I was going to say. You're so angry at the army, I don't see how…"

"My anger is my business."

"I know it is. But how could going there possibly…"

"Look, you said yourself that I need to come to terms with my anger. And this trip is supposed to be healing. I think it makes sense for me."

Pam paused so long, Trish was about to ask if she was still there.

"Is that the only reason you want to come?"

"No," Trish replied. Her voice faltered. "Maybe somehow, I don't know, I can help keep you safe."

"Oh, Trish." Pam's voice softened. There was unmistakable love in her voice, and it nearly melted Trish.

Tears escaped from Trish's eyes. She could barely speak. "I couldn't keep Laura safe, but maybe you…"

"Honey, you can't keep me safe, just as you—or I—couldn't keep Laura safe either. It is what it is. I'm doing this fully aware of the risks."

"Let me come."

She could picture Pam shaking her head, biting her bottom lip in that adorable way she had when she was worried. "You're sure?"

"Yes. I am."

CHAPTER SIXTEEN

Trish's suitcase lay on her bed between her and Rosa, symbolic, Trish supposed, of the fact that there was always something dividing them in spite of their close friendship.

Rosa had come over on the pretense of helping her pack for Afghanistan, but Trish expected her friend to start lecturing her any minute on how she was making a big mistake.

"Okay," Trish muttered, figuring she'd make a preemptive strike. "Go ahead and tell me I'm being foolish. That this whole thing is a bad idea."

"I never said it was."

"No, but you're about to."

"Clairvoyant now, are you?" Rosa said with a smirk that indicated she wasn't amused. "Boy, you sure are a woman with a plethora of talents."

"You can stop with the sarcasm any minute now."

"Fine. Sorry. I'm not quite sure I understand why you're doing this. Why it's worth risking your life."

"Because maybe it will help me understand what Laura was doing over there. Why she was so goddamned committed to the army and her fellow soldiers. Why they always mattered more than me or her own family."

"What if Afghanistan doesn't give you those answers?"

"Then I'll never understand any of it. And that'll be the end of it."

"You might find tiny remnants of Laura there, but you won't find *her* there, if that's why you're going."

"No, that's not why I'm going. I'm not looking for her. Or for her ghost. Some answers, yes, but that's all."

"What about Pam?"

"What about her?"

"Are you doing this just to follow her? So she doesn't get away?"

"No. Pam's a big girl. She has her own reasons for doing this."

Rosa's eyes were implacable. It was that damned, disbelieving look she had, practiced during years of teaching. Well, Trish was a teacher too. "I think you're afraid of losing her. Literally and figuratively."

Trish leaned heavily against the headboard. Why did they always have to have this stubborn little dance, this wielding of words like fencers jabbing with swords, before they got to the truth?

"I think I might be falling in love with her," Trish confessed.

"Oh, dear. It's serious, then?"

"Yes."

"How did it happen?"

"I don't know. Really, I don't. I mean, we were incredibly distraught and grieving together over Laura, then we were needing each other, and then…"

"You found comfort and solace and a kindred spirit in one another?"

"Yes. And more. I mean, all those years when I was with Laura, Pam was just a kid. The little sister who tagged along, you know? I never gave her much thought, other than feeling familial affection toward her. I knew she had a crush on me, but big deal. She's not the first baby dyke to have a crush on her older sister's girlfriend."

"So when did you become attracted to her?"

Trish thought back to the moment when her heart unexpectedly lurched the first time Pam held her in her arms, when she'd shown up unannounced at the funeral home. "When she first held me. When I first looked into her eyes and saw a grown woman. A woman who still loved me, only deeply this time. A woman I had absolutely no good reason *not* to consider that way."

"And why aren't you with her now? What happened?"

Slowly, Trish shook her head, remembering the withdrawing of emotions, the gulf between them since they'd nearly made love. They still had not discussed what had happened, nor whether they could salvage their budding relationship from these ruins Pam had made in her quest for her identity. Ruins they'd both had a hand in making.

"I don't really know." Her declaration was insufficient as an explanation, but it was the truth.

Rosa was frowning at her with that typical Rosa skepticism. "Come on, *something* must have happened."

"It almost did."

"Huh?"

They'd come so close to making love, Trish ached at the memory. Pam's breasts were so perfect, the flesh so soft and yet firm beneath her hands and against her lips. She remembered how they rose and fell with each breath, stiffened with every touch. The sweet memories flashed through her mind…Pam's stomach quivering as Trish ran her fingers across it, Pam's mouth open and silently begging for more as her eyes squeezed out the world, the arching of her back to give Trish more access.

"Oh, God," Trish whispered, her breath caught up in her throat. She would do almost anything to have that moment back, to have Pam in her bed and in her arms. Simply to have Pam. "I think I've lost her."

"Then don't chase her, that's the worst thing you can do. Let her know you're here, but for God's sake, don't go running after her to Afghanistan."

"No." Trish stood, began pacing the plank floors of her bedroom. "That's not what I'm doing. I'm not chasing her."

"Are you going there to try to protect her?"

"What are you talking about now?" *Rosa and her damned questions!*

"Are you afraid she's going to get hurt or killed? Like Laura? Or that she's going to stay there?"

"Don't be ridiculous." She couldn't admit that all of those things were in large part fueling her motivation. Admitting it to Rosa would make it sound as ridiculous as it probably was.

"It makes sense to me. You couldn't protect Laura from getting hurt, and you sure as hell couldn't get her to stay here. You're not going to make those same mistakes with Pam, are you?"

Trish's anger and frustration rose in her like a mushroom cloud expanding slowly outward. "Goddammit, Rosa! You make me sound like some possessive, crazy bitch. Or just plain possessed. You really think I would risk going to a war zone so I could somehow protect Pam or force her to come back to me?"

Rosa couldn't seem to keep the tiny victorious smirk from her lips; Trish wanted to slap it off her.

"I think this is it for you. That you gave your heart to Laura and lost it. Pam's the last time you'll risk your heart on anyone again, and you want to make damned sure it doesn't get broken. And yes, even if it means going to a war zone. In fact, you have to admit there's a certain serendipity to it. You couldn't snatch Laura from the jaws of war, but with Pam, there's a good chance you can do exactly that."

Trish collapsed on the bed, dragged a hand across her face. Rosa was damned exhausting sometimes. Damned annoying too. But she was almost always right. "Fuck. I don't know what the hell I'm doing. But it feels like I should go. Like I need to go. I feel like Pam and I are in this thing together, wherever it takes us."

Rosa slid an arm around her shoulder. "Then go, okay? No matter what the reason. Just come back with your heart and your body intact. And with some answers."

"I'll try."

"Oh, and if anything happens to you over there, I'm going to kick your ass when I see you again. And Pam's too."

Trish smiled. She knew Rosa meant every word.

* * *

At the airport gate, Pam waited for Trish, despising the anxiety blossoming in her stomach. She had flown from Chicago to Detroit, where they had agreed to accompany one another to New York City for the trip to Afghanistan by way of Amsterdam, then Dubai. It was going to be a long trip, about twenty hours. Twenty hours in which she was sure Trish would try to coax her to open up about all the things on her mind, about where they stood with one another. Well, what the hell could she say? She had no more light to shed on any of it...not on her search for her own identity nor on the obstacles that stood between them. As far as she was concerned, nothing had changed since the last time they'd seen each other.

Maybe Trish had changed her mind about going, she thought with faint hope. It would be easier if she went alone— no one else to worry about, no one else worrying about her. And yet, she was going to the last place where Laura was alive, the place where she'd spent the last few months of her life. It would be her final connection to Laura, the last chance to say goodbye to her.

She felt guilty for wishing Trish wasn't coming. Trish had been with her almost every step since she'd found out about Laura's death, and she knew deep down it would be wrong now to cut her out of the grieving and the reconciling of Laura's death that was still to be done. They shared a unique bond. And they needed one another, in spite of the complicated mess they'd made of their relationship.

"Hi there."

Pam looked up even as her heart twisted at the sound of Trish's voice—the voice that never seemed to leave her consciousness, or her dreams, all these years. Even now, after everything they'd been through together, Trish's voice was like a warm, welcoming caress. Pam couldn't imagine her life without Trish in it. Even if they were destined to be nothing more than friends.

"Hi," Pam replied, hearing the gladness in her own voice.

Trish dropped into the plastic sculpted seat beside her and pulled Pam's hand into her lap. "If you don't want me to…"

"No," Pam said definitively, momentarily stunned by Trish's uncanny ability to read her mind. "I need you to come with me."

"I guess we should probably set out some ground rules."

"Like?"

"Separate rooms or at least separate beds. No pressure, no coming on to one another, nothing physical."

"No pressure to talk about things if one of us doesn't want to?"

Trish pressed her lips together, sighed. "Fine. I'll give you all the emotional space you want, but we have to talk someday, you know."

Yes, they did. But not now, when things were so confusing, so raw. Pam simply nodded, then sat back and watched the gate area fill up with fellow passengers. She could see their plane outside the floor-to-ceiling windows, its metal cladding gleaming like a shiny nickel. She wished the plane were taking her to Laura and not to where Laura had once been. Moments like these, she still couldn't believe she would never see her sister again.

"That's us," Trish said, tapping Pam's thigh before rising to her feet.

Pam hadn't heard the announcement. She was thinking about the first time she'd ever flown. She was six, and it was the summer after her father had been killed while learning to pilot a small plane. Later, she'd been told that learning to fly had been his dream, but living the dream had ended his life in the middle of a cornfield just across the state line in Indiana. Their mother, still grieving over her husband's death, sent Pam and thirteen-year-old Laura to a cousin's in Dallas so she could be alone with her grief. On the plane, Pam was afraid that they too were going to die; strapped into her seat she clutched Laura's arm so hard that she left bruises. Laura was patient with her, reading her storybooks throughout the entire two-hour flight until Pam pretty much forgot they were on a plane. They didn't talk about her fear or whether Laura carried the same fear. If Laura did, she hid it well, assuming her role as protector and nurturer with fierce determination.

It was astounding, mind-blowing now, to think that Laura too had died in an air crash. As she snugly fastened her seat belt, it occurred to her that she wasn't so much scared as unwilling to battle fate. If crashing was her destiny too, then so be it.

As the plane sped down the runway, Pam reached for Trish's hand.

CHAPTER SEVENTEEN

Laura's journal held Trish spellbound. It was like reading a great thriller novel, never knowing what was coming next. The writing was so superb, she quickly forgot the journal was about Laura. The Laura she knew and loved. The Laura she fought with so many times about her choice to make the military her life.

During the long flight, she filled Pam in on the parts she'd missed, then asked if she could read out loud.

"Of course," Pam said. "But will you stop if something is too hard for me?"

"Just say the word." Trish slipped on her dark-framed reading glasses.

"Before you start, can I ask you something?"

"Anything."

"How come reading about Laura's experiences over there doesn't upset you?"

"I don't know. The writing is so good, I forget it's her. I get lost in her stories. And if I think of it like a novel, maybe the ending will be...you know, different than the real-life ending."

Pam shot her a wink. "I forgot you're a wannabe novelist."

Trish shook her head. "Laura's stuff is far better than anything I've ever written. She's the one who could have been a bona fide writer. God, it's gripping stuff. Listen to this:

"It's sickening how many schools the Taliban have closed or destroyed, and the ones that remain open are taking a terrible risk. Kidnappings, assassinations, bombs, any assortment of violence and threats of violence. Teachers, students and parents are not spared. Education or any forward progress is the enemy of the Taliban, and they are nothing if not brutal with their enemies.

"There is an Afghan medical clinic within sight of our forward operating base here in Helmand Valley. Three others further away have closed because of violence or threats of violence. The one that remains open manages that rare feat only because it is close to our base. It offers the only medical care for Afghan civilians in the region. When I look at that one-story adobe-style building through my binoculars, I feel a resolve harden around my heart like a plaster cast. The Taliban must go. They do not want to educate their people or provide basic medical care. They are barbarians.

"Yesterday I was manning the clinic at the FOB. Two Afghan children were rushed in (they were too severely injured to be taken to the civilian clinic). They were playing along the road and accidentally set off an IED in a plastic bottle. The one child suffered only minor injuries, but the other, a nine-year-old boy, had his legs turned to hamburger meat and his skin sandblasted by the explosion. He was in terrible shock—his BP bottomed out. All I could do was hydrate him through an IV, swathe his legs in pressure bandages, medicate him with antibiotics and sedatives. I intubated him right before they evacuated him by helicopter to Kandahar. I've heard he's still hanging on, but if he lives, I doubt he'll ever walk again. What kind of monsters do this to their own people, especially children?"

Trish closed the journal, Laura's frustration and anger finding a foothold in her own psyche. "Doesn't it piss you off? I mean, how *can* those animals do things like that to innocent people?"

"It's a different world over there, clearly. But living in the middle of all that tragedy, the way Laura was, I can understand why she wanted to stay and do her part to make some kind of a difference. And she was, I think."

"I don't know. I mean, can one person really make a difference?"

Pam smiled with satisfaction. "Sure. Look at Gandhi."

"All right, you got me there. But I mean one soldier. Or a doctor. Over there in Afghanistan or Iraq. God, it just, I don't know, seems so futile sometimes. Like we're banging our heads against the wall over there, and for what?"

"I ask myself the same things with my own job lately. Every day, as a matter of fact. Sure, I'm helping sick people get better, but is it really a difference in the global sense?" Pam's smile faded. "Am I really doing enough?"

"Is that what you want to do, make a difference globally?" Now they were getting somewhere. Back to Pam feeling as though she was never as good as Laura. "Look," Trish said. "I'd love to educate the whole world, but I can't. I can only help educate one student at a time. And yes, sometimes I wish I could do more, of course I do. Everyone feels the frustration of their limitations some of the time. Reading this journal, clearly Laura wished she could have done more too."

Pam chuckled softly. "I know what you're trying to do."

"You do, huh?"

"Yup. And I wasn't comparing myself to Laura, honest."

"Okay, fine. But I wanted to remind you that you aren't the only one who gets frustrated in their job, who wishes she could do more."

"You're right. Hell, I forgot that you're also a frustrated writer."

Trish chewed on her bottom lip. "Damn, I wish I'd never told you about those corny romances I try writing."

"Ever thought of writing something more real? More important?"

"Like what, a biography of Gandhi?"

Pam grinned. "I deserved that." She tapped the closed journal on Trish's thigh. "What about that?"

"Laura's journal? What do you mean?"

"Exactly. Laura's journal. Make it into a book or something, I don't know."

Trish was momentarily speechless. It was a crazy idea. She didn't know the first thing about war or about writing non-fiction. "I...Seriously?"

"Why not? I tend to agree with that reporter in Ann Arbor who said Laura's story deserves to be told. Who better qualified to tell her story than someone who loved her?"

"Jesus, Pam, I don't know. There's private stuff in there. I mean, Laura meant for that journal to be private."

"We don't know what her plans were for that journal some day. And yes, agreed, some of the private stuff isn't for public consumption. But the things that she wrote about—the mission, her job, her colleagues, the Afghan civilians. They deserve a voice, don't they? And who better than through Laura, who cared so much about what she was doing over there."

Trish remembered her bitterness toward the army and its war. "I wouldn't want to be an apologist. Or a defender of our foreign policy over there. I couldn't."

"No one's asking you to. Just think about it, okay? Don't decide anything right now, but see how you feel after spending a few days there. You have my full support if you decide that's what you want to do."

As much as Trish's creative side was intrigued by the idea, she wasn't convinced. What would be the emotional toll of writing a book about Laura? And wouldn't her own biases make a mockery of the project? "I'll think about it." The leather cover of the journal felt soft and worn, comforting. Could she even do justice to Laura's words, to Laura's war experiences? Even if she wanted to, was she up to the task?

Trish turned and studied Pam's profile; she was lost in her thoughts and staring out the window. Trish smiled. "Nice job."

"Huh?" Pam replied, distracted.

"Changing the subject from talking about you."

"I don't want to talk about me right now. There isn't much to say."

"Oh, Pam." Trish reached for her hand and gave it a squeeze, wishing the gesture would somehow convey the love she felt for Pam and the regret that they were at an impasse. Her heart ached at being shut out like this. They were sitting so close together, yet emotionally they were a million miles apart. Haltingly, her voice thick with emotion, she whispered, "Don't you know that I'm here for you? That'd I do anything for you?"

Pam looked at her for a long moment, her eyes full of sadness. And perhaps regret. "I know, Trish. I know. But I'm giving all I can right now."

It would have to be enough, Trish knew, even though she desperately wanted to take Pam into her arms and press her tightly to her, then kiss and caress away her sadness and confusion. Would she ever have Pam in her arms again? Would she ever get another chance to make love to her? To prove to her that they could have a life together, if only they'd take the chance?

She had to look away, knowing her despair was written all over her face.

* * *

In spite of her words to Trish, Pam knew she *wasn't* giving all she could. Hell, she was giving almost nothing. She told herself she was too emotionally exhausted, too distraught over Laura's death, that there simply wasn't anything else left to give. But she was also smart enough to know that she needed to give, needed to share and to take from Trish, because closing herself off was a slow slide toward emotional death. Living with grief, with gut-wrenching loneliness, was not the time to put up walls. Intellectually, she knew that doing so would only make things worse for her in the long run.

She looked at Trish's sleeping form in the seat next to her and felt a familiar tug at her heart. Trish was so beautiful. So serene. Such a calming, level presence. Solid in every way. Dependable, smart, talented, warm, generous. And oh, God, so incredibly sexy. Trish was everything she could ever want in a woman, in a partner. Had *always* been everything she'd ever desired. But now that the prospect of Trish being hers was finally at hand, it scared the shit out of her. What if, after all these years of fantasizing, daydreaming, longing for Trish, it didn't work out? What if this love for Trish was simply some juvenile form of a crush that she'd held on to, nurtured, molded into something that it wasn't? In her mind, she'd crafted theirs into a perfect union, but there was no such thing as perfection in real life. As a couple, they could never live up to Pam's fantasy. And what if she wasn't enough for Trish? What if she turned out to be the Wright sister who was all wrong for Trish?

Pam closed her eyes, pictured Laura. She knew they strongly resembled one another, everyone said so, although Laura had shorter hair and, in her uniform, looked more masculine. Laura had also been an inch shorter and slightly stockier. A better athlete by a notch or two, maybe even a better doctor too. But Laura hadn't seemed truly capable of love, of being a good partner to anyone. She loved her army, her friends, her career, her sports, her short-term love affairs. But since Trish, it seemed she'd never really tried to give herself to another woman, at least as far as Pam could tell.

That's not going to be me. I am not going through the rest of my life without love, without a true companion. I will not be a loner who devotes absolutely everything to my career. I want so much more, Pam realized. So much more, in many ways, than Laura had ever been prepared to risk.

She remembered Laura and Trish as they'd been in high school—innocently in love, madly attracted to one another, spending all their time together, not caring about the other kids and teachers knowing the nature of their relationship— of course, that all changed in college as Laura drew closer to joining the army. But in high school they spent evenings doing their homework together in Laura's room, although sometimes, when Pam would press her ear to the door, she heard a lot of moaning and groaning and muffled giggles in what she guessed were heavy makeout sessions. Sunday dinners, Trish was always the fourth. Laura's basketball games, hockey games, track competitions, Trish was always there, cheering her on. Then things began to change between them. It was subtle, but there was less hand holding, less fooling around when they thought no one was looking, less laughter, more worried expressions, more serious tones to their voices. It was clear Laura had begun pulling away, planning her exit from Trish, even before medical school graduation and joining the army. Perhaps the army had been a handy excuse for staying single.

Dammit, Laura, I wish we'd talked about this! I wish I'd known you better.

And yet Pam knew in her heart that Laura had loved Trish. Had probably loved her as much as she was capable of loving anyone. But that wasn't enough, not for a woman like Trish, who wanted a true partner in every sense of the word. There had always been love, but as they became young adults, Pam had observed that their relationship began to take on the appearance of trying to fit a square peg into a round hole.

Well, big sis, what would think now about your little sister taking your place in Trish's heart? In her bed?

What hurt was that she'd never be able to ask, and would never be granted, Laura's permission to be with Trish. It was crazy, stupid, but she wished somehow for Laura's blessing before she moved forward with Trish. *Maybe then I wouldn't feel guilty.*

Pam's gaze returned to the cloudless sky outside the airplane window. They were in Afghanistan airspace and were beginning to descend. A small stream of fear raced through her. It was dangerous here, but she reminded herself that she needed to see where Laura died, needed to move in her world for a short time. Maybe there were answers here to be had. And maybe there weren't. But she'd been compelled to come, and for that, there must be a reason, she decided. Whatever it was, she vowed to keep an open mind and an open heart.

She glanced back at Trish, raised her fingers to Trish's cheek and stroked gently until she stirred. Big brown eyes took a moment to fully focus, before a lazy smile spread across Trish's face. Pam swallowed against the wave of longing that swelled her heart. How she'd love to wake up to that smile, those sleepy eyes, every morning. *Not yet though*, she told herself. It wasn't their time yet.

"It's almost time to land," Pam whispered.

"Bagram Air Field already?"

"You've been asleep for a couple of hours."

"Sorry about that."

"No, don't be. I wish I'd been able to sleep."

"Are you okay?" Trish asked, her voice still scratchy from sleep.

Pam took a deep, quiet breath as Trish's voice sent a pulsing warmth down her middle. "Yes. Are you?"

"I'm a little scared. Okay, quite a lot scared."

"I know, but they'll look after us. I expect Camille and the rest of them will make sure we're as well protected as can be."

"I know, but nothing's guaranteed, is it?"

Pam thought about Laura and how being a doctor was supposed to be one of the safer vocations in a war. But then, nothing and no one was truly safe when there was a war on. Hell, even when there wasn't a war, nothing about life was guaranteed. As someone who worked in an emergency room, she knew that lesson all too well.

The plane drew sharply lower. Trish's hand snaked into her own, squeezed tightly. Their fused hands felt good, familiar, as though they'd done it a million times before. Pam had to shut her eyes tightly against the sudden threat of tears.

"This okay?" Trish asked warily.

"Yes. Definitely okay." She squeezed Trish's hand tighter. She wouldn't let go until after they landed.

Mountains split the desert from the sky. Pam was surprised that some of the peaks were snowcapped, it being summer and all. She'd been warned to expect temperatures well past one hundred degrees, and even now she could see heat shimmering up from the ground, making the brown earth below look blurred.

The plane descended lower. Below looked nothing like flying into a typical American airport. There were no skyscrapers, no paved streets, no rush hour of traffic. The buildings were one-story and made of brick or mud or wood, with clay walls around most yards. A few brown faces looked up at the plane, some waved. *Talk about a strange land*, Pam thought, tensing. She'd been told that if she went off base she should not be too friendly with people because it wasn't always clear who the enemy was. Taliban fighters sometimes disguised themselves or used women and children as suicide bombers. Pam shivered at the thought.

"You okay?" Trish asked.

"Yep."

The seat belt alarm chimed its reminder. Pam could see they were almost at the base, with its barbed wire fencing and its crowded collection of small buildings. The stark difference at this airfield was that there were no passenger jets with the usual names across them like British Airways or American Airlines, only military aircraft lined up like toys. There were fighter jets, big bulging cargo carriers, bombers and helicopters of various sizes.

A fighter jet screamed down a parallel runway before lifting off and circling in a clockwise pattern.

"Jesus, we're not in Kansas anymore, that's for sure," Trish whispered dramatically.

The plane touched down with two bumps, not unlike the dozens of other landings Pam had made in her lifetime. She always said a silent prayer with every safe landing. With both her father and her sister dying in air crashes, Pam couldn't help but feel a little spooked about flying.

"Welcome to Bagram Air Field," the captain said over the speaker as the plane cruised to a near stop.

Pam looked around her. The large plane was nowhere full. A smattering of a couple of dozen passengers anxiously began unhitching their seat belts, even though they were supposed to wait until the plane came to a stop. A few were in uniform, but most looked like civilians. Private contractors, Pam guessed, or government workers.

The heat was like a brick wall when they stepped out of the plane's doors and on to the metal stairs that had been wheeled into place. Pam nearly choked trying to gulp enough air. Trish was doing the same, her hand reflexively moving to her throat. It was hard to breathe.

"Relax," Pam finally managed to whisper. "Slow, shallow breaths at first."

It was a dry, steady heat, like hot glowing coals. The smallest exertion of walking down the steps and across the shimmering tarmac made Pam break out in a sweat. Two soldiers in full battle dress uniform handed each of them a flak vest and helmet and warned them to wear them at all times when they were outside.

"Even on the base?" asked a pudgy man in a rumpled short-sleeved shirt and tie.

"Yep," the male soldier replied in a southern accent. "The base comes under attack several times a year. I can't force you to wear it, but it's to your own peril if you don't."

The man took the offerings and shuffled along, grumbling. Pam and Trish accepted theirs like they were life jackets in a sinking boat and began putting them on immediately. It earned them a trace of a smile from the soldier.

"Ladies, over here."

Pam turned to see Camille Chavez patiently waiting a few yards away, also wearing camo BDUs, complete with a flak vest, although she held the helmet in her hand. They hurried to her as quickly as the heat would allow and were each greeted with a warm hug and a wide grin.

"Lieutenant, it's so nice to see a familiar face," Pam said with relief.

"Please. I won't answer to anything but Camille from you two. And sorry about these vests and helmets. They're a pain, but wear them whenever you can, okay?"

"The heat," Trish said in a strained voice. "How do you stand it?"

"You get used to it. Your body adapts somewhat after a couple of weeks, of course, not that you'll be here that long. Just make sure you drink lots of water."

Pam looked around, struck by the simplicity of the buildings—all low-slung, hastily thrown-together structures of metal or wood, including many large, army green tents. The two runways were the only paved roads. Everything else was dirt or gravel, all of it surrounded by twelve-foot-high fences topped with barbed wire, dotted occasionally by watchtowers. The snow-peaked mountains looming in the background lent a small sliver of beauty to the ugliness of the base. It was almost the polar opposite to Chicago, with the lake serving as a backdrop to the tall, majestic skyscrapers. Worlds apart in many ways, the two were.

"I know," Camille said. "It's not much to look at. But it's home. Come on, I'll show you where you're staying."

"It is air-conditioned?"

The desperation in Trish's voice made Camille chuckle. "Yes, your hut is air-conditioned. I'll let you two settle in for a couple of hours, then how about a tour of the hospital?"

Pam brightened. "I would love that."

As they walked, Trish asked, "How do you come to think of a place like this as home, when everything looks so temporary?"

Camille shrugged beneath her flak jacket. "It's the nature of the military. You wouldn't believe what can feel like home. When you're out on a long march or a convoy, sleeping under a truck can feel like home. Or a tent."

How much we take for granted in our lives, Pam thought, remembering television images of refugees from Syria and the Sudan living in tent cities, happy to have escaped death and violence. How could living like this not change you? How could it not affect your outlook on life? She and Laura were not much alike at all, save for their physical similarities, their shared background and early family life, their medical degrees. *Why didn't we really talk about any of this? Why didn't I know you better, Laura? We were different, but I would have liked to have known how you felt about what you were doing, about how you were living, about how it had affected you.* The journal helped clarify some of Laura's thoughts, but not as much as a heart-to-heart discussion would have.

Trish fell into step beside her. "You okay?"

"Sure. Why?"

"You looked a little sad. Like you went somewhere."

"I'm good." Pam felt like a shit for walling off her emotions from Trish. Trish loved her, of course she did. Maybe she was not entirely in love with her—it was too early for that—but Trish cared for her more than anyone else in her life now. *So why can't I accept it? Why can't I accept what I've wanted for so long?*

She grew more despondent with each step. Camille deposited them at a wooden hut and told them their luggage would be delivered from the plane soon.

"It's not much, but at least it's private. And yes." She winked at Trish. "There's an air conditioner."

"Thanks," Trish said. "It'll almost feel like home."

"I doubt it, but enjoy and get some rest. I'll come back for you two in a couple of hours."

Camille was right, it sure wasn't like home. Spartan came to mind. The hut was only about eight by ten feet, with two very narrow single beds shoved against the walls and separated by about three feet of space. At the end of each bed was a wooden trunk for their luggage. There was a fine coat of dust on the floor, even though it had probably been swept this morning. There was dust everywhere in this place, its grittiness even finding its way to her tongue and teeth.

Trish sat down on the one of the beds. She patted the space beside her for Pam to join her.

"I know this isn't easy. Want to talk about it?"

Pam sat down. *God*, she thought, *the mattress is awful thin. This is going to be like camping*. "It's not easy for you either."

"No." Trish shook her head, smiling. "They teach you that in medical school? That when someone asks you a personal question, you turn it around on them?"

"That obvious, huh?"

"Let's just talk, okay? I miss not talking with you."

Oh, God, I miss it too, Pam thought with despair. There was a catch in her throat. When had she become so afraid to talk to Trish? Stupid pride or fear was keeping her from the very thing she wanted. "I got cold feet, didn't I?"

"Sorry?"

"About us. I got cold feet as soon as true intimacy became a reality. My dream was coming true before my eyes, and I chickened out."

Trish's forehead wrinkled adorably as she concentrated on Pam's words. Pam wanted to kiss the lines smooth.

"Yes," she said softly. "You did. And it hurt."

"I know. And I'm sorry." Pam closed her hand over Trish's. "I got scared of so many things. Of you, of me, of Laura's ghost."

"I know, Pam. And you're not Laura. Nor do I want you to be Laura. Do you believe me when I say that?"

"I think so, yes."

Trish reached into her shoulder bag on the other side of her and pulled out Laura's journal.

"I think it's time you realized how different the two of you really were."

CHAPTER EIGHTEEN

As an only child, Trish couldn't relate to the way Pam had looked up to her big sister. Pam did almost everything Laura had done before her, from playing the same high school sports, to going to medical school, to crushing on her girl.

"You know," Trish said. "When you were a kid, I used to wonder sometimes why you didn't do more things on your own. Things Laura never did. But she was a big presence, wasn't she? And she was so damned good at everything she did. Who wouldn't want to be like her?"

"I guess I was young enough and stupid enough to try to compete. Or at least to try to be as good as her. I mean, what wasn't there to want that she had? All those trophies stacked up in her room, the glowing report cards, seeing how much everyone adored her. And she had the most beautiful girl in the whole school."

"Okay, I was agreeing with everything you said until you got to that last part." There were plenty of girls who were better looking, but not in the Wright sisters' eyes, it seemed to Trish.

Pam laughed, and when she stopped, her eyes glistened with something beyond mere happiness. It struck Trish that there was love there. Genuine, full-fledged love, and not the puppy dog I-have-a-crush-on-my-sister's-girlfriend kind of love.

"Pam." Trish couldn't keep the quiver from her voice. "When did you really, truly start to love me?"

Pam swallowed visibly, never taking her eyes off Trish's. "When you came to be with me for the funeral. That's when I knew you weren't a fantasy. Because you were there for *me*, not for Laura."

It was true. She'd been miserable at the sight of Laura's flag-draped casket, distraught at knowing she'd never see her again. But it'd been Pam she wanted to comfort, Pam whose friendship she had quickly and desperately come to need. As she looked into Pam's eyes now, she realized that all she wanted was to be in Pam's arms. To be in her future. And it had absolutely nothing to do with Laura.

"I love you, Pam, and I'm sorry if you're not ready to hear it or if you don't believe it. But nothing has ever been more true." Tears suddenly sprang to the surface. "And not because you look a lot like Laura, and not because you're her sister, and not because you adored me all those years ago." *Oh, God, I am so in love with you*, Trish thought. *Please, please don't let me lose you too. I couldn't survive it.*

Pam pulled the journal from her hand and tossed it to the other bed, then took Trish into her arms and kissed her. The heat from her lips, from her body, ignited Trish's desire like a match set to a fuse. God, how she wanted Pam. But not yet. It was too soon.

Pam's lips moved to her jaw, her neck, back up to her lips. So sweet, so soft. The hunger was there, like a low background hum, but the kissing…

Oh, yes, the kissing was what fluttered Trish's heart, made her moan deep in her throat. The kissing was enough for now, and she never wanted it to stop.

It could have been hours but had probably been only minutes when Pam gently pulled away. "If we don't stop now," she said, every bit as breathless as Trish, "we won't be able to."

"Dammit, I know. But there's more of this later. Right?"

Pam grinned, and Trish was pleased to see that the gray-green hue of her eyes had darkened to the deep colors of a turgid sea. *Yes*, Trish thought with satisfaction, *you're as aroused as I am.*

Pam moved closer, her mouth so close that Trish could feel her warm breath against her ear. She shivered pleasurably. "I plan to kiss you so much that you're going to have bruised lips."

In a voice husky with lust, Trish said, "You mean that, don't you?"

"Yes, but I'll let my actions speak for themselves."

Pam began suckling Trish's earlobe, her tongue capturing the delicate flesh. It was a dance that was erotic, demanding, but patient too. Trish's thoughts headed straight south. *Oh, God, that tongue, that mouth. The things it could do to me!* A steady, rapid pulse began to beat in her groin, like a second heart.

Pam pulled away again. "Sorry, I'm torturing you."

Trish fell back on the bed, pretending faintness. "Oh, but it's such a sweet torture."

"Don't worry, I'm torturing myself every bit as much. Now... you were going to read to me?" Pam retrieved the journal from where she had tossed it earlier.

Trish opened her eyes. God, she wanted to kiss Pam again. Was it bad not to care much about Laura's journal right now? *Shit. Laura.* What *would* Laura think of the two of them kissing? Would she be appalled? Indifferent? No, Trish decided, taking the journal from Pam. With what she had discovered in the journal, Laura would probably give them her blessing. If nothing else, it turned out Laura had been clear-eyed about her own shortcomings, what she called her failings as a sister, a daughter, a lover. And there was comfort in that.

* * *

Pam noticed the slight trembling in Trish's hands as she opened the journal and began to read out loud.

"Feb. 23:

Today is a day for thinking of Mom, the sixth anniversary of her death. I miss her as much or more than ever. But worse than her absence is the guilt I have never shared with anyone. Everyone felt sorry for me because I was on tour in Iraq when she died and that I had to rush home for the funeral. The truth was, I avoided Mom those last months when she was so sick. I took refuge, comfort, in staying in Iraq, because somehow war seemed so much easier to handle than my dying mother…"

Pam felt her chest constrict. Her hand flew to her mouth at the shock of Laura's words.

"Pam, I'm sorry. We don't have to…"

"No. Go on." She needed to hear the rest of what Laura had never shared with her.

"The truth is, I'm a coward in the face of death. Oh, I can stare down an RPG or a rifle, can operate on somebody with a steady hand while splinters of wood and dust are raining down on me from an explosion. But I could not and cannot deal with watching someone I love die. Completely selfish and childish and weak of me, yes. But better to hide my weakness by looking selfless, by appearing committed to serving my country at any cost, including the cost of not being there for Mom when she died. And that is the truth. I can't speak of it to anyone, even after all this time, but maybe writing it out like this will help me not feel like such a shit."

Laura had never before discussed her fears and weaknesses like this. It was unsettling, like the earth had shifted off its axis a little. Laura had always been the bravest person Pam knew, her moral guide, her role model. But this was a side of Laura she had no idea existed. This was a fallible Laura.

"Are you okay?" Trish asked. "You've gone all pale on me."

Pam nodded, unable to speak.

"Shall I go on?"

Another nod.

"The real rock has always been my little sister Pam. I couldn't admit that before, but I can now. It's hard to come to terms with the fact that my much younger sister has more balls and more heart than I will ever have. She's a better woman than me. There. I've said it. And it's the truth."

Pam felt her eyes widen the tiniest bit, then moisten. Thankfully, Trish was too engrossed in the journal to notice that she was on the verge of tears.

"Pam was the one who put her life on hold for months to look after Mom. She was there for Mom, physically and emotionally, and there to pick up all the pieces of the estate, of Mom's things, after the funeral, while I had to rush back to Iraq. It was all Pam, and it's not the first time my baby sister has bested me. The truth is, Pam is the kind of person I only wish I could be, but never will be. She's kind, loving, selfless, and most of all, she's not a coward about anything. Well, okay, she probably wouldn't like getting shot at, but she's not a coward about matters of the heart, that's for sure. And you know…"

"Wait," Pam interrupted.

"What's wrong?" Trish reached over, squeezed her thigh reassuringly.

"She's wrong. I am a coward. I'm every bit as scared of things as she apparently was."

"Like what?"

"Scared to figure out what to do with my career, for one thing."

Trish made a face of disbelief. "That's not fear. That's being brave. You feel there's something more you should be doing, and you've got the guts to try and figure out what that is. That's why you're here in part, isn't it?"

"Yes, but not in the way you might think. It's not to see if I have what Laura had to make it as an army doctor."

Trish visibly relaxed. She smiled for the first time since their hot kissing session. "I was a little worried about that, since we're being honest."

"Don't be. I want to understand what she was doing here and why it was so important to her. I thought—hope—it might give me some clarity. But not because I want to follow in her footsteps. I want to make my own path, but through her drive and commitment and sacrifice, I hoped to find some answers."

"I understand. I'm here looking for answers too."

Pam's jaw tightened. "You're still trying to figure out how much she loved you, aren't you?"

Trish turned away, retreating into herself. *Damn*, Pam thought. She hadn't meant to redirect the conversation and certainly not to make some veiled accusation. *Christ, am I always going to be jealous of her and Laura?*

"I'm sorry," Pam said. "I didn't mean that the way it sounded. The truth is, I'm a terrible coward when it comes to you, Trish."

"No." Trish turned steely eyes on her. "Your sister was the coward with me, not you."

Deep down, Pam was incapable of labeling Laura a coward, even though Laura had labeled herself a coward in her journal. As long as she lived, she'd never be able to think of her big sister as a coward. She and Laura simply had different strengths, that's all.

"There's a big difference," Trish continued. "You've been cautious with us, and I completely get that. I'm cautious too. Laura was a huge presence in both our lives, and we need some time to put that in the right place."

"I've been scared that I'll never measure up." Pam shook her head, angry with herself for having so little self-confidence. But she knew how much Trish had loved Laura. How could she not feel inferior in the face of that? How could she ever hope Trish might love *her* as much one day? Whether Laura had deserved that kind of love from Trish and whether she had ever been capable of returning it was moot in Pam's mind. The salient point was that Trish had loved her sister so much that she'd mostly put her life on hold all these years.

Trish cleared her throat to get her attention. "Listen to this:

"And you know what else? She'll make somebody very happy some day. She'll be a far better partner than I've ever been or ever could be. Those same qualities that make her such a good doctor—her empathy, her patience, her selflessness—are the same qualities that will make her a great partner. If she ever finds the right woman, she'd better not hesitate and make the mistakes I made. Ah, who am I kidding? She won't make my mistakes; she's too smart for that. What I really think is that Mom and Dad got it right when they made Pam. She's the true gem in this family. I'm only sorry she had to spend so much of the early part of her life in my overbearing, attention-seeking shadow."

Trish closed the journal in her lap, and for a moment neither woman spoke.

"You okay?" Trish finally asked.

Numbed, Pam could only shrug. How could she possibly realign the dynamics of three decades of being the little sister who'd blindly looked up to her big sister, three decades of ignoring or excusing Laura's faults and shortcomings? Three decades of convincing herself she'd never hold a candle to Laura no matter how hard she tried? All these years, she'd been trying to live up to a mythic figure that had never existed.

Pam dropped her face into her hands and cried. Instantaneously, Trish's arms were around her.

"I know," Trish whispered soothingly. "I too thought she was perfect, and when she wasn't I tried to remake her image into something she could never be. I'm not sure I can forgive myself for that."

Pam wiped her eyes with the back of her hand, tried to gather herself. "Maybe that's exactly it. Maybe we need to forgive ourselves for not being perfect either."

CHAPTER NINETEEN

The colonel, a seasoned veteran with a craggy face and a battle-hardened gaze, seemed surprised by Pam's question. She thought she saw a crack in his stiff composure, but it was gone in a flash.

He quickly deflected the question back at her. "Do the things you see in the ER make you angry?"

"Yes." Drunks and drug addicts with their self-inflicted damage didn't cause her nearly the frustration, sadness, and, yes, sometimes anger as an innocent victim brought in from a drive-by gang shooting or a child killed or severely injured by a hit-and-run driver or the abusers who were violent with their spouses or children. "On a regular basis, as a matter of fact."

The colonel, Mike Davidson, leaned back in his chair and propped his feet on his desk. He wore camo pants and a scrub shirt. It was the end of a long day. "And does that anger prevent you from doing your job?"

"No, of course not."

"Same here. Our work trumps our emotions, whether you're an army doc or a civilian doc such as yourself."

"And at the end of the day, after the work's done?"

There was a bit of ego in his smile. "Our work here is never done. Your shift never truly ends until you catch a transport plane out of here. So the bottom line is, there's little time to think about what you're doing or why because the next damned thing you see is probably going to make you even angrier, if you let it." This time his smile was purely cocky. "So you don't."

Pam had seen doctors wear this same badge of honor many times, usually crusty older docs who'd paid their dues and were proud of it. "What about when you do get that transport plane out of here. What happens then?"

He studied her for a moment, his dark eyes unblinking. In spite of his tough demeanor, Pam liked him.

"Sounds like this question is meant more for yourself than for me," he finally said.

Okay, so she'd underestimated him, Pam realized. "You're not a colonel for nothing, are you?"

He laughed, and she could see he liked her too. "I can see some of your sister in you."

"Nah. She was much tougher than me."

"Probably. But I'm reading between the lines that you think maybe that toughness is not such a good thing?"

Pam hadn't intended on being so honest with Laura's commanding officer, and yet he was easy to be around. Callous and stern, yet honest and transparent. Mike—although everyone called him Colonel Davidson or just plain Colonel—had spent a couple of hours yesterday showing her around the base hospital and introducing her to everyone. He'd called her in for a chat this afternoon after saying he wanted to help her any way he could. "Anything for a family member of Major Wright's," he'd said with a curtain of sadness in his eyes. "She was one of my best. Ever."

"I used to think," Pam told him now, "that being a good doctor and doing right by your patients meant owning your emotions. Not being afraid of them. But I got to a point where my work was beating me down. Like it wasn't worth it. Like no matter how pissed off or sad I got or how much I cared, nothing ever really changed. People went on with their lives. Or they didn't. And little I did was making a difference. I don't want to wind up bitter."

"Being a good doctor, first and foremost, means saving the life of your patient. *That's* what you're there for. That's your job. You're not their mother, their spouse or their social worker."

He was right. Those who were able to keep their job in perspective probably never ended up emotionally frustrated like her.

"There must have been times when Laura—when the rest of you—got angry with what you saw here."

"Of course. We're human. But we can't do it all, and we sure as hell can't fix all the evil in the world. I'll tell you something though. The work we do here helps show the Afghan people, as well as our enemies, that we're trying to do good. Politics and religion aside, we're trying to help. And I damned well have to believe that the arc of justice and humanity eventually bend in our favor."

"Laura had that figured out, didn't she?"

"Yes."

But I need more than that, Pam thought. *I need more than the immediate reward of saving someone or patching them up. And I certainly need more than some philosophical belief that my good work will somehow, in the end, make the world a better place.*

"But you're not Laura," he continued. His tone wasn't judgmental. "Can I ask why you went into emergency medicine?"

Pam had asked herself this hundreds, maybe even thousands of times. "The adrenaline rush, the immediacy. And because I'm good at making order out of chaos."

The colonel gave her a conspiratorial smile. "Now you're talking. That's exactly what the army does and the staff at this hospital. We make order out of chaos."

"But it isn't enough. Not for me."

"You see," he said in an authoritative tone, like a professor lecturing a student. From anyone else, she would have resented it. "*Your* problem is you can't let go. You can't move on."

Was she that easy to figure out? Maybe he'd simply sized her up as Laura's opposite, because Laura had certainly proven in her life that she could let go. That she could move on. It had been a common theme with her.

Mike removed his feet from his desk and scooted his chair closer to Pam, his air of authority replaced by something more pleading. "I want you to do something for me."

Whatever it was, Pam instantly trusted this man, just as she knew her sister had. "What is it?"

"I want you to go spend a couple of days at the NATO hospital at our base in Kandahar."

"Why?"

The colonel frowned at her for an instant, probably used to giving orders without them being questioned, she supposed.

"It's mostly used now to treat the Afghan population, though it's still the trauma center for our casualties in the field. It will give you a better idea of some of the work that we're doing here. A broader perspective." More gently, he said, "It might help answer some of the questions you have about practicing medicine right now."

Mike stood, not waiting for her reply. "There's a chopper leaving for Kandahar at oh-six-hundred tomorrow."

A chopper? Pam's mouth went dry.

"I'd like you to be on it," he said, looking at her as if throwing down a challenge.

Pam stood, equal in height. She had the urge to salute. "I'll be on it, Colonel."

* * *

Trish had so many questions for Camille she hardly knew where to begin. If she was going to write a book based on Laura's experiences here—and that was a big *if*—there were only about a thousand questions she'd need answers to.

"Did you read Laura's journal before you sent it to Pam?" Might as well start with the most obvious.

"No," Camille answered, and Trish believed her.

"Not even tempted just a little bit?"

"We all have similar experiences here. I imagine she wrote about some of the specific things she witnessed here, the things she did, things she was frustrated or pleased about. If I'd read her journal, it would have been like reading my own."

They were sitting in the dining hall drinking coffee that Trish imagined was strong enough to peel paint. "Jeez, I think this coffee is your biggest enemy, not the Taliban."

Camille laughed at her joke. "You're not the first to suggest that."

"Do you keep a journal?" Trish asked.

Camille tapped on her temple. "Nah. It's all up here."

"Would you ever write a book someday about your experiences here? Lots of soldiers do."

"I doubt it. Why?"

"I think Laura might have wanted to. Did she say anything to you about it?"

"No. But it wouldn't surprise me. She was always scribbling something down. Took a lot of photos too. I jokingly asked her about it once, but she just made a joke back and didn't really answer."

Camille's mouth moved silently, and she narrowed her eyes. "Are you thinking about doing something like that with her journal?"

Trish drank her coffee as a stalling tactic. "Maybe. I don't know yet. I don't want to do it if she would have been opposed."

Camille's face was stern as she concentrated. "I don't think she'd mind," she finally said.

"You two were close, weren't you?" Trish wasn't sure she wanted the full truth.

"Yes. But only to a certain degree. There was a line that I don't think anyone was allowed to cross with her."

"Can I ask you something personal?"

Camille smiled at her teasingly. "Isn't that what you've been doing?"

Trish felt herself color a little. "Sorry."

"Don't be. It's refreshing."

"The army's not very conducive to relationships, is it? I mean, you're single, aren't you?"

"I'm single by choice, but lots of people here have someone back home."

"But what I mean is, being in the army, it makes it a lot harder, doesn't it?" What she couldn't come right out and ask—mostly because Camille had no way of knowing—was whether it was Laura or her way of life that had prevented her from committing to Trish. Or anyone else, as far as she could tell.

"Sure, but you can do it if you really want to."

All those years she refused to believe Laura—the grown-up Laura—could want something other than the little house with the white picket fence. A life with *her*.

"I wish," Trish said, a catch in her throat, "that I'd been enough for Laura." As soon as she said it, she knew it was a lie. It was Trish who didn't want the army lifestyle, every bit as much as Laura didn't want the homebody lifestyle.

Camille looked at her kindly. "It's never simple, is it?"

"No. Did she ever talk about me?"

"She mentioned you a few times. I got the impression you were always the one she let get away. You know, her one regret. We all have one. Just because things didn't work between you two doesn't mean there wasn't a lot of love there."

She didn't know why Camille's words gave her such solace, just that they did. "Yes. There was a lot of love. But now I understand it was a selfish love on my part." Oh, how she'd been so full of self-righteousness in those days. How sure she'd been that *her* way was the right way.

Camille quirked her head at her.

Trish laughed suddenly. "Are you sure you even want to hear all this?"

"Of course I do. In war, there's not a lot of time to sit and figure things out with people over a long period of time. You get to know people—and their stories—quickly. Laura was like a sister to me over here."

"You see, I loved her in a such a way that I wanted her to fit her life around what I wanted. I wanted her to have the same dream for us that I had. But she wasn't wired like that, and I tried to force it anyway. That's what I mean by a selfish kind of love. I think I need to learn to love people as they really are."

"Hmm, that's funny, because selfish was how she described herself when it came to you. Said she was too selfish to give what she needed to give you."

"I guess we were both selfish."

"Being selfish is part of human nature," Camille said. "And so is wanting love."

Trish looked around the spacious dining hall, big enough to seat several hundred soldiers at once. It wasn't the only dining hall on base, but it was the biggest. It was mostly empty this time of day—midafternoon.

Trish took a deep breath. She wanted to understand exactly what Laura had chosen over her. And why. "Camille, will you explain to me what you and the others like you, like Laura, love so much about…" Trish gestured around her. "All of this? About being here and doing what you're doing?"

Camille smiled, set her empty cup down. "Sure, but I think we'd better get a second cup of coffee."

* * *

With her index finger, Pam traced Laura's name in the concrete wall. It'd been hastily engraved, then painted red, like the other fourteen names in the same part of the stone, all of them soldiers from the base who'd been killed in action so far this year. Dozens of other names represented past years. Next year's was blank, and Pam wondered how many names would end up there.

Trish stood beside her and traced Laura's name too after a moment. "When her name's on a veterans wall in D.C. someday, we'll go see it together," she promised.

"That's all we have left of her," Pam said glumly. "Just her name engraved in walls."

"No, it isn't," Trish said sternly. "She's much more than a name chiseled in concrete. We both know that. It's up to us to keep her spirit alive. In our work, in our memories."

"And in loving each other?" Pam intentionally sharpened her tone.

"Loving each other and taking care of each other is probably the best way we can honor Laura."

Will it be honoring her when I fuck you? Pam said to herself, the ferocity of her sudden anger surprising her. *Hey, Laura, big sister, check this out. I'm going to fuck your ex-girlfriend one of these days. Fuck her until she comes she like she's never come before. Fuck her until she pulls my hair and screams my name and begs me for more. Is that honoring you enough? Huh?*

"Hey," Trish said sharply, snapping her back to the present. "What's wrong? You look like you want to kill somebody."

"Nothing." Pam turned and began marching back to their hut. She could feel Trish hot on her heels.

"Dammit," Trish said, breathless from trying to keep up with her. "What the hell is going on? Talk to me."

Pam shut the flimsy plywood door and dropped on to her cot. Her heart pounded. For a moment, she dropped her head into her hands, but she remained dry-eyed.

"Sweetie, please?" Trish sat down beside her but didn't touch her.

Pam refused to talk about her anger. It wouldn't help. "The colonel at the hospital has asked me to go to Kandahar to check out a hospital. It was started by the military but it's mostly for Afghan civilians now. The military doctors have begun mentoring Afghan doctors. Eventually it'll be their hospital. At least, that's the plan."

"Why does he want you to go?"

"I don't know, really. He didn't say, just that it might help me."

"You talked to him about your career struggles?"

"Yes."

Trish exhaled loudly, a sign of nerves. "Okay. That's good, right?"

"Maybe. I hope so."

Panic edged into Trish's voice. "He's not trying to get you to stay here, is he?"

"No, nothing like that." Pam tried to soothe her with a smile. "Besides, I'm not interested in staying here. I told you that."

Trish exhaled again, slumping her shoulders. "Good. Thank God. So how does this work? When do you go and for how long?"

"I'll be gone two, three days, max. I leave in the morning." Pam knew her next words would send Trish through the roof, such as it was. "By helicopter."

"What?" Trish leapt off the bed, began pacing furiously. "No, no, no. You can't be serious. Not by helicopter."

"It's safer than a road trip."

Trish wasn't listening. She was stomping around the tiny room, arms crossed tightly against her chest. She was shaking her head back and forth, like one of those dolls on a car dashboard. "No. Anything but that."

Pam stood, went to her, placed a steadying hand on her arm. "It'll be fine."

Trish halted, looked her square in the eye with fury, hurt and fear. "Don't go."

"I want to go. It might help me in some way. It might help me understand my purpose, and it might give me some direction. God knows I need it right now. And it will let me see some of the good work our troops have done over here. Things they've done to make this country a better place."

Trish was not to be mollified. "You might die for it."

"I'm not going to die for it."

"You don't know that, and in any case, you're prepared to risk your life for it, aren't you?"

"I don't know what else to tell you, Trish, except I feel a strong need to do this."

"You're trying to punish yourself, aren't you?"

"What? What are you talking about?"

Trish began her furious pacing again, head down. "It's like you're taunting the gods, or Laura, or *something*, by flying in a helicopter. Are you daring the universe? Is that what you're doing?"

"No, of course not. Now please stop this pacing and tell me what you're talking about."

"Fine." Trish stopped in front of her. "You're punishing yourself for being in love with me. For stealing Laura's girl.

And you're punishing yourself for being the one who's alive. It's survivor's guilt, and it's guilt for loving me. And this—this flying-in-a-helicopter nonsense—it's like you're daring the universe to take you too."

The words were like cold water thrown in her face. Pam sucked in her breath against the shock. She shook her head, unable to form words, unable to even consider that there might be some truth to Trish's words.

"It's okay," Trish said pointedly, then softer. "It's okay." She began crying, quietly, standing erect, arms limp by her side.

Pam took a step toward her, engulfed her in her arms, and felt her own sobs geyser up through her chest. They held each other through their tears, their sobs, as their thoughts spun furiously, trying to break through the wall of pain.

"I never thought," Pam said haltingly, the words stalling in her swollen throat, like hitting speed bumps on a road. "All those years I was secretly in love with you…"

"Yes?"

"All that time, loving you from afar, I never thought…"

"It would happen for real?"

Pam shook her head. "I never thought it was meant to be. Laura…she was supposed to come back for you some day, dammit."

"I don't think she ever was." Trish led them to her bed, where they sat down, holding hands. Their faces were soaked with tears. "I couldn't see that part before, or I didn't want to believe it. But I can now." She took a deep, shaky breath. "She was never coming back for me, Pam."

Pam straightened, pulled away from Trish. "Right now, I hate her."

"What? Why?"

Anguish burned in her face; her skin felt like it was on fire. "I hate her for letting you go. I hate her for making me take care of Mom by myself when she was so sick. I hate her for making me think she was such a goddamned perfect God all my life when clearly she wasn't. I hate her for leaving everything unfinished, for not seeing things to completion."

Trish's eyes shone with fresh hurt. "Like me?"

"What?"

"Am I one of the jobs you have to finish for Laura?"

Pam knew she'd gone too far. She sucked in her breath as though by doing so, she could take back her words. "No, Trish, no." She reached a hand out to touch Trish's face, but Trish pulled away, her posture stiff with anger.

"I am not Laura's hand-me-down. And I'm most certainly not a project you have to take on because Laura couldn't finish it." Her words were blunt, like hard punches meant to bruise. "Your duty to me, to Laura, is over, okay?"

Pam froze. No, no, that wasn't right. That's not how she thought of Trish. She loved Trish, was *in love* with Trish, and had been for years. And not because Laura couldn't or didn't want Trish for herself. Not because Laura had broken promises to Trish and had broken her heart. No, that's not what this was about. This was not about cleaning up Laura's mess, and it was not about trying to *be* Laura, to emulate her. Hell, she was done with that and had been for a long time. She hadn't fully realized it until dissatisfaction with her job had begun to creep in. Yes, she'd chosen medicine largely because that's what Laura had chosen, and yes, emergency medicine was full of the testosterone and thrill seeking that Laura had thrived on as an army doctor. But she finally understood now that it wasn't her calling. She was not a carbon copy of her sister, and there was no longer a need to try to keep up with Laura or to compete with her.

Trish had moved to the wall, her back to Pam. She stood stock-still, but her shoulders were stooped, resigned. She looked small, defeated.

Pam went to her, slowly, and gently placed a hand on her shoulder. "Trish, honey, I love you. And not because I feel some obligation to, and not because I'm trying to be some kind of better version of Laura. You're not the grand prize in a competition between me and Laura. Or between me and her ghost. Okay?"

Trish turned around, leaned against the plywood wall, her hands at her side. She said nothing, but her face was full of despair.

Pam stepped closer, her face inches from Trish's. "I admit, I was confused about us at first. I felt guilty for having the chance to love you when Laura couldn't because she's dead. I felt like I was taking something I had no right to take."

Trish spoke softly. "I'm not anyone's property to take or own."

"I know. I'm sorry. Bad choice of words. I was afraid I was only in love with you because Laura had been in love with you, and that's not fair to you or to me."

"Laura gave up on me a long, long time ago. She couldn't commit to me or to anyone. Is that the way you want to be too?"

No, Pam wanted to shout. She was not like Laura in that respect. She would never give up on someone she loved. "I was also afraid," Pam continued, "that you might only be loving me because I reminded you of Laura. That if you couldn't have her, then at least you could have me."

A wry smile twitched on Trish's full lips. "Like you're the consolation prize?"

"Something like that."

The smile disappeared and the clouds rolled in. "When are you going to start believing how wonderful you are? How deserving, how loving, how giving, how good and decent you are? When are you going to start believing that it's *you* I want? It's you I always should have wanted, not Laura."

Pam expelled a short laugh. "Except you would have been thrown in jail."

Trish rolled her eyes. "You know what I mean. God, Pam, it's you who will be the last thought in my head when I die. It's you I'll always feel I was meant to be with. And if you decide…" She blinked hard, visibly swallowed once, twice. "If you decide you don't want me…or if anything happens to you…*you* will always be my greatest loss, not Laura."

The force of Trish's words pushed Pam back a step. They took a moment to register, like a stone sinking slowly, steadily, to the bottom of a lake, finally landing with a hard, final thud.

"Are you sure it's me you want?" Pam said it more to herself than to Trish, as though she still couldn't quite believe it.

"Yes," Trish said, stepping up to her. "You were the one I was waiting for all this time, Pam. You. I made a mistake with Laura. I realize that now."

Tears pricked at Pam's eyes. Someone—no, not just someone, Trish—wanted her, had always wanted her. *Her*! Not her brash, brave, dashing, adventurous, handsome, smart, athletic, charming older sister.

Trish touched her lips to Pam's for an instant. "Are you sure about all of this?"

Pam returned the quick kiss. A wave of heat had begun sweeping up her body. She felt fevered. "Am I sure of what?"

"Me."

"Oh yes." She felt Trish's arms move around her, felt her hands loosely drawing circles on her back. Heat flashed hard and deep through her. "Yes, I'm most definitely sure."

Trish's lips pressed softly against her neck, her throat. *Oh, God*. Pam closed her eyes, feverish in the glow of Trish's touch. Trish's lips moved north, to the underside of Pam's jaw, and her tongue flicked out, tracing the outline of Pam's lips. *Oh, God*.

"Do you want me?" Trish said quietly, breathlessly.

The vibration of her lips against Pam's ratcheted her heat up another dozen degrees. "God, yes."

Trish wound her fingers through Pam's hair, then pulled her head closer and kissed her hard, deeply and with a surprising urgency. They were both breathing hard, both kissing with a level of desperation and hunger Pam had never known before. Her skin, her lips, were on fire. Her hands itched and burned to touch Trish's bare skin, which she imagined to be cool and impossibly soft.

"How much?" Trish whispered.

Pam's mind labored to decipher the words. "How much what?"

Trish kissed her again. Their mouths fought a battle of complete conquest—pressing, occupying, exploring, remembering. *Oh how sweet is victory*, Pam thought. *Defeat too*. Hell, one was as good as the other in this case. She wanted to take and be taken, receive as much as give.

"How much," Trish said between searing kisses, "do you want me?"

Oh, Jesus. How much do I want you? Is there a way to describe how much? No, she decided, there wasn't, because she wanted her as much as she wanted to breathe, as much as she wanted to live. She'd wanted her this way for a long time, but now it meant everything, because Trish wanted her too. "I'm not going to tell you."

Trish pulled back and looked at her quizzically.

"Nope," Pam said, suddenly scooping Trish off her feet. "Not telling you."

Trish squealed, threw her head back and laughed as Pam carried her the few feet to one of the beds. "Showing me, then?"

Pam deposited her on the small bed, stood and looked down at her for a long moment, wanting to savor this dark-haired beauty who looked up at her with desire, with love, with a chest heaving and straining against a tight shirt, the top two buttons undone, inviting her, tempting her. *Oh, God,* Pam thought again. *I want you so much, Trish Tomlinson. So much it hurts.*

She fell to her knees, reached over and brushed Trish's wavy hair from her forehead. "I will never," she said, looking deeply into Trish's eyes, "want another woman the way I want you. You are the only woman I've wanted, who touches me to my very core, whose love and friendship gives my whole life meaning. And…" She rose up slowly, climbed on the bed beside Trish and leaned over her until her face was mere inches from that luscious cleavage. She breathed Trish in, licked her lips teasingly. "I've never wanted to rip the clothes off a woman the way I do you." She let her eyes wander over every inch of Trish's body. "God. The way I want to kiss and taste and suck every inch of your body. The way I want to make you tremble and shake all over. The way I want you to cry out my name and beg for more." She smiled at Trish. "And a few other things along the way."

Trish gasped. Pressed her legs together. "God, you're killing me, Pam."

"Oh no. The torture's only just begun." She moved her palm to the flat of Trish's stomach, felt it quiver in anticipation. That gorgeous chest heaved harder too, and Pam couldn't wait to get her first real look at those full breasts, her first real touch. They looked like perfect round sculptures, stiff peaks where her nipples rose majestically, and Pam imagined them almost melting inside the velvety warmth of her mouth.

Shit, she thought. *Now I'm the one who needs to press my legs together before my clit explodes.*

"You're not..." Trish pushed up on to her elbows, breathing hard, her brown eyes nearly opaque with lust.

"Not what, sweetheart?" Pam whispered, stretching out and pressing her body against the length of Trish's.

"Not." Trish spread her legs, allowing space for Pam's hips to settle. "Not going to stop, are you?"

Pam smiled, feeling a little evil. "Do you want me to?"

Trish's eyes widened. "God, no!"

"You want me to make love to you." It was a statement, not a question. As an exclamation mark, Pam reached inside Trish's shirt to stroke her stomach. It was taut and quivered in response, like harp strings vibrating against the plucking of expert fingers.

Trish nodded twice, squeezed her eyes shut. Her chest rose and fell quickly, the middle button of her shirt—the next one down that was still closed—nearly popping under the strain. Her nipples looked so damned tight, hard as nails. Pam needed to touch them, and automatically her hand slid to the clothed, soft underside of Trish's breast.

"How much?" Pam said, turning up the heat, the torture. Her thumb brushed against the edge of Trish's nipple, and her whole body twitched at the simple touch.

"Oh, God. How much what?"

This time Pam's thumb began to draw circles around the base of Trish's nipple. Harder, then faster. "How much do you want me to make love to you?"

Trish moaned, moved her hands toward the buttons of her shirt in an attempt to expose her breasts. Pam caught her hands, halted them. "Oh no you don't. Not until you tell me."

"Jesus," Trish said, her eyes narrow slits, her mouth fighting for air. "I'm going to fucking die, right here, right now, if you don't make love to me, Pamela Wright. Do you understand me? You're killing me, baby. *Killing* me. I need you to make me come. I need you to make me come so bad, it hurts."

Pam smiled, pushed Trish's hands against the thin mattress, and roughly popped the remaining buttons.

"Oh, God, yes," Trish said, arching her back to give Pam better access to her breasts.

Pam didn't need the hint. She asked and was given permission to remove the necklace with Laura's ring on it. Next, she pulled at Trish's bra, but it wasn't budging. The clasp was somewhere in the back. *Dammit!* She didn't have time to screw around with it, so she tore the bra, ripped it right down the middle. And oh, how it was worth it! Freed, Trish's breasts rose up toward her, straining for Pam's touch. Pam dipped her face into the soft valley between them, closed her eyes, breathed in the earthy, floral scent of Trish's skin, felt Trish's hands in her hair, pressing. Like jail wardens, Trish's hands were not about to let Pam's mouth her stray from her chest. Not yet. Not until she got what she wanted, and oh, how Pam was going to give her what she wanted.

Pam's mouth claimed a breast—sucking, licking, devouring, sucking again. With her right hand she cupped the fullness and pushed it deeper into her mouth, heard Trish moan in response. Her tongue sprang into action. Stiffly, precisely, quickly, she licked the hardened nipple, flicked her tongue hard against it, felt Trish's fingers dig into her scalp, felt Trish's body heave against her. She sucked again, stroked with her tongue, sucked, nipped with her teeth, stroked and sucked some more.

"I've never," Trish said between gulps of air, "wanted… anyone…so…very much. Oh, Jesus…I want you, Pam."

Pam stopped to look into Trish's eyes, wanting to be sure she heard correctly. "Not anyone?" *Not even Laura?*

Trish thrashed her head from side to side. "God, no. Not anyone. Never like this."

Pam felt her clit stiffen, felt herself become impossibly wet and turned on. "Oh, darling. I love you so much."

"I love you too," Trish blurted out before pushing Pam's head back to her breasts.

Priorities, Pam thought with a chuckle. She took turns with each breast, lovingly, hungrily, suckling them, cupping them, stroking them with her tongue and her fingers. She loved the fullness of them, how they were both firm and soft at the same time. Much more interesting than her own small breasts, she decided. She could spend all day making love to these breasts, but there was more to explore. Much more to love.

She trailed her tongue, her lips down Trish's stomach, stopping to kiss the soft skin there. Trish's hands were still tangled in her hair, and it wasn't long before they were urging her further south. Pam was happy to oblige, but first she needed to get those canvas cargo shorts off of her. Her hand dove between Trish's legs, cupped her firmly. A little teasing before getting down to bare skin, she thought with a streak of mischief.

"Oh!" Trish gasped.

Pam grinned, feeling naughty. She increased the pressure from her hand, palmed Trish in a circular pattern. Trish's legs began to buck and her hips tried to levitate off the bed. She didn't want her coming like this, through her shorts. No. She wanted her to come in her mouth.

"Wait," Pam commanded, desperately pulling at the button and zipper of Trish's shorts.

Trish's hips were still undulating. She'd moved a hand to her mouth to clamp down on it with her teeth, probably to keep from screaming out past the thin, cheap plywood walls.

Urgently, Pam pulled Trish's shorts and damp panties from her hips and down her legs, then settled herself between Trish's legs. "God, you're beautiful, sweetheart."

Trish pushed her hips off the bed, trying to close the gap between herself and Pam's mouth. "Please, Pam," she mumbled. "I need your mouth on me."

Pam's own desire raced through her with hurricane-like force. She would have to fight not to come while making love to Trish, she knew, because she wanted Trish's touch bringing her to orgasm. She pressed her mouth to Trish's engorged clit, felt Trish jerk against her in response. *Oh, yes*, she thought. *So ready*. Gently she took Trish into her mouth, sucking her lightly. Too much pressure and Trish would come instantly, she knew, so for as long as she could she kept it low and slow. Light and tight. But Trish was so wet, so hard, that she knew it wouldn't be long. Trish's hands began pushing against the back of her head, signaling more was needed. Pam pressed her mouth harder against her, stroked her hard and deep with her tongue. Faster and faster too, until Trish's hips gyrated against her and Trish's hands mashed her face harder against her. Oh, she could do this forever, she thought deliciously. Consume, devour Trish. Even when Trish trembled and cried out sharply, her body flailing in orgasm, Pam continued to press her mouth against her, continued her loving ministrations. She slipped a finger inside and instantly felt Trish tighten around it.

"Oh, God," Trish cried as the orgasm continued to rip through her. "Oh! Yes, please don't leave yet," she commanded just as Pam was about to pull out of her.

"Never. I'll never leave you."

She stayed inside Trish, one finger, then two, moving them ever so slowly. She marveled at being inside this woman she loved and had loved for more than half of her life. Making love with her was much more than she'd ever expected, ever dreamed or fantasized about. Making love was an extension of her love for Trish, a deepening of it. And none of it would have meant a damn thing if Trish hadn't looked at her the way she did now with so much love in her eyes. Sex was nothing without love, and Pam realized now how empty and one-dimensional her past sexual experiences had been and how she'd never want to make love with anyone other than Trish again for the rest of her life. No. She was home now.

She crawled up the length of Trish, still inside her, and kissed her tenderly on the lips. "I love you, sweetheart. You were wonderful. You're everything I could ever ask for in a woman. In a lover. In the love of my life."

Trish's eyes instantly moistened. Her smile faltered.

"It's okay," Pam soothed. "You don't have to talk right now."

"No." Trish cleared her throat as a tear shimmered in her eye. "You need to know right now. This feels so right. So wonderful. I couldn't love you any more than I do right now."

Pam slipped her fingers out of Trish and hugged her tightly. They lay silently for several minutes in each other's arms, the sweat from their skin intermingling. The room's overworked air conditioner barely kept it below eighty degrees.

"Darling," Trish said after a few moments. She rolled them both over until she was on top of Pam. "There's a problem here."

"There is?" Pam had grown groggy from the adrenaline and exertion of sex.

"Yes. You still have your clothes on."

Pam smiled lazily. "There's a solution to that."

"Damn right there is." Trish smiled wickedly, then began pulling Pam's US Army T-shirt from the waistband of her shorts.

Pam quickly re-energized. She hauled the shirt over her head, then yanked off her sports bra. Trish's eyes lit up as she surveyed Pam's breasts, shoulders and neck.

"So beautiful," she murmured. But her eyes didn't feast for long before she got busy pulling at Pam's belt and zipper, then sliding her shorts down her long legs. Pam reached down and started to remove her underwear, but Trish stopped her.

"No. I want you to leave your underwear on for now."

"Seriously?" Pam couldn't decide between being intrigued or disappointed by the request.

"I want to prolong some of my explorations. Like taking your time with a really great meal instead of gobbling it up." Her grin was carnivorous.

Pam's heart beat harder. She could already picture Trish's head between her legs, Trish's mouth bringing her exquisite pleasure. *Yes*, she thought, *let me be the meal you devour slowly. Just not too slowly!*

She threw her head back against the pillow as Trish's tongue began circling her nipple. She felt paralyzed beneath Trish's touch, like helpless prey, but in the most pleasurable way imaginable. She would do anything Trish wanted, would let Trish do anything she wanted to do to her, because in this moment, she felt entirely at one with Trish. It was consummate pleasure, complete love.

Pam easily lost track of time, had no idea how long Trish had been going down on her when she felt her orgasm gather in her toes and shoot straight up her legs in rumbling, powerful waves. She rocked with them, gyrating into Trish, reaching for more, for every last drop of pleasure. Colors and indefinable shapes flew past her vision, and while she wasn't a religious person, she felt almost at one with everything that was beautiful in the world at this cresting of physical and emotional pleasure.

"Oh, sweetheart," she said breathlessly as she pulled Trish up beside her. "God, I love you. That was incredible."

Trish chuckled softly against her shoulder.

"What?" Pam smiled but kept her eyes closed, reliving every last second of pleasure she'd just felt.

"I was thinking. They say new sex gets better with time, but if it gets any better than this, I think I might not survive it."

"Hmm, that's exactly my conclusion too. But we could die trying."

"Yes." Trish snuggled closer. "We could."

Pam felt her body slacken with exhaustion and happiness. She'd just made love with the only woman she'd ever really loved, something she'd had no right to think would ever happen. But it had. And marvelously so. She wondered, as sleep beckoned, whether she should feel guilty. Whether *they* should feel like they'd somehow betrayed Laura by making love and professing their love for one another. By wanting to be together. No, she decided without a shadow of hesitation. Nothing this right, this perfect, could be wrong.

CHAPTER TWENTY

Dusk was deepening into night when they finally emerged from their tiny room, Trish joking that they should hang a sign on it—The Love Shack.

"Aren't you hungry?" Pam asked.

"Nah." Trish leaned against Pam, took her hand and affectionately squeezed it. "I don't care if I ever eat again."

Pam chuckled. "Feeling like a teenager too, I see?"

"I never felt this good as a teenager. Or any other time."

Trish felt Pam stiffen at her side, just a little. She knew they needed to talk about Laura and how she was going to fit into their lives now. "Come on. Let's go for a walk. But not too far. It's getting dark and I don't want to get lost."

Holding hands, they threaded their way along the dirt track surrounding the other small living quarters. This sector was a small village of wood and metal huts, housing mostly officers and medical staff. Skyward, the occasional jet or helicopter took off or landed, their twinkling lights an understated contrast to their screaming engines. The smell of diesel fuel permeated the air, along with other unpleasant smells Trish didn't want to think about. It certainly wasn't the most romantic place on earth, but it was all they had.

"I love you," Trish whispered. "So very much."

"I love you too, sweetheart. God, it feels so good to be able to say that out loud. I feel like going up to that control tower and shouting it out."

Trish smiled. She'd never imagined feeling this full before. This happy. With Laura, there'd been so many ups and downs, stress and disagreements, as they'd tried to weave their way through their problems. There had always been love between them, but a large part of their relationship had consisted of trying to make things work, Trish realized. Nostalgia, and Laura's absence in her life, had dulled that sense of failure over the years.

"Are you okay?" Trish ventured. "About us?"

"Yes. More than okay. You've always been the woman of my dreams, and I feel like I've finally reached the mountaintop."

"Yes. It's our time now. But I thought we should talk about Laura."

Pam slowed their pace but remained silent.

Trish pressed on. They needed to get this part behind them. "She's always going to be a part of our lives. She brought us together, after all."

"It's true. I never would have known you existed if Laura hadn't started dating you in high school. Unless you'd become my babysitter. Now *that* would have made for some interesting fantasies."

Trish lightly smacked Pam on the shoulder. "I'm sure you had plenty of fodder for fantasies about me once you became a hormonal—or should I say, horny?—teenager."

"All right, I admit it, I did have more than a few fantasies about you. Especially once you finished college and came back to teach at our high school in my last year. I ached to have an after-school detention where I'd have to…Oh, never mind. It's kind of dirty."

Trish laughed, halting their progress. She put her arms around Pam's neck and pressed her body against her lover.

"After what we just spent the last couple of hours doing, I think I can handle a little dirty talk."

Pam bent her head and kissed Trish on the mouth. It was a long, deep kiss that promised a lifetime of more. "I'd rather show you," Pam said after ending the kiss. "Matter of fact, I'd rather be inside you when I tell you."

A jolt of lust shot through Trish's belly. Instantly she was hard and wet, the thrumming inside her a constant drumbeat. She couldn't get enough of this woman, couldn't get enough of the exquisite pleasure Pam gave her. "We have all night, you know."

Pam growled against her throat and kissed her once more. "I know and I can't wait."

"Come on." Trish grasped her arm and gave a tug. "The dining hall is open all night. Let's replenish ourselves first."

"Do you always have to be so practical?"

"When it comes to looking out for you, yes."

The lighting was dull but they trudged along slowly, following the maze of walkways toward the large wooden dining hall.

"You know," Trish continued, "when I said Laura brought us together, I wasn't just talking about before. I also meant now. Through her death."

Pam slowed to a stop and turned to look at Trish. "I guess we owe all of this—us, I mean—to Laura. Do you think she would be okay with it?"

Trish thought for a moment, remembering how much Laura had loved and admired her younger sister, even though she never verbalized it much. She was proud of Pam, always had been, and after reading Laura's journal, it was entirely clear how much she respected Pam. If only Pam would believe it.

"She thought of you as a more perfect version of herself," Trish said. "I didn't exactly know that before I read her journal, but I always saw it in her eyes and heard it in her voice when she talked about you."

"What about you?" Pam looked deeply into her eyes. Even in the near dark, Trish could see a trace of fear in them. "Do I measure up?"

"Do you measure up?" Trish pulled Pam into a tender hug. "Oh dear God, Pam. When are you going to believe that it's *you* I love? That it's you I've been waiting for all my life? You don't have to measure up to anyone. You are you, Pam, and I love you."

"Thank you. And I'm sorry," Pam mumbled against her. "It hasn't been easy living my whole life in her shadow."

"I know that, sweetheart. But this is your time now. *Our* time. And we have Laura to thank for it. She gave us this gift of finding each other again. I believe that now."

They held each other in silence for a while. Quietly, Pam said, "She loved us both, didn't she?"

"More than anything. And yes, she would approve. How could she not?"

"Yes," Pam whispered, softly kissing Trish's lips. "How could she not?"

* * *

They made love again through the night, held each other on the narrow bed meant for one. They slept little, Pam especially, because she knew Trish was terrified of her flying to Kandahar in a helicopter in a few short hours. Trish hadn't said more about it, but she often trembled when Pam held her.

They rose with the sun.

"Hungry, my love?" Pam asked.

"Not really."

"Well, I'm starving. Must be all the calories we've been burning in this little room."

Trish deflected her attempt at humor with a frown. "Pam..."

"I know, sweetheart. We need to talk about me going to Kandahar."

They sat across from each other on the two beds. Trish looked like she was trying so hard to hold it together and only barely managing it.

"I know you don't want me to go," Pam continued. "But I am going. It's only for a couple of days, okay? I will be all right, I promise."

Trish looked away, didn't speak for several minutes. "You can't make a promise like that."

"No, you're right. But I will do everything in my power to come back safely to you."

Trish swiped at a tear on her cheek. "Aren't you afraid, even a little?"

Of course she was afraid. Of course she couldn't help but think about the tragedy that had befallen Laura. "I'm not going to lie to you, Trish. Yes, a part of me is afraid. But I don't want to live my life being afraid. And I don't want to avoid doing something that might make a difference in my life, that might help me figure out my future. Our future. I'm finding my own way now, and that means doing this trip to Kandahar. Hell, it's why I needed to come to Afghanistan."

"To banish Laura's ghost?"

"Yes," Pam declared. She had to admit there was some serendipity to flying in a helicopter in a war zone, a little bit of tempting fate. Maybe Trish was right in accusing her of testing herself this way. If she survived, then she could go on to be her own woman.

Pam stood, held out her hand. "Come on. Let's go eat breakfast, then you can see me off. And please." Pam's voice broke. "I need your love and strength right now, okay? More than ever."

"You have that, my love. Always." Trish smiled through her tears and took her hand.

* * *

Trish clutched Camille's arm as the Chinook helicopter roared slowly up into the sky. It was slow, like a cumbersome bird, its massive twin blades, front and back, beating a thunderous beat that reverberated through Trish's chest. Dust and sand billowed outward in fine, brown clouds, creating their own little dust storm.

Trish fought against the fear that it might be the last time she would ever see Pam. It wasn't healthy to think that way, might even be some kind of jinx, but she couldn't help it. She couldn't lose anyone else she loved, especially not Pam, and especially not after they'd finally found each other again.

"It's going to be okay," Camille said through the receding noise.

"It better be."

"Today I'm going to take you on a proper tour of the base and introduce you to some people who worked with Laura."

"I'm all yours. And I need to be busy right now, so thank you."

"Tomorrow evening is the weekly remembrance ceremony for the fallen. Someone says a prayer and reads out all the names of the soldiers who've died in this campaign in the last twelve months. You won't want to miss it, especially if you're thinking of writing a book."

Trish shook her head. The helicopter was the size of a pinhead in the sky now. "I don't entirely know if I'll write that book. Part of me wants to put all of this in the past. Permanently."

Camille began leading her away from the airstrip and toward a waiting jeep. "You'll know the right thing to do."

"Well, whatever it is, I know Laura won't be forgotten."

Later, with a little time in her room before lunch, Trish pulled out the journal. There was only one more entry to read... Laura's last. She'd been putting off reading it, not quite ready to face the end of it, the end of Laura's daily presence in her life. But she wanted to read it alone, in case Pam wasn't ready to face it.

April 6:
I can't really explain my mood today. I have the day off, because tomorrow I'm off to Takhar to fill in for the FOB doc there for a week or two. With nothing to do, I'm falling into a philosophical mood. I've been lying around reading the novel Matterhorn, and it's got me thinking about war, about the good and bad of it, the purpose it serves. Only history determines whether a war was right or not. And by right, I mean, did it serve a useful purpose? Did it accomplish anything? Did some good come of it? Did it move the

world a little closer along the spectrum toward justice and fairness? And who gets to be the judge of it all? Not me, that's for sure. But I'm doing my part in it and hoping like hell I'm doing the right thing.

I've been thinking too about the human instinct of wanting to leave a mark behind. A legacy, or something that indicates we were here, like, hey, look what I did, and please don't forget me. I think about this kid Ryan Jackson, arrived at the base last week. He was only nineteen, his first tour. He was killed three days later by a sniper outside the wire. What mark did that poor kid get to leave on this earth? Probably not much. But hopefully, he stays in somebody's memory and in somebody's heart. And that has me thinking, really, is there anything better than that? Isn't the love that someone will always feel for us in their heart the best thing we can leave behind? The special memories of us that they will take to their grave? Paper disintegrates, computers break, history misinterprets and alters people's stories. I just hope that somewhere out there— Pammy, Trish—that I'm loved and remembered, and always will be. Anyway, enough of this maudlin crap. I need to pack now for the trip tomorrow.

Trish closed the journal and wept. She wished she could say to Laura that she was loved and would always be remembered. *And if you're out there somewhere, Laura, if you can hear me now, please look after Pam.*

CHAPTER TWENTY-ONE

After the initial takeoff, Pam's anxiety gradually eased. Having the fierce-looking Black Hawk helicopter escort her Chinook helicopter helped. So did the relaxed and confident poise of the dozen or so soldiers who were catching a ride with her. She even looked to mathematics for a little solace. Her father had died in a plane crash, then her sister. What were the odds it would happen to a third member of the family? Almost nil. The Wrights were not so special that they might defy forty-five million to one odds, she figured. Hell, it's not like they'd ever won the lottery or anything like that. She would be fine.

From above, Kandahar Airfield looked very similar to Bagram, with its long runways, its gaggle of jets and helicopters parked at angles, two large hangars and a smattering of low-slung buildings, all protected by tall barbed wire fencing. Like Bagram, it was a small city—home to 26,000 soldiers, mostly American and British, and it was being expanded to include Afghan National Security Forces and the Afghan air force. She'd read up on the base online yesterday after learning she'd be paying it a visit and discovered that it was largely the

Canadians who snatched it from the Taliban in late 2001, then rebuilt it. But Canada and many other NATO countries had significantly cut the number of their troops in Afghanistan over the years, and now it was mostly the Americans doing the work on the ground. She didn't know much about the hospital, but arrangements had been made that would allow her to be fully embedded at the hospital for a couple of days as an expert observer. Security clearance and passes had been expedited, which spoke volumes to her about how much Laura had been respected by her colleagues and superiors. They knew she was here because of Laura, and they were eager to help her in any way.

As soon as Pam stepped off the helicopter's metal steps, a hand reached out to shake hers.

"Dr. Wright?"

Pam shook the woman's hand. "Yes, that's correct. Hello."

"I'm Captain Meg Atwood. A nurse at the hospital here."

"Ah, that explains the scrub shirt."

"I'm not really one for wearing military garb. I like casual." She had warm blue eyes, and they lingered over Pam. "Seems you're stuck with me while you're here. I, on the other hand, don't consider you a burden at all."

Pam laughed, not at all offended by the flirting. It was harmless, as far as she could tell, and besides, being crazy in love with Trish left her immune to anyone else's interest in her.

"C'mon," Meg said, taking Pam's duffel bag and leading her to a jeep that was coated with about an inch of dust. "I'll show you the hospital and get you settled in."

"What branch are you?" Pam asked as they bumped along the dirt track.

"Army. Canadian."

"Oh. Well, that explains the accent, then."

Meg frowned, raised her chin defiantly. "Now, why do you Americans always say Canadians have an accent? I don't get it. To me, I sound exactly the same as you."

"Nope, not true. Canadians sound more clipped, more precise, more, I don't know, *correct*. Almost British, but not quite. More like the way Americans should talk, if you ask me."

Meg smiled. "Dr. Wright, I think I'm going to like you just fine."

"And it's Pam, by the way. And I think I'm going to like you just fine too, Captain."

"Not Captain. Just Meg."

"Okay, Meg from Canada. You caught me by surprise. I thought the Canadians were pretty much gone from Kandahar?"

Meg smiled enigmatically. "I'm a relic they can't seem to get rid of around here."

Another career military gal, Pam thought. *Like Laura.*

"So they told me you're a doc in Chicago. Emergency medicine. I was also told you're in Afghanistan to see where your sister served. My condolences, Pam. Your sister sounds like she was a tremendous doctor. And soldier, even if she was American." Meg glanced sideways and slipped Pam a wink to show she was kidding about the American part.

"Thanks, and yes, I've heard nothing but good things about her army career. Did you know her?"

"No, I'm sorry, I didn't, unless it was in passing. But I wish I had, if she's anything like you."

"You're very kind. I forget how big these bases are and how many troops from all over the world are posted here." Pam wished the nurse had known her sister, if for no other reason than the instant connection it might have provided. It was lonely here, among so many thousands of strangers.

The jeep's trail of dust caught up to them when Meg braked to a stop in front of the hospital, momentarily shrouding them in a brown cloud.

"You can leave your bag in the car," Meg instructed. "I'll show you around the hospital first, then take you to the dorm."

The career military nurse knew the hospital intimately. She'd done several tours, dating back ten years, she told Pam, but she was able to adapt easily to Pam being a civilian. She explained things in a way Pam would grasp easily and did so without sounding patronizing. Pam couldn't help but like Meg, who seemed to have an unmistakable streak of wildness behind her flashing eyes and quick grin.

"You'll see our patients are a real mix of International Security Assistance Force soldiers, civilians and yes, even some Taliban."

"Wow, that must be hard," Pam said in a whisper as they squeezed past a dark-bearded man on crutches. "Are you frightened?"

"No. They're not generally in very good shape by the time they get here, and we strap them to the beds if we need to and keep an armed guard on them."

"Are they grateful?"

Meg scowled. "No. I think most of them would rather die a martyr."

A little girl in a pink robe wheeled past them in a wheelchair, her left leg missing from the knee down. The stump was freshly bandaged, and Pam felt her eyes widen in surprise. "You treat kids here too?"

The girl smiled up at them, the wheels of the chair cheerful in their squeaking. Her expression was innocent, almost gleeful. She looked like a kid from America, not from this war-torn country.

"Looking good, sweetie," Meg said happily to her and tousled her hair. Of course, the girl couldn't understand a word of it, but she nodded back enthusiastically.

"Civilians injured as a result of the war, yes," Meg said to Pam. "Sometimes even civilians who are just really sick if we have the room. But kids…it's hard to say no."

"What's that little girl's story?"

"Leg blown off while she and her older brother were playing with what they thought was an empty pop bottle."

Pam shook her head. How sick was that, blowing up little kids. "Did the brother make it?"

Meg shook her head grimly. "Peter, hey." She nodded at a youthful-looking doctor coming their way. He looked barely old enough to be a med school freshman, let alone a full-fledged doctor. "This is Pamela Wright. She's an ER doc from Chicago."

The young doctor shook Pam's hand. "Pleased to meet you. I'm Peter Milson. You going to sign on with us for a civilian tour? That's what I'm doing. Got three more months here."

"He's our pediatrician," Meg interjected.

"Wow, pediatrics too. You guys do everything here." Pam turned to Peter. She didn't try to hide her relief. "And no, I'm not planning to do a tour here. Sorry, not my cup of tea."

Meg succinctly told the young doctor about Laura.

"I'm sorry," Peter said. "I'm sure she was a fine doctor and a fine soldier. We'll miss her for sure."

"Thanks." Pam smiled, surprised by the effect the stranger's words were having on her. Her eyes began welling with tears.

"Why don't we go to the staff room and grab a cup of coffee," Meg said helpfully, reading the situation. "Care to join us Peter?"

"Don't mind if I do," he said, smiling at Pam in a way that made her a little uncomfortable. He wasn't creepy, far from it, but his signals were telling her his interest might be somewhat romantic. "I'll go on ahead and start brewing a fresh pot."

"He's cute, don't you think?" Meg said after he was gone.

Pam hesitated. She wasn't sure how the Canadian military—or Canadians in general—felt about homosexuality, although she remembered gay marriage had been legal in Canada for about ten years now. "I, ah…wouldn't really know. About the cute part, I mean."

Meg looked at her quizzically, although there was a hint of a knowing smirk twitching the corners of her mouth. "Not interested?"

Pam took a deep breath. "I'm gay."

Meg laughed as though it was the funniest thing she'd heard in at least a week.

Shit, is she laughing at me?

"Sorry," Meg finally said. Her eyes roamed appreciatively, inappropriately, over Pam, but it was flattering. "I think it's spectacular that you're gay. Perhaps it's my lucky day after all."

It was Pam's turn to laugh. "If that's a come-on line, sorry, but I'm happily taken."

"Damn. How unlucky for me." She pretended to swoon. "Oh well. Someday my princess will come."

"Are all the staff as funny as you?"

"Hell, no, but they're not half bad. They put up with me, after all. Come on, let's go check out our CT scanner before we get that cup of coffee."

* * *

Meg and Peter joked around only as close colleagues could. Meg was laughing at the teddy bears on his scrub shirt, Peter countering that she was jealous. They were easy to be around. Pam didn't hesitate to answer when they asked her why she'd come to Afghanistan. She told them more about Laura, about her own dissatisfaction lately with being an ER doctor, about how her disenchantment with work had multiplied after Laura's death.

"Life's too short to be in a job that doesn't leave you fulfilled," Meg said.

"So you both love what you do?" Pam asked.

Meg grinned widely. "Love it. Maybe I like living a little on the edge, but the military, the war, it's in my blood now. I don't know what I'll do when it's over. Probably go a little crazy."

Peter took his time answering. He had a thoughtful, methodical way about him that contrasted with his boyishness. "I love working with kids. Of course, what else would you expect from a pediatrician, right? But here...they need help so badly, you know? And they're so incredibly grateful. *That's* what keeps me doing this. You help them, even if it's in a small way, and they look at you like you've just given them a million dollars. Medical help is gold to them."

"Yes," Pam said. "That's what I want too. I don't need thank-you cards and flowers, but I want to feel useful, appreciated, like I'm truly making a difference. That's all I've ever wanted."

"So," Peter said quietly. "What are you going to do?"

Pam concentrated on her coffee cup. It was chipped ceramic with a Vancouver Canucks logo on it. She thought about the colonel in Bagram, how he'd told her that her dissatisfaction stemmed from not being able to let go. "I think," she finally said, "that I need to get out of emergency medicine. I need to work with people I'm helping for a longer period of time."

"What about another specialty?" Peter asked. "Cardiology, oncology, obstetrics, psychiatry." He flashed her a winning smile. "Or pediatrics."

Pam shook her head. "No. I don't want another two to four years of training right now. I want to get started right away. I just don't know the direction."

"Would you consider," Meg said, "working for Doctors Without Borders? Or spending a year or two in a developing country? They certainly need help from people like you." She rolled her eyes. "Like us. If they ever boot me out of this joint, that's what I'm going to do."

Her love for Trish swelled her heart, and she smiled at Meg. "Nope, not me. I have someone special I want to settle down with."

"Oh, right," Meg said. "Lucky girl."

"Am I missing something here?" Peter looked from one to the other.

"Yes," Meg replied smugly. "Our lovely Dr. Wright is happily—what, betrothed?" Meg waggled her eyebrows teasingly.

"Something like that," Pam answered, a little embarrassed.

"Damn," Peter said with a frown. "Just my luck."

Pam and Meg shared a secret smile.

"Okay," Meg said pointedly. "Back to your career. You're in Chicago, but you're from Ann Arbor, right? Are you going to stay in Chicago?"

"I'm not sure. I haven't discussed it yet with my, um, *betrothed*." The idea of marrying Trish made her nearly hiccup with a joy so sweet, it was almost painful. Should she ask Trish to marry her? Was it too soon? Would Trish even say yes?

"Earth to Pam," Meg was saying.

"Sorry, daydreaming. What were you saying?"

"There's a great VA hospital in Ann Arbor. Chicago too. Have you considered working with veterans and their families? If you don't like emergency medicine anymore, they provide tons of other medical services. You could do family medicine, take shifts at outlying clinics. There's even programs for veterans who are homeless and have substance abuse problems."

Peter nodded his agreement. "So many of our veterans suffer from PTSD and mental health issues, and a lot of them end up homeless or abusing drugs and alcohol. They need help, and so do their families. I've heard some of the VA hospitals have outreach programs that try to get shelter and medical help for the ones on the streets."

Wow, thought Pam. She hadn't known. Laura had never said anything about VA programs and hospitals, and now Pam found herself wishing they had discussed it. "Yes, I'd be interested in that." It also might be a great way to honor Laura, she realized, and to pay tribute to Meg, Peter, Colonel Davidson and Camille and everyone else doing their part in this war. "How can I find out more?"

"Well," Meg said with a satisfied smile. "I just happen to know a great gal who served here with me a few years ago. Dr. Logan Sharp. Lives across the border in Canada, splits her time between a hospital there and the VA hospital in Detroit. Why don't I email her and hook you guys up when you get home?"

"All right, thanks."

Meg winked. "Logan is one of the best people I know. You'll love her. She's about the best friend I ever made in this outfit. She was a major once, just like your sister."

"Well," Pam said, pushing her empty coffee cup aside. For the first time in weeks, she felt a new sense of peace and purpose. "Looks like this little therapy session with you two might have done the trick. I feel much better, thank you."

Peter grinned at her. "Wait until you see my bill."

* * *

Camille bounced on the balls of her feet, looking as though she could barely contain a happy secret. She clutched Trish's arm companionably as they strolled across the tarmac to where the short ceremony would be held in an empty hangar. It was nearly dusk, and while it was still hot as hell, evening had cooled things a couple of degrees.

"So when are you going to let me in on it?"

Camille grinned enigmatically. "Let you in on what?"

"Fine. I'll play along. But it better be good."

"Oh, it is, I promise."

Whatever it was, she longed for Pam. She missed her. She'd gone years without Pam in her life, and now a day away from her felt like forever. God, how were they going to handle going back home and living two hundred miles apart? They would need to talk about it, settle some things, like where they were going to live. Perhaps on the long flight back.

There were at least three hundred soldiers gathered in the hangar, quietly at ease. The colonel who ran the hospital was present. A few others Trish recognized as well.

A soldier with a Bible stepped on to a small wooden box that served as a podium. He recited a brief prayer for all of their lost brothers and sisters, singling out the most recent—a soldier killed a few days ago in a suicide bombing near Kabul. He talked about sacrifice, what it meant, and how freedom wasn't truly free. "Amen," some of the soldiers mumbled.

Colonel Davidson stepped up next.

"Many of us had the pleasure and honor of working with Major Laura Wright before she was KIA in April. And for those of you who didn't know about her attributes, I'm going to share a few."

He flashed a quick look at Trish. She nodded in acknowledgment.

"Major Wright was not only a good doctor, she was a great doctor. There was no one finer at this hospital in skill and competence. I watched her save the lives of many soldiers on many occasions. She never complained, never slacked off. No, wait. I take that back about not complaining."

There were a few muffled chuckles in the crowd.

"She complained if she didn't have anything to do. She complained when she wasn't able to spend time at a forward operating base or when she wasn't able to go into the nearby towns and villages to administer help to women and girls. In fact, it was her goal to set up a mobile clinic that would go out to some of these places weekly or monthly and offer help to the female indigenous population. Major Wright had one other complaint. She complained bitterly about the enemy, especially when she saw firsthand what they did to our troops and to their own people.

"Because of her passion for her work, for her fellow soldiers, and for the Afghan people, and because of her talents, her kindness, and her tireless efforts for the United States Army and for freedom in this country and elsewhere, I have a special announcement to make."

Trish held her breath and squeezed Camille's arm in anticipation. Camille beamed back at her.

"Starting next week, our hospital unit is fulfilling Major Wright's dream with the new Wright Mobile Medical Unit. Henceforth to be known as the WMMU."

Trish exhaled in relief. Her heart thumped with pride. She was so proud of Laura and incredibly proud to witness this moment. The crowd was clapping and whistling and stomping enthusiastically. Camille hugged her. "Damn, I wish Pam were here," Trish said. "I should be recording this for her with my phone."

"I was the first to volunteer for the new unit," Camille said proudly. "I'd have done anything for her. We go out next week."

"She was so lucky to have had you as a friend," Trish said.

Camille looked at her with moist eyes. "Laura was blessed with some wonderful women in her life, wasn't she?"

"Yes, she was." Trish looked around the room at the men and women in uniform and at how they were embracing the news of the new medical unit. It was clear they wanted to help change this country, that they wanted to be much more than witnesses to the violence. They wanted to leave their mark on Afghanistan. And though Laura was gone, she was still leaving her mark. *Finally, I understand why you were here, Laura.*

This, Trish thought, *is how I will end my book about Laura, because it's also a beginning.* She was convinced now that writing a book about Laura was the right thing to do.

"What?" Camille said, eyeing her.

"Nothing, just thinking. Pam's going to be so excited about this. I need to text her about it right away."

She did want to text Pam, but she also wanted to be alone for a minute. She wanted to cry but tried not to. As magnificently as Laura was being remembered and honored now and as much as her dream would live on in the new medical unit, Trish was struck by the permanency of Laura's absence. She was gone from all of their lives, forever, and there was a hollowness in Trish's soul that she knew would never heal. Somehow, life had been easier knowing Laura still walked this earth, still breathed and looked up at the night sky as Trish did, even though they'd been apart so long.

She thought back to their senior high school prom. It was 1993. They'd gone as a couple, not caring what anybody said. Laura was popular enough that no one ever said anything negative to their faces anyway. They danced to the last song of the night, Whitney Houston's "I Will Always Love You." Trish had melted into Laura's body as they danced, had felt so loved and so safe in her arms. So hopeful for the future, too, and so completely blind to anything bad ever happening to either of them. The future was an open road before them, the last time in their lives before the world, before life's problems, closed in on them. It was a sweet moment in their lives, but it was gone now. Trish could not go backward in her life. Nor did she want to.

As she quietly exited the hangar, she let herself briefly miss the innocent girls she and Laura had once been. *I will always love you, Laura Wright. Rest in peace, my love.*

CHAPTER TWENTY-TWO

Pam sat with the little girl in the pink housecoat, helping her assemble a puzzle. They didn't speak the same language, but Pam found it surprisingly easy to communicate anyway. She smiled a lot, made exaggerated facial expressions, touched the girl affectionately, and she lapped up the attention. Pam read a children's book to her, pointing to the pictures to try to explain the meaning, then tucked her in for the night.

"What's going to happen to her?" she asked Meg a few minutes later.

"I hear she has an aunt and uncle she can live with."

"What about school? Was she going to school?"

"She had been, but it was hit with rocket fire a few months ago. Our troops are repairing it, and I understand it's going to open again soon. But it's damn hard to keep those schools going. The Taliban make it their mission to keep people here back in the Stone Ages."

An alarm went off over the loudspeaker. A code red, it was announced.

"What's going on?" Pam asked as she rushed to follow Meg down the hallway.

"Incoming casualties," Meg yelled over her shoulder. "I'll go find out the details."

Pam didn't know what to expect, but the place sprang to life like a busy anthill. Medical personnel rushed around, quickly gowning up, speaking in rapid tones. It reminded her of a multi-victim car crash coming into her emergency room in Chicago. It was tense but eerily calm at the same time, every action having a purpose. People looked at the wall clocks, glanced anxiously toward the hospital's doors. They were ready.

Meg returned and thrust a pair of rubber gloves and a gown at Pam. "Here. Just in case we need to press you into action."

"Sure. What's happened?"

"A platoon ambushed on foot patrol about thirty miles from here. Five casualties, two extremely serious. They're all being medevaced in. ETA is about three minutes now."

* * *

At first Pam tried to stay out of the way, but out of habit, she followed the second gurney down the hall. Like the first, it too left a stream of blood, like some kind of grisly trail marker. The doctors, nurses and medics spoke in a verbal shorthand which Pam couldn't entirely decipher.

From the first trauma room she could hear the mechanical beep of the soldier's heartbeat flatlining, followed by the defibrillator machine trying to shock him back to life. She remained in the second trauma room, where the situation was slightly more optimistic.

A medic stood to the side, his job done for now. With both of them on the edge of the fray, Pam asked him what had happened. An insurgent had detonated a bomb planted beneath a bridge just as troops had begun to cross it, he told her. The injured soldier's name was Ross, though Pam didn't know if it was his first name or his last name. She glanced at him on the table, his uniform torn and bloody, his head soaked in sweat.

His legs had taken the brunt; they were shredded. His right hand too. His legs resembled raw, bloody ground beef. It was a shocking sight in spite of Pam's experience treating car crash victims and gunshot trauma. He was semiconscious, moaning, his eyelids fluttering. The team worked efficiently on him, getting a tube down his airway, inserting an IV through the vein near his elbow. Tourniquets applied in the field were still attached to his upper thighs.

"His abdomen's been compromised," one of the doctors said. "Let's get X-ray in here."

Pam stepped a little closer.

"We're going to have to get him out of here as soon as we can stabilize him," Meg said, joining her along the wall.

"Where?"

"Bagram, then they'll transfer him to Landstuhl, Germany."

Pam stepped back, heard more commotion outside. She stuck her head out to see what was happening. More stretchers were being whisked by. More blood, someone loudly groaning that he didn't want to die. Shit, Pam thought, was it never going to stop? It was like a massive pileup on the expressway, except that this was the only hospital that could treat the victims. There was no diverting patients elsewhere. This was it.

Pam asked how she could help. A gruff-talking surgeon told her to clamp off the artery in another soldier's leg while he sewed it back together. She did so and watched the surgeon's painstaking work even as her back began to ache from standing and bending over the patient.

It was at least an hour before the urgency plateaued, then dropped, and everyone seemed to take a collective breath. Bloody gowns and gloves were dropped into trash cans. Mops and buckets were pulled out of closets.

"Thanks for helping out," Meg said to Pam, looking exhausted.

"Any time. How many were lost?"

"Just one. There's still hope for Ross, the one with the mutilated legs. He's stable enough to transfer to Bagram. A couple of others are getting ready for transport too."

Pam knew well the mixed feelings of losing some but having saved others. It was the saves you had to concentrate on, especially during the moments when the lost ones haunted your thoughts, made you second-guess your actions. "You guys did great work in there."

Meg shook her head lightly. "I wish we'd done a little better, but we did what we could. Sometimes…"

"I know. Sometimes it comes down to needing a miracle."

"Yeah. And they're in short supply in this country. Listen, can you do us one more favor?"

"Sure, anything."

"I know you were going back to Bagram tomorrow anyway, but would you mind going tonight? We need to chopper out these three casualties as soon as we can, and we're short of flight nurses. Plus they should have a doc onboard anyway. Can you do it? You'll have a couple of medics with you, but that's all we can free up right now."

Pam didn't have to think twice about it. She'd help in any way she could. "I'm happy to help, Meg."

Meg smiled, touched Pam's arm lightly. "Thanks. And I'll get you my friend Logan's email address. I'll let her know you'd like to meet her."

"You've been a great help, Meg. More than you know."

Meg squeezed her arm, turned and headed back toward one of the treatment rooms. Pam pulled out her cell phone. She'd felt it buzz in her pocket earlier. She read Trish's text, pride bringing a grin to her face. Yes, Laura and her comrades had done great work over here, under such physically and emotionally trying circumstances. Naming a new mobile medical unit after her was the ultimate honor, Pam thought with satisfaction. Far more so than a folded flag or a medal.

Quickly she texted Trish that she would be returning tonight on a medical transfer.

* * *

Trish set her phone down, drained her cup of tea.

"You look like you've just won the lottery," Camille said with raised eyebrows.

Trish was already thinking about how they'd spend the rest of the night. "Pam. She's coming back early. Tonight."

"You look relieved."

"I am. I'm crazy worried. I know no place here is truly safe, but I'll feel much better having her back on base. With me."

"I can see that you love her very much, don't you?"

Trish thought about how long she'd loved Pam. Decades. She'd loved her as the kid sister of Laura. They were family. But she marveled at how that love had transformed so quickly from familial to romantic. And how right that transition felt. Maybe, she thought, it was always meant to be this way. That Laura had always been a conduit to finding her future with Pam. Strange how life worked out sometimes.

"Yes," Trish said simply. "More than I ever knew was possible. What about you? Have you ever been in love, Camille?"

It was several moments before Camille answered. "Once." When clearly it was all she was going to say on the matter, she tipped her near empty cup at Trish in a salute. "You're lucky to have loved two such wonderful women."

Yes, Trish thought. *Lucky. Please God, let my luck hold a little longer, until Pam is safely back in my arms.*

* * *

They were packed into the Black Hawk medevac helicopter like sardines—three casualties laid out on metal fixed stretchers, two medics, Pam, the pilot and co-pilot and a gunner, who kept careful watch from the half-open door of the helicopter. The twin engines were loud, along with the wind rushing through the door—both sources of noise making conversation nearly impossible. Pam hoped like hell one of these casualties didn't go into cardiac arrest or start bleeding out suddenly. She was a doctor of emergency medicine, but she was at home in a well-equipped, well-staffed trauma room in a modern hospital.

Certainly not in an army Black Hawk helicopter, where everything was bolted down, where the sliding metal stretchers were stacked one on top of the other, and where you couldn't turn around without knocking your elbows or knees or head into something or someone.

She looked down at her patient, who was still a patient in need of advanced medical care, no matter what his surroundings. She marveled at the fact that a soldier could be badly injured in the field and within an hour be diagnosed via X-ray, MRI or CT scan and be on an operating table. It was no wonder the mortality rate of soldiers in the First and Second World Wars was so high, when it could be hours or even days before they received any sort of expert help. Today, the mortality rate for soldiers injured in the field was exceptionally low, all things considered. If a casualty made it alive to a base hospital, he or she was likely to stay that way.

Ross—she still didn't know if it was his first or last name— opened his eyes and stared at her with what looked like a mix of awe and panic. He had an oxygen mask over his face.

Pam bent close to him. "It's okay," she yelled over the din. "You're going to be all right, Ross. You're on your way to Bagram, where they'll take good care of you."

The fingers of his good hand moved, first in a tremble, then more frantically, as though he were signaling something. He moaned too, like he was trying to speak through his oxygen mask.

"What is it, Ross?"

He moved his hand in a motion of holding a pen and writing.

Pam asked the medic across from her for a piece of paper and a pen, and he quickly supplied both from a cargo pocket in his uniform. Carefully she placed the pen in Ross's left hand, held the small pad of paper for him.

My legs?

Pam knew they were a lost cause. They were heavily bandaged, and most of his body was covered with a thermal blanket to help keep him from going into shock. She simply shook her head. There was no sense in shielding him from the truth. If it were her, she would want to know.

Tears pooled in his eyes. He looked away for a long moment, probably trying to envision what a future might look like without legs, without being whole for however long remained of his life.

"You're alive," Pam said simply. "That's what you have to focus on now, okay?" She'd treated patients before who'd lost limbs in terrible accidents. She knew what the shock and devastation of it meant, the stages of denial and disbelief, helplessness, and finally, acceptance.

He looked back at her, nodded slightly. He began to write again on the paper, in ragged block letters.

Baby. Soon. Wife.

"Your wife's having a baby?"

He nodded. His eyes brightened.

"Then you have a lot to live for, Ross."

He nodded again, looking momentarily pleased.

Moments after he'd drifted off to sleep, Pam too began to feel exhaustion seeping into her. Physically, she'd not done anything strenuous on her short trip to Kandahar. Mentally, it was a different story. She wished she could nod off too, but too many images and memories floated through her mind—the doe-eyed little girl in the pink housecoat, the blood of the soldiers as they were rushed into the trauma rooms, the methodical but hurried actions of the medical staff, the controlled tension in their voices. She supposed they got used to this sort of on-again, off-again chaotic maelstrom, much as she did working in a hospital emergency room. But the danger here felt so much riper, so close, as though it might reach out and snare everyone all at once. Any feelings of safety and security were fleeting and certainly not to be taken for granted, Pam had quickly realized. Every moment of being alive was a blessing.

It was pitch-black through the tiny windows, but she could sense that the helicopter was descending. They ought to be close to the Bagram base now, probably only minutes away, she guessed.

"Fuck!" It was the pilot or co-pilot, she wasn't sure which.

The gunner a few feet away from her echoed the same epithet. He dropped to his knees, braced himself, pointed his heavy automatic weapon through the half-opened door toward the ground, though how he could ever find a target in the blackness, she had no idea.

"What is it?" Pam shouted, her heart thundering in her chest like a herd of galloping horses.

And then she heard what the others must have. Firecrackers, although of course they weren't firecrackers. Something hard and metallic pinged off the roof above her. Another ping hit the outside of the door next to her.

"We're going dark," somebody from the cockpit shouted, and in an instant, all of the helicopter's internal and external lights blinked off.

Pam tried to settle her heartbeat, then her voice. "We're okay," she said to Ross as he stirred in his stretcher. One of the earliest bedside manner rules she'd learned was to make the patient feel calm, as though events around them were under control, even when they weren't.

"Motherfuckers!" the gunner said through his clenched jaw before he began firing off rounds. It was a staccato *crack-crack-crack* in bursts of ten or twenty, Pam couldn't be sure exactly how many rounds he was letting loose, but each burst made her jump. She'd never been near gunfire before.

More clunks and metallic pings rang off the helicopter's outer shell. There was no doubt in her mind that they were being fired at. Everything about the helicopter, even the glass, was bulletproof, she'd been told before. It could withstand rocket attacks too, apparently. It was a veritable fortress with rotor blades, she'd been led to believe, and she hoped like hell it was true.

The Black Hawk suddenly jerked hard to the left. Pam sucked in her breath, the damned wild horses active again in her chest. It banked to the right in a dodging move, except now one of its engines began making a high-pitched screeching noise. There was a faint smell of smoke. Alarms from the cockpit were sounding, the ominous bleating giving Pam more reasons to quietly freak out. Everything tensed in her body, adrenaline and fear gushing through her in waves. She felt slightly nauseous and dizzy.

Fuck, this can't be happening. We can't go down. We cannot go down, goddammit!

"We've got to set this bird down!" the pilot yelled. "We've been hit. We're not going to make it to the base."

Okay, focus, she told herself. *Focus and function through the fear. You can do this.*

She glanced at the medic across from her. He nodded and blinked reassuringly at her. They were all in this together, and they were all going to be okay, she decided. It was the only outcome possible, she truly believed. She'd found love, she'd found the happiness she'd been searching for all her life. It would not end this soon. It would not! Laura, God rest her soul, was her angel now. Laura would help her. Laura *had* to help her.

The helicopter bounced along, as though there were giant potholes in the air. One of its engines had gone silent, the other was struggling, she could tell.

Had Laura panicked silently inside when her helicopter was going down? Had she been brave on the outside, as Pam was now? Trying not to show fear, when inside, she recited a list of regrets she didn't know she had? Pam couldn't help but compare her situation to Laura's, as unbelievable as it all was.

Ross was squeezing her hand, pulling her out of her morbid reflections. She looked at him. He smiled beneath his oxygen mask. Her heart rate began to settle, her body relaxing a little. There was a baby to look forward to for Ross. Trish was waiting for her just a few miles away. It was going to be okay.

They bumped along through the air, Pam wishing she could see how far they were from the ground. At least she couldn't hear any more firecrackers and things pinging off the helicopter. The gunner had stopped firing and settled back in his seat for the landing.

"Landing hard in thirty seconds," the pilot yelled.

Pam double-checked the tension in her seat belt, then checked the straps keeping Ross on his stretcher. They were both ready.

They hit ground in two hard thumps. Then everything stopped. The engine noise, everything.

Without a word, the gunner released his belt and quickly slid the door fully open, his weapon in the ready position. One of the two medics had retrieved a rifle from under his seat and followed him out. The pilot and co-pilot were still in the cockpit, shutting things down, radioing somebody—hopefully somebody at Bagram, Pam prayed.

The remaining medic told Pam to stay where she was and look after the patients. "We're going to set up a guard perimeter outside the helicopter while we wait for help."

Pam swallowed. "Is help coming?"

"Yup. We're only four miles from the base. They have our coordinates and they're on the way."

Oh, thank God! Pam squeezed her eyes shut and gave silent thanks. A few minutes and they'd be rescued. She felt giddy with relief. "Hear that Ross? Help is on the way."

* * *

Trish knew something was wrong as the wait on the tarmac stretched out. Camille was with her, and they both kept scanning the dark sky for the incoming Black Hawk.

"Shouldn't it have been here by now?" Trish asked impatiently. She knew the answer; Pam's helicopter was at least ten minutes overdue.

Camille gave her some feeble excuses, but it was useless. Something was wrong. She could feel it in her gut—a cold, clenching feeling—and she shuddered.

"I need to find out," Trish implored. "Please, Camille. Find out what's wrong."

Camille nodded. Trish could see in her eyes that she thought something was wrong too. She turned on her heel and hurried away, leaving Trish shivering in the hot night air. Please, she said under her breath over and over again. *Come back to me, Pam. Come back to me. Please.* She wanted to cry, but didn't. If Pam was in trouble, she didn't need a blubbering, emotionally crippled girlfriend. She'd need her to be strong.

Camille returned with the colonel from the base hospital. They both looked solemn, and Trish's stress level spiked another notch.

"Please tell me what's wrong," she said. No point in pretending everything was going according to plan.

Colonel Davidson sighed, concern creasing his forehead. "Their helicopter came under attack just a few miles from here. It wasn't a serious attack, just small arms, but it did enough damage that they had to set down."

Trish's stomach tightened, the word "attack" echoing in her mind. Jesus, Pam had come under attack? How could that be? She was a civilian, for God's sake. This wasn't her war. She was supposed to be observing, not getting involved in anything like being fired at.

Trish's anger shot to the surface. Her jaw felt like steel. "How could this happen, Colonel?"

He blinked at the question. "It's generally a pretty safe route the choppers take back and forth. There hasn't been an incident in months." His brown eyes softened considerably. "I'm sorry, but these things can be unpredictable."

"Where are they now? Is Pam okay?"

"A convoy of armored vehicles is leaving the base now to retrieve them. There were no injuries in the attack." He flashed a quick look at Camille, and in that instant, Trish realized that Pam was still in danger.

She kept her voice steady. "What are you not telling me, Colonel?"

"The situation is under control, Ms. Tomlinson. They'll set up an armed perimeter around the chopper until help arrives, which should only be another twenty minutes or so."

Twenty minutes! The longest twenty minutes of my life, Trish thought ruefully. If they made it through this ordeal, she would make damned sure they got the next flight out of this God-forsaken place. She steadied her voice. "If they were fired at, it means there are enemies in the area, right?"

"That's a possibility, yes, but we're putting a couple of Apache choppers in the air as we speak. They'll fly over and scare off any insurgents. As far as these things go…" He smiled for the first time. "This one's pretty good."

Camille nodded assurance, and Trish's relief was instant. "Can I go on the convoy to retrieve them?"

"Afraid not," the colonel said, not unexpectedly.

Camille turned to Trish. "C'mon. It'll probably be close to an hour before they're back. Let's go get a cup of coffee."

Trish scanned the inky, empty sky one last time. It was going to be okay. It *had* to be.

CHAPTER TWENTY-THREE

The bumpy ride back to base in the armored vehicle was quiet; nobody spoke, and that was fine with Pam. She needed time with her thoughts, needed to come down from the adrenaline high of coming under attack and having to crash-land in the desert. The fear hadn't paralyzed her, but it had shaken her badly. She couldn't let Trish see her like this. She hadn't come as close to death as she'd initially imagined. It was nothing as dramatic as what Laura had encountered in her death, she was sure, and she needed to get a grip. She was okay, and so was Trish.

Pam closed her eyes, lulled by the rattling of the mammoth vehicle and its diesel engine. She wanted to contribute, wanted to help in a meaningful way, but not here in a war zone. She wasn't cut out to handle the futility, the volatile highs and lows, the feeling of living a parallel life out here that was so different from the way people lived back home. It was no wonder that soldiers returning home had trouble adjusting. Maybe that's why Laura never came home for long. Staying in a war zone for as often and for as long as she could meant she didn't have to try to live a normal life. Maybe there was some comfort in that for Laura, but it couldn't have been healthy for her, Pam decided.

God, she thought with a shiver, *I do not want to be like that*. Nor did she want other soldiers like Laura to feel that they didn't belong back home. She wanted to do something to help them. And not just because she appreciated the sacrifices they'd made, but because they deserved to be happy, to be productive members of their community. She might be woefully inadequate in her skills to make a real contribution, but she had to try. She'd get in touch with this Logan Sharp when she got home, see if there was a way she could help.

When the convoy pulled into the base, the vehicles drove quickly into an empty hangar. The doors all clanged shut behind them. It was for a debriefing, she was told. They were all asked privately to describe exactly what had happened, in chronological order, of course. Pam, as a civilian, didn't technically have to cooperate, but she did. She told the major asking her questions that she didn't want anyone to get in trouble for the fact that she was on that helicopter. Nobody did anything wrong, she said, and she'd willingly taken the ride. In fact, the soldiers on the helicopter with her had remained very calm and professional. She owed them her life.

Trish was waiting outside for her, alone and looking small, standing stock-still as though she were afraid to move. Pam hesitated for a moment, drinking her lover in. It was the most beautiful sight she'd ever seen—the woman she loved waiting for her. She gave a silent thanks to Laura and whichever higher powers had brought her and Trish together and had kept her safe tonight. Then she ran to Trish, threw her arms around her and lifted her off the ground as they clung to each other. Pam let her tears spill on to Trish's cheek and shoulder as she twirled her through the air.

"Oh God, I'm so glad you're safe," Trish muttered. She was crying too. "Please. Please don't ever leave me again."

"I won't, I promise you."

Trish's shoulders shook, and Pam held on tighter.

"I thought I'd lost you," Trish choked out.

"I know, I know, baby. I'm so sorry." Pam kissed the top of her head. "It's okay now. Everything's going to be okay."

"Can we leave this place now? Go home and start our lives together?"

"Yes. Definitely." Pam cupped Trish's cheeks with her hands, gazed into her tear-filled eyes. "I'm ready to say goodbye to this place. To Laura. Are you?"

Trish nodded before taking a step backward. She reached behind her neck and unclasped the necklace with Laura's ring on it, settled it in her palm and closed her hand around it. She shoved it in her pocket. "We'll find a special place for it later, but that place isn't around my neck anymore."

Pam smiled, stepped toward Trish and planted a soft kiss on her lips. "Are you sure about that?"

"Yes." Trish gave a final swipe to brush the tears from her cheek. She looked at Pam with love in her eyes, but also a resoluteness Pam had never seen before. "I loved your sister. But it was a long time ago, and it was during a time in my life I'll never have back again. And I don't want that time back again. This is my life now. *You* are my life now, and this is exactly how I want it to be. It was how it was meant to be. I believe that now."

Pam looked up at the sky and the bright stars that looked much closer here than they did back home. They were closer to heaven somehow in this awful place. "It feels like we have her blessing."

Trish nodded silently.

Pam knew Trish was thinking the same thing, that Laura had been her angel an hour ago. That she'd kept her safe so she could live the rest of her life with Trish. "It feels like she's given us a gift," she whispered.

"Yes. I believe that too. And I feel like I know her so much better now, after coming here."

Pam looked around one last time, then took Trish's hand. "I think I know what I want to do now."

Trish took in the gravity of her statement, and smiled at her. "Good. I want you to tell me all about it while we pack."

"I'd love to."

* * *

Their lovemaking was gentle, loving, patient. Every touch, every kiss, was as soft as a caressing breeze. Their climaxes dissolved in tears—tears of joy, relief, reward. They held each other for a long time. After a while, Pam told her all about her visit to the Kandahar base—the hospital and its dedicated staff, the little girl in the pink housecoat, meeting the indomitable Meg Atwood, the pediatrician, the soldier Ross (she still didn't know his full name) with his shredded legs and his hope for the future, anchored by his unborn child. She hoped he'd be all right.

"Sweetheart." Nestled tightly in Trish's arms, Pam moved back enough to look into her eyes. "I've figured out what I want to do."

"Whatever it is, you know you have my full support."

"I know that, thank you."

"Well? You're killing me here."

Pam smiled in the dark, her heart light. She knew she was making the right decision. "I want to work with veterans. Veterans trying to adjust to life back home. I don't know how exactly yet. I mean, it'll encompass my training as a physician, but it's all very much in the embryonic stage. Meg has a friend, a doctor who works in Detroit with veterans, and she suggested I get in touch with her."

Trish kissed the tip of her nose. "Honey, that sounds wonderful, and I know you'll do a terrific job. I'm so proud of you."

"You are?"

"Yes, and Laura would be too."

Pam rolled on to her back, stared up at the dark ceiling. She hoped Laura would be proud of her decision, but of course she'd never know. And that was okay. It was *her* life, and the only people she had to please now were herself and the woman she loved. This was where her life was taking her now, and she was fully ready to move forward with it. And maybe that was always the way it was meant to be—to go where life takes you, to embrace it fully, to give it all you have and be prepared for the next bend in the river, she realized.

"What about you?" Pam asked, turning back to Trish. She began stroking her dark, wavy hair. Silk on her fingers.

"I want to write that book. About Laura's life here, using her journal entries. But I want it to be more than that. I want it to be about other soldiers too. Maybe some of those veterans you want to work with. What their life is like now, because working in a war zone is such a small part of who they are, isn't it?"

"Yes, it is. And there's so much more to their lives than a place like this, even though it seems to define them for such a long time afterward, maybe forever. I'll help you with the book any way I can."

Trish kissed her again, yawned. "Thank you, my love. That means so much to me. But I figure I'll work on it during summer holidays for however many years it takes. I don't want to give up teaching."

"Good, I'm so glad to hear you don't want to stop teaching. You're too good at what you do."

Trish chuckled. "How do you know I'm a good teacher?"

"Well, you see, in my fantasies, you're absolutely incredible." Pam lowered her voice, growled playfully. "Especially the part where you keep me after school for detention. And you're wearing this tight white blouse with the buttons nearly popping. I'm sitting at a desk, you see, and you lean over me…"

"Okay, wait," Trish protested, then burst into laughter. "You're incorrigible, do you know that?"

"Yes, now kiss me!"

Trish pressed her lips to Pam's. They were tender, pliable, and in direct contrast to her tongue, which grew persistent and playfully demanding. She parted Pam's lips, pushed inside, where her tongue danced wildly, instantly teasing a moan of pleasure from Pam.

With all the willpower she could summon, Pam wrenched herself away. Breathless from her burgeoning desire, she said, "There is one more thing I want to talk to you about."

"Hmm, let's see. How about we talk about how I'm going to ravage your body again? And then again just for the fun of it!"

Pam laughed. "I would love to talk about that. But first things first. Seriously."

Trish groaned. On her side, she leaned on an elbow, her other hand resting on Pam's naked hip. "Okay, sweetheart. What would you like to talk about?"

"Us."

She could see Trish's eyebrows dart up. "But I thought…"

"Yes, you thought right. Everything is wonderful, and I've never been happier in my life."

Trish's voice dipped ominously low. "But?"

"But nothing. There is no 'but.'"

Trish exhaled, relaxed her body. "God, you had me worried."

"Sorry. It's just…"

Trish's hand slid up Pam's body and began stroking her face. "You can talk to me about anything, you know that."

Pam did know that. There wasn't anything she was afraid to talk about with Trish. But she was worried about her reaction to what she was about to say. After a deep breath, she plunged ahead. "My entire family is gone now. And you're an only child, and…"

"Yes, my love, we're each other's family now. We're all we've got, aren't we?"

"Yes. But I want more. I want to us to grow our family someday."

For a long moment, Trish said nothing. "Do you mean…?"

"Yes." Pam swallowed. *Oh, God, what have I done? I've scared the crap out of her*.

"Okay, but shouldn't we talk about living together first?"

Pam searched Trish's face in the dark for clues about whether she was kidding or not. Trish didn't make her wait long. She burst out laughing, and soon Pam was laughing too.

CHAPTER TWENTY-FOUR

Pam was nervous, though she had no reason to be. She had every expectation that Dr. Logan Sharp would be a nice woman and helpful too. But Pam couldn't help feeling like a kid on her first day of school—excited but completely out of her realm. She really had no idea what she was getting into, but her desire to do something to help veterans propelled her forward. It was something she knew she had to do.

Trish, of course, had offered to go with her to Detroit to meet Logan Sharp, but Pam had tactfully declined. It was the first day of classes for Trish, and they'd just finished moving Pam into Trish's house the week before. No, she had told Trish, she could handle this herself, and she'd give a full report to Trish over dinner tonight.

A tall, willowy waitress directed Pam toward a table for two in the corner of the restaurant. Pam hesitated for only a moment, watched the fit-looking woman with the perfectly erect posture glancing over a menu. She definitely looked ex-military.

"Hi," Pam said, trying to sound breezy, as though she met strangers in restaurants all the time.

The woman looked up with pleasant, hazel eyes. She rose quickly and gracefully to her feet, offered her hand.

"Pamela Wright." Pam smiled and shook her hand warmly.

"Logan Sharp. Very nice to meet you, Pam."

"The pleasure is all mine. Thanks so much for agreeing to meet me."

"Have a seat." Logan gestured to the empty chair across from her, and Pam sat down. "I'm just thrilled you want to help. I won't lie to you. I plan to twist your arm, bribe you, do whatever it takes to convince you to work at one of our VA hospitals, either here in Detroit or the one in Ann Arbor."

"Well, since we're being honest, you probably won't have to work too hard to convince me."

Logan smiled, and Pam couldn't help but smile back, immediately drawn to the woman's warmth and genuineness. "Good to know. My wife will be relieved to hear it too. She figured I'd have to ply you with the most expensive dish they have here."

The word "wife" made Pam smile again. Meg hadn't mentioned that Logan was married to a woman. "She sounds like a sensible woman."

"She is. You should meet Jillian sometime. She wanted to come today, but she figured she'd be intruding."

"Funny. My partner Trish wanted to come too. Guess we should make it a foursome next time?"

Logan's instant laughter was deep and warm, like liquid honey. "Deal. So I understand you met Meg in Kandahar a month or so ago?"

"Yes. She was a great help. I wish I'd had more time to get to know her."

"Is she doing well? We email occasionally, but I only see her once every year or two."

"Yes, she seems happy. She told me she loves the military."

Logan shook her head lightly. "God bless Meg. They don't make many like her."

The waitress came by again, took their order—grilled salmon for Logan, a portobello quesadilla for Pam.

"Meg said you live across the border in Windsor?"

"Yes, I'm Canadian. Served two tours in Afghanistan and didn't re-enlist when my commitment was up." A faint frown settled between her eyes.

It wasn't a stretch to imagine Logan in a war zone. She had the look of a capable, brave woman who'd seen everything there was to see, but had come to a peaceful acceptance of it. Well, mostly peaceful, anyway.

"May I ask why?"

Logan glanced away. For a moment, she was somewhere far away. "It's a tough life, and not for everyone. I realized after I came home that I was having some PTSD symptoms. I got some help. Having a stable, loving relationship helped a lot too. I took a few months off work, and when I came back, I decided to split my time between ER work at a hospital in Windsor and working a couple of days at week at the VA hospital here."

"Well, I'm glad you made it back okay. And more than just physically made it back."

Logan nodded. "I'm sorry your sister had to pay the ultimate price. Her sacrifice will not have been made in vain. I know the kind of work she was doing, and I know the kind of difference it makes in peoples' lives over there, both soldiers' and civilians'."

"I'm starting to see that now, but I admit, when she died, my attitude wasn't quite that enlightened."

"I understand. I've been through all the doubts and second-guessing myself."

Pam told Logan about her and Trish's trip to Afghanistan to find some closure.

"And did you find it?"

"Yes." Pam was mildly surprised at how easy Logan was to confide in. "Afterward I felt like I knew Laura better, or at least understood her, and understood what she was trying to do there. By seeing other medical professionals in action there, it made me appreciate Laura's sacrifice all the more. And it convinced me that I could do something to help too."

"Well, I'm glad you came to that conclusion. We can use all the help we can get. Working with veterans may not seem as glamorous by comparison, and it doesn't pay as well as private practice, but it's incredibly awarding."

"Then it sounds perfect."

Their food arrived, and Pam, her nervousness long ago evaporated, took a ravenous bite of her quesadilla.

They talked more about their backgrounds, Pam explaining why she'd begun to drift away from emergency medicine even before her trip to Afghanistan.

"You might find yourself more inspired about medicine once you do this kind of work," Logan suggested.

"That's what I'm hoping for. I'm just not sure where or how to get started."

Logan talked about her VA work, about the programs and the veterans. She recited a few statistics about substance abuse and depression that many veterans, especially the younger ones, often experienced. Veterans had high rates of homelessness and suicide too, she said, as well as divorce. "A lot of them suffer silently from PTSD. What areas do you think you'd be interested in working in?"

"I don't really know, to be honest. I'm open to suggestions."

Logan signaled the waitress for the check. "I've got an idea. Why don't you leave your car here for an hour or two and come with me?"

* * *

The John D. Dingell VAMC was one of the newest VA centers in the country, Logan explained during the drive. It served more than 330,000 veterans from four counties, or about forty per cent of all veterans in the state's lower peninsula. She'd worked at the hospital part time for three years now, she said.

Pam asked her about support at the VA hospitals from the state and federal governments.

"Yes, it's there," Logan replied. "More than even just a few years ago. Our programs are expanding every year. Of course, there's still so much more we need to do, but we don't have to resort to the same degree of begging for funding that we once had to."

"What about when the war is over?"

Logan sighed loudly. "I do worry that once the last of the troops come home—if they ever do—that veterans will sort of fade from the picture. That it won't be sexy for politicians or the media to pay attention to them and their needs anymore."

Pam told Logan about Trish's plan to write a book—how the first half would be about Laura's life at war, the other half about veterans who've returned home.

"Tell her I'll help connect her with people and do anything I can to help," Logan said. "Sounds like exactly the kind of project that will help people understand veterans better. And," she added triumphantly, "she needs to meet my wife Jillian. She's a photographer. Maybe they could collaborate."

"That sounds perfect." As they pulled into a parking area reserved for hospital staff, Pam asked the question she'd been dying to ask. "This work you do here." Pam gestured through the windshield at the large, sprawling complex. "How do you feel about it? At the end of the day, the week, the month? Do you feel like you've made a difference?"

Logan smiled, her eyes bright with joy. "Oh, yes. I feel I'm doing as much good here as I was in Afghanistan. Except that I don't have to worry about getting shot at or a rocket landing in my lap. And the best part?" She parked and shut the engine off. "I get to come home every night to my wife and daughter."

An idyllic vision flashed in Pam's mind. She and Trish cooking dinner together. A baby in a high chair, laughing, watching them, squirming with excitement. The three of them in the kitchen. A family.

"Sounds like you have exactly the life I'm trying to build for myself," Pam said.

"Then you're a very lucky woman. As am I. C'mon, let me show you what I do here."

Logan toured her through a couple of wings and several floors, showed her where programs such as addictions counseling, physiotherapy, cardiac rehab and sexual health were conducted. There were other areas of the hospital they wouldn't have time to look at today, Logan explained. There were one hundred and eight beds in the full-service hospital, plus a nursing home of equal size. A program for homeless veterans took up part of another building. "We'd need the right paperwork to get you through those areas, but there's one more place I can take you to."

Logan led the way down a hall, stopping in front of a closed door. "This," she said with a grin, "is our music room. I swear it's the most popular place of all." Gently, she pushed the door open.

Instruments of every kind hung on the walls. On the floor were a couple of drum kits, a piano, a large conga set.

A man in a wheelchair, his back to them, quietly strummed a guitar.

"They can come in anytime and use the room, the instruments," Logan said. "There's also piano lessons, guitar and drum lessons. Musicians volunteer their time to come in and teach. It's great. The vets love it, everybody loves it."

The man in the wheelchair swung around to face them.

I know that guy, Pam thought.

"Doc?" He squinted at her. "That you?"

Logan watched them with mild amusement.

"Ross? My God, it *is* you!"

Pam rushed across the room to him, bent down and hugged him, guitar and all.

"It's so good to see you. How are you, Ross?"

"A hell of a lot better than I was, last time you saw me."

"Afghanistan?" Logan prompted.

Pam nodded, quickly summarizing their experience together.

"She was my angel," Ross said, emotion thick in his voice. "I don't know that I would have got through it if not for this woman. Christ, I don't even know your name, doc."

"Pamela Wright. And I hate to admit this, but I don't know your full name either." She smiled helplessly. "We missed the formal introduction. Things were a bit crazy at the time."

Ross laughed. "That's an understatement. Rory Ross, but everybody calls me Ross. And it's a pleasure to formally meet you, Pamela Wright."

"Do you know Dr. Sharp?" Pam asked.

"Afraid I don't. It's a big place here."

"Sure is," Logan said. "You're doing okay?"

He looked down at his lap, at the stumps he had for legs now. "Been better, but I'm here."

"Well," Logan said with empathy, "that's the main thing. Very few of us make it back undamaged. We have to rebuild our lives with what we have."

Ross set the guitar down, fumbled around in his back pocket. He pulled out a cell phone, tapped it a couple of times, handed it to Pam. "My little boy, Marty. Only three weeks old now."

Pam smiled at the picture. A father couldn't look more proud than Ross did, cradling his baby son. "Beautiful."

"Yeah," he said, stuffing the phone back in his pocket. "I've got one more surgery to go, then I'll be able to go home for good. What about you? You still in Chicago? Wasn't that where you said you live?"

"Ann Arbor now."

"Sweet. Just down the road. You should come for dinner sometime, meet Marty and my wife Kelly."

"That'd be nice."

"One more thing, doc." He tilted his head at the guitar. "You know how to play this thing? 'Cuz I can't play worth a shit. Not anymore, but I still love to hear it played real good." He raised his right hand to show Pam. It was scarred and missing two fingers. Remembering how mangled it was, she was surprised he'd managed to keep most of it.

Pam picked up the guitar and sat down on a nearby stool. She hadn't played in months, but she didn't think Ross would mind if her skills were rusty. She thought of Laura, how Laura loved to listen to her play the guitar when they were younger. By her own admission, Laura had never possessed the patience to learn how to play an instrument. Too much sitting in one place, she'd scoffed, and yet she was supportive of Pam learning and playing.

Pam began the opening bars of "Ain't No Sunshine When She's Gone." The song came back to her more effortlessly than she expected; it was one she'd spent hours—weeks—learning when she was a teenager and despairing over her unrequited love for Trish. Now she thought, fingerpicking her way through the song, it was about Laura and Laura's absence. Not Trish. Never Trish again.

"Damn," Pam said after Logan and Ross applauded her. "Seems like all the good songs are about women breaking your heart, doesn't it?"

"How about something happier, doc? Last thing I need is to sit around here listening to sad songs." Ross was grinning around his words.

"Okay," Pam said, then began the opening notes to Jack Johnson's "Better Together."

When she was finished, she set the guitar down, and turned to Ross. "How would you feel about being in a book one day?"

EPILOGUE

It was warm for November—spring coats and light shoes weather. The pungent scent of distant burning leaves permeated the air, and Pam breathed in deeply. She loved fall, loved the four seasons of the Great Lakes. She loved living in Ann Arbor again, loved the city's refinement, the signs of learning and teaching everywhere. It felt like a city of possibilities, with the continuous promise of bright futures rolling out from it like a red carpet. She loved the autumn weekends too, when the city was bathed in yellow and blue as alumni swarmed in to watch the football games. The party atmosphere made her feel young, happy, weightless again. She and Laura had been to the Big House a handful of times to see a football game, and they'd acted as silly as the rest of the young fans, painting their faces, drinking beer, yelling and stomping their feet in wild cheers. It was Laura who'd taught her how to throw a football. How to spread the tips of her fingertips over the string, how to spin, release, and arc the ball, using her wrist.

Beside her, Trish held her hand—strength and love in their entwined fingers. It was Veterans Day, and Laura's name had just been pasted on a plaque for the memorial wall downtown. A shaky version of "Taps" was being played on the trumpet by a nervous, young cadet. There were veterans from many wars here, some old and stooped and nearly blind, others more youthful, but they too stooped with a weariness that hadn't been delivered by age.

Pam thought of her own weariness, wondering if it showed in her face, in her body. Laura had been gone seven months. And while Pam had found incredible happiness in those months, the loss hadn't left her. Probably never would, she guessed. She'd filled some of that space with her work at the VA hospital in town—the new health program for women vets—and of course with Trish. They hoped in the next couple of years to fill more of that space with a child too, and Pam couldn't wait. But she knew, deep down, that something would always be missing from their lives. *Laura*.

She squeezed Trish's hand as a minister, then a priest, recited a prayer.

"You okay?" Pam whispered.

Trish smiled at her, nodded. There was pride in her eyes and a sense of peace that had finally supplanted her anger. They'd both come to an acceptance of Laura's death, its heartbreaking permanence. And yet in some ways, Laura was more alive to them than she had ever been. With Trish it was through the book she had begun writing about Laura and veterans returning home. With Pam it was through her work at the VA hospital. They weren't ready to completely let the army off the hook— it wasn't a perfect institution by any means, and it had made its share of mistakes—but at least now they understood the necessity for its existence, respected and appreciated the tireless sacrifice its servicemen and women had made. Freedom and justice came at a price. And while she hated that her sister had paid the ultimate price, Laura had certainly not been the only one. Many other good men and women had paid that price too, and they all belonged to the stars now, Pam thought with hopeful determination. *They are part of everything now, all of us.*

Silence, heavy as a blanket, hung over the ceremony. An army colonel in full dress uniform stepped on to the podium, his polished boots making a thudding sound in the quiet. He cradled a small red velvet box in his large hands. He cleared his throat nervously, but when he spoke, his voice was strong and clear. He spoke about Laura and her army career, listed all her impressive accomplishments. He opened the box to reveal four medals, to be presented posthumously. There was an Iraq campaign medal, an Afghanistan campaign medal, a Purple Heart and a commendation medal. He called Pam to the podium. She tugged Trish along, and together they accepted the medals.

These pieces of ribbon and precious metal would not magically heal their hearts, Pam knew. But they would be a reminder of Laura's excellence, of her commitment, and they would be symbols of what Laura had believed in. They would be symbols of her quest to make the world a better place, and for that reason, they were precious to Pam.

The gathering disassembled quietly, people peeling off alone or in small groups. Pam and Trish lingered, touching Laura's newly affixed plaque on the wall.

"Hmm," Trish muttered. "What do you think Laura would have thought of all this?"

Laura hated pomp and circumstance, but in her heart, she was a proud woman, a proud soldier. "She would have liked it, I think."

"I think so too. You ready to meet the gang?"

"Yes, let's go," Pam answered. They were meeting Logan and her wife Jillian and their young daughter Maddie for dinner. Rosa and her new girlfriend were joining them as well. They would celebrate and have a good time, and they'd give one hell of a toast to Laura, Pam thought with a smile. She tucked the box of medals inside her jacket. She'd bring them along and put them right in the center of the table, as if Laura herself were joining them, smiling in that way of hers that was both cocky and humble at the same time.